I0757507

Every Hex You Take

CRESCENT MOON MYSTERY #3

TARA LUSH

COVER DESIGN
LOU HARPER/ COVER AFFAIRS

EDITED BY
THE AUTHOR BUDDY

Copyright © 2024 by Tamara Lush

All rights reserved.

No part of this book may be reproduced in any form or by any electronic or mechanical means, including information storage and retrieval systems, without written permission from the author, except for the use of brief quotations in a book review.

To my mother, who always loved Masterpiece Mystery. How I wish she could've read my books.

One

The morning of January tenth had me bopping around the house, a strange tingle coursing through my bones. This wasn't a caffeine-fueled frenzy, but rather, one more sign that the day would not be normal.

First up, it was a full moon. No explanation required there.

Second, it was the anniversary of David Bowie's exit from this earthly plane, an event that shook my Gen X self to the core when it happened in 2016. He'd been a particular favorite of mine as a teenager, especially the *Let's Dance* album. I was a sucker for a man who could play guitar.

Still was, in fact. Personally, I believe the universe broke when Bowie died, and things have never been the same since.

I was listening to that very album as I got ready for my lunch meeting on January tenth, singing and dancing along to "Modern Love." Every so often I'd glance at my pet, Freddie Purrcury.

Pet was the wrong word, honestly. He was more like permanently retired royalty.

The slightly oversized orange feline was snoozing on the

bed, uninspired by both Bowie's baritone and my harmonizing.

"Did you know it's Peculiar People Day?" I mused aloud.

Freddie didn't move a whisker.

I hadn't mentioned the Peculiar People Day to anyone in my new hometown, but I secretly thought folks here should embrace the milestone a little more publicly. It was a selling point. Almost everyone in Cypress Grove — official slogan: Discover Your Destiny — was peculiar.

Including me, I guess.

Cypress Grove was known as The Psychic Capital of the World, drawing folks from across the globe who were seeking... well, they were seeking all sorts of things. Truth, justice, peace, advice, love, eternal happiness, you name it.

All of this is why I found myself pondering life's mysteries as I primped. I sifted through the jewelry box until I found what I was looking for: a moonstone ring. The stone itself was a substantial, rough-cut gem, set in platinum. Not only was it my birthstone, but it held deep personal significance.

It had been my Aunt Shirley's ring.

Before I slipped it on the finger that once held my wedding band, I brought it to the window, inspecting it for dirt, cracks, or loose prongs, but it was as perfect as the last time I'd worn it during a quick trip over the holidays to see my daughter. She hadn't noticed the flashy stone, and I didn't bother to explain where it came from, or how it gave me a subtle surge of energy.

She also hadn't detected the change in me since I left my former home in California.

I was now the kind of person who believed in crystals and magic. In witches and ghosts. In the universe and the unknown.

This was the new Amelia Matthews, at the age of forty-seven: innkeeper, empty-nest divorcee, and possessor of a quirky-yet-still-baffling psychic power. My Aunt Shirley had left me the historic Crescent Moon Inn, and I now lived in her old apartment on the first floor of the three-story Queen Anne Victorian.

The new version of myself retained some familiar habits from my past life, such as baking — a nod to my previous venture running a cookie delivery business in California. However, it now also included a mix of new pastimes: investigating murders, participating in seances, and conversing with spirits.

As one does in midlife, white fighting off hot flashes. At least here in Cypress Grove.

The people from my old existence on the West Coast — namely, my family — didn't know about my unusual new one here in Florida yet. They didn't know of my powers or my confidence. I hadn't told them about the murders, the seances, and definitely not the ghosts, worried they'd have me committed.

All my twenty-one-year-old daughter Jenny said over Thanksgiving was, "Wow, Mom, Florida's been good for you. It's like you're ten years younger."

Ahh, kids.

Jenny and my family would, in time, learn about my new powers. Once I got more comfortable, and once I figured out how exactly to break the news. As far as they were concerned, I'd inherited a quirky place of lodging from our long-lost paternal aunt, and was having something of a Jimmy Buffet-inspired romp in the Sunshine State, complete with fruity drinks sporting umbrellas and midlife muumuus.

My brother even teased me about buying a golf cart.

Nothing could be further from reality here in Cypress Grove. In my short time here, I'd solved two murders, made a bunch of wonderful new friends, and found myself unexpectedly drawn to a handsome and charming history professor who also happened to be a paranormal researcher. His name was Oliver Everhart, and even the mere mention of his name made several of my internal organs flutter in the most delicious way.

After my divorce, I'd hung out with a few men casually, but no one grabbed my heart or imagination. Dating after forty was like trying to find the least damaged thing at the thrift store that didn't smell weird.

Because I knew how rare Oliver was (he smelled amazing), I was trying to take that relationship slower than a manatee swimming through a dense patch of seagrass. He seemed to feel the same, which was just peachy with me.

And, if all that wasn't enough, there was my newfound power: I had the gift of psychometry, which meant I could touch objects and glean emotion, information, even facts.

I was like a human DVR, in a way.

Quite shocking for a slightly introverted, divorced mom of a college student, a woman who had always considered herself another face in the crowd. I was still getting used to it, honestly, and was learning to tune out unwanted visions and details.

I'd also been asked to join a coven, a fact that made me sound far cooler and more interesting than I actually was. Today I was meeting the coven leader — was that what they're called? I wasn't sure — to discuss membership requirements. This was why I was carefully choosing my jewelry and outfit. Part of me was a little worried I wouldn't look the part.

What did people in covens wear, anyway? It seemed so cliché to wear black, so I refrained.

The ring was so sparkly that it practically winked at me in the sunshine. When I slipped it on, I immediately felt a little surge of power.

The ring hugged my finger snugly, its weight a familiar comfort. I checked my reflection one last time, making sure my appearance matched the seriousness of the day's appointment. Today I wore a professional yet relaxed hunter green dress, with short sleeves and a flattering V-neck. I topped it off with a long, gauzy ecru-colored scarf.

While I'd dressed preppy in California, now I embraced my inner Stevie Nicks.

But the crowning achievement of the outfit were the shoes: a riotous mix of green leather and velvet floral print, with brogue details, lacy trim, a low heel, and excellent arch support. I'd spent way too much on them, but they were both comfortable *and* conversation pieces.

I felt a thousand times hipper than I really was when I wore them. Which is why I only pulled them out for special occasions, when I needed a confidence boost.

Like today.

I paused to say goodbye to Freddie. He'd now parked himself near the window and was soaking up all the sun's rays as they peeked through drapes. As I scratched his formidable orange belly, he let out a *mrrrrap.*

"Be good," I murmured to him. He swatted at me with his paw when I stopped scratching, barely missing the back of my hand with his razor-sharp mittens.

I stepped out into the cool January air, happy to find the temperature was practically perfect. I'd had a hot flash this morning while getting ready that had left me drenched in sweat and near breathless. Florida's winter breeze washed over me and cooled my skin.

I cast a glance at the Crescent Moon Inn and wrinkled my nose. I'd done a few cosmetic renovations inside, but the exterior was sorely in need of a paint job. The earliest I could schedule anything was for March, two months away.

My new friend Liz's voice echoed in my mind: *You can't do everything all at once, Amelia. First things first.*

It was a quick drive to Cypress Grove's historic downtown. Normally I'd walk the six blocks from the inn, but it was a tad warm today and I didn't want to show up sweaty and disheveled.

Even the fact that I didn't get a parking spot on Main Street couldn't dampen my excited mood. I pulled into the city lot near the police station and power-walked to the meeting point.

The town's quaint charm boosted my mood even more. I'd come to learn that it was a perfectly preserved example of "old Florida," meaning Key West-style wooden homes, Spanish-revival municipal buildings, and brick storefronts along Main Street. The place was charming as all heck, and Cypress Grove wore its uniqueness like a badge of honor.

From a handful of unusual roadside attractions to the offbeat, New Age characters strolling the streets, this town whispered secrets and spun tales of its own. I adored everything about it.

With every step toward Haunted Hearth — a local cafe known for its chicken salad that could rival ambrosia — I felt a surge of both excitement and apprehension. And not only for the Hearth's food, which was always a treat.

I'd been invited here almost three months ago by Julia Torricelli, the leader of one of the main covens in town. The group, named the Sisters of Hecate, catered to witches and witch-adjacent women of Generation X.

Julia wanted to discuss my coven membership. This invite had baffled me since Julia had asked me to lunch. Although I had newfound psychic powers, I didn't consider myself a witch, just someone with particularly sharp extra-sensory perception.

Having a group of witchy friends, though, was appealing, so I figured I'd hear Julia out. I'd come to adore most everyone I'd met in town and was eager to meet more.

The bell above the café door chimed a happy greeting as I stepped into Haunted Hearth. It was packed, and the aroma of roasted garlic and fresh bread instantly made my mouth water. I was glad Julia had chosen this place. Not only was it my favorite casual eatery, but it was somewhere I felt extremely comfortable.

Important for lunch with a coven leader.

I spotted Julia. She sat at a corner table, her demeanor exuding a sense of absolute and total control. Everything about her looked expensive and refined.

I'd only met her once, during an Agatha Christie-style dramatic reveal of a murderer. But from that brief encounter, I gathered that she was a woman who got stuff done. I admired that, since I tended to be a bit more scattered and impulsive. At least it seemed that way since starting perimenopause; in the past year I'd felt like I was pinging around like a pinball in a machine.

"Amelia, so glad you could make it," Julia greeted me with a smile. She appeared professional, as if we were here for a job interview. I guess we kind of were. Her eyes fell to my feet. "Great shoes."

"Thanks. Wouldn't miss this for the world," I smiled as I sat across from her, trying to match her nonchalant tone while my curiosity percolated beneath the surface. "Plus, I never pass up a chance to have the chicken salad here."

"Me neither." She smiled.

A basket sat between us on the table, a few inches from the salt, pepper, ketchup, and hot sauce bottles. Actually, it wasn't a basket, not exactly. It was an oval rattan handbag, approximately the size of a football. Unusual, elegant, and not at all in style. Yet I recognized what it was immediately.

"Wow, I haven't seen one of those Nantucket lightship baskets in years," I said, recalling the time my ex-husband and I took our then-five-year-old daughter to the island off the coast of New England. It had been one of our best trips together, prior to my ex's affairs, and I remembered ogling the expensive, handmade baskets in several shops. I'd settled, and splurged, on a woven bracelet for twenty-five bucks that my ex had insisted was made in China.

My daughter colored it with a hot pink permanent marker two days later.

"Those handbags are quite rare, especially here in the South. I've always wanted a purse like that." I leaned in to get a better look at the impressive treasure.

This particular basket looked vintage. The cherrywood-hued rattan was in excellent shape, practically shining in the soft light of the café. You could tell that it was handmade, well-crafted, and wildly expensive.

It matched with Julia's understated luxury vibe — today she wore an elegant, stretchy gray dress that complimented her silver hair, a strand of silver pearls, and scarlet red lipstick. She seemed to be the kind of midlife woman who could both afford Eileen Fisher and wear it without looking like she'd rolled out of bed in her jammies.

The handle was a smooth wood, probably rosewood, oak, or walnut (I'd read a lot about the baskets during my mini obsession with them following my trip to the island).

Like many of the baskets, it had a lid. Usually, they had a wooden decorative inlay on the top, and this one did — but it also appeared to have a detailed and delicate ivory design inlaid into the wood. Possibly scrimshaw even, if it was truly vintage.

"This, my dear, isn't a purse. It's your basket of clues."

Two

Julia rotated the basket, and that's when I saw the clasp that held the entire thing shut.

It, too, appeared to be scrimshaw. At first glance, it looked like a bony finger. *Hunh*. I'd never seen one like that. Weird.

I pointed. "Is that a real—"

"Bone?" Julia smiled. "No. We've had it tested. It's scrimshaw."

I let out a breath and my shoulders inched away from my ears.

"But let's not focus on this right now," she said, sweeping the thing off the table and into a sturdy canvas bag that sat on a chair to her right. She clapped her hands together. "Let's get to know each other and have some lunch, yes? We've got a lot of ground to cover, Amelia."

She went on to explain that another woman would be joining us.

"Renee Zinn is the co-leader of the coven. She's running a bit late because of work. That poor woman, she's always so busy." Julia paused to take a sip from the glass of ice water in front of her. "She teaches piano, she's in the town band, she leads online workshops about astral projection, and does gig work delivering food. I don't know when she sleeps."

It always surprised me to hear things like this about people in town. They had the most extraordinary powers, and yet their day jobs were so mundane. I smiled.

A server came over, and Julia ordered for herself and Renee. Of course, I got the chicken salad croissant, the café's specialty. When tall glasses of sweet tea arrived, Julia and I chatted about what we'd done over the holidays, the weather, and the new bookstore in town. Normal stuff, like any midlife ladies during lunch.

Julia was telling me about the bookstore's owner, a man known for his Reiki ability, when a flustered-looking woman with wild and wavy salt-and-pepper hair approached.

"I'm so sorry, oh my gosh. That last food delivery was something. The customer wanted this certain brand of olives and I couldn't find them, then I had to haul everything all the way to her back door, through her garden. She had a giant tortoise." She shook her head and plopped down at the empty chair to my right. "Hi. I'm Renee Zinn. Apologies."

"I'm Amelia Matthews." We shook hands. Her skin was warm and her touch firm, and something about her friendly energy made me instantly like her. "I want to know more about that tortoise."

Julia and Renee laughed.

"I ordered you the usual," Julia said to Renee, as the server set a third tea on our table.

"Yay. I'm starving."

Renee blew out an exhale and her shoulders relaxed. She turned her attention back to me. "A tortoise in Cypress Grove, can you imagine? Only here, I swear. It was one of those big ones. The thing's probably a hundred years old." She brushed back a strand of hair, revealing an earring that looked like a tiny, silver moon.

Our food came quickly, and while eating, we theorized about the tortoise, laughing and swapping obscure facts about the giant creatures. It was the kind of strange yet endearing conversation I'd found myself in dozens of times here in Cypress Grove. Even without the coven membership, I was grateful to be sitting with two women my age who seemed like they could be future friends.

Conversation turned to Freddie, my cat, with Julia calling him an "old soul." She'd met my feline exactly once, and I sensed they shared a bond that I didn't quite comprehend yet.

Renee had ordered a delicious-looking brie and cranberry sandwich, and even cut off a slice for me to sample.

"The food here is incredible," I said between mouthfuls. "And the new hand cut potato chips are something else."

After we finished, we lingered over coffee, the conversation naturally drifted towards the reason we were all here. Renee, between sips, broached the subject that had been flitting around my mind since I woke up this morning.

"So, Amelia, about the coven. Julia tells me you're quite the sleuth. And with your skills, I think you might be just the person for our group, and for one particular mystery."

"Before we allow anyone into the coven, we ask them to complete a task," Julia explained. "We try to match the task with the person's ability, and since your powers appear to be quite strong, we're throwing you into the deep end, so to speak. Of course, that is, if you want to join the group."

"Have you given her the rundown?" Renee asked Julia. "The nuts and bolts?"

"Oh! No. Hold on. We should start there. I'm getting ahead of myself." Julia flashed an apologetic smile and twisted in her seat, extracting a brochure from her bag. "Here's a bit about us."

I wanted to giggle, but didn't, for fear it would come off as rude. But the fact that the coven had a brochure struck me as funny. I accepted the folded, glossy paper and studied it.

It was like something you'd expect from a high-end spa or an exclusive club, not a witch coven. The front cover featured an abstract design, a swirl of deep purples and midnight blues that seemed to move if you stared long enough, with the name "Sisters of Hecate" elegantly written in script.

Opening it, I spotted a headline: "Embrace Your Inner Enchantress in the Company of Kindred Spirits." There was an introduction that read more like a manifesto, calling to the women born between 1965 and 1980 who felt the pull of the mystical and the magical in their everyday lives. It spoke of empowerment, sisterhood, and the exploration of the meta-physical, all wrapped in the comforting nostalgia of our shared Gen X culture.

"Totally rad, but in a modern way," it read.

I was all in from the first paragraph.

The brochure outlined the group's goals: to create a supportive community where members could explore their psychic and magical interests, to foster personal growth and self-discovery, and to engage in philanthropic efforts with a metaphysical twist. I nodded as I read, excited I'd been asked to join.

It seemed like a sorority, but without the binge drinking, hazing, or cattiness. I'd never been in one of those in college because those groups never spoke to me. This one did, however.

There were regular meetings that included workshops on various subjects, guided meditations, yoga, and opportunities for socializing and networking. Nice.

One section, titled "Magical Mentorship," caught my eye. It detailed a program where newer members could learn from more experienced witches. I certainly needed that, since I felt as though I was bumbling along with my new powers.

The brochure also highlighted community projects the Sisters of Hecate were involved in, such as a local garden they maintained using permaculture principles infused with a touch of earth magic, and a volunteer program at the community center where they offered free psychic readings and healing sessions once a month.

"Wow," I murmured as I read, glancing up at Julia. "You all do a lot."

"We're an active coven, but we're not one of the bigger ones in town," Julia said. "We are open to all in our age range, regardless of ability. We offer mentorships for those who are learning their powers."

"Yeah, the Boomers and the millennials." Renee sighed, then shook her head. "Those groups are far larger, and kind of unwieldy."

I wasn't sure what that meant and figured I'd find out in time. I read on, unable to contain the smile from spreading on my face.

Tucked towards the back was a calendar of events. Full moon gatherings, seasonal celebrations that honored the pagan wheel of the year, and special events for solar and lunar eclipses. Each event was described in a way that made it sound both deeply spiritual and casually fun, like an otherworldly cocktail party.

If I joined this coven, I'd never be at a loss for things to do. I briefly flashed back to how lonely I'd been in California.

"Ooh, goat yoga happy hour, I like the sound of that," I said.

"The baby goats are the cutest," squealed Renee.

These were absolutely my people.

The final page was a heartfelt invitation to join their ranks, to add one's own energy thread to the tapestry of their collective power. It was signed, "In Solidarity, The Sisters of Hecate."

I looked up from the brochure, my mind swirling with possibilities. The idea of being part of something so welcoming and empowering was both thrilling and a little daunting.

"This is incredible," I said, meeting Julia's gaze. "It's like the metaphysical Junior League. I had no idea covens could be so...organized. So fun."

Julia chuckled, a warm, vibrant sound. "Well, we like to think of ourselves as a modern coven for women dealing with the challenges and opportunities of midlife. A support network. We're a little bit of everything, Amelia. Tradition meets innovation. And we'd love for you to be a part of it. Some of our latest projects include a medical fund for under-insured members, and we're forming a pickleball team this year."

"You can keep that," Renee said, pointing to the brochure.

I thanked her and slipped it into my tote. "I would very much like to join. It seems right up my alley. My new alley." I laughed. "I never imagined I'd be, well, doing all this."

Renee nodded. "The powers, they come at midlife for many of us. It's often a surprise, especially on top of peri-menopause."

I took a sip of my iced tea, curiosity piqued. Maybe this group could explain why I hadn't experienced any of my abilities in California. "I'm all ears. What's the project you'd like me to work on?"

I hoped it was something to do with baking. I'd knock their socks off with one of my cookie recipes. Maybe they want me to organize a fundraiser. Back in California, I was the go-to woman for bake sales at my daughter's school.

Julia leaned in, her voice dropping to a whisper. "It's about Marigold Wentworth. You've heard of her, haven't you?"

I tilted my head. "That name sounds familiar. Wait. Perimenopause brain. Why? Oh! I know. There's a park named after her here in town. I still haven't memorized all the names of the parks, there's so many."

Both Julia and Renee nodded. "The one where the bridesmaid was murdered recently. That's why we think this is perfect for you," Julia said.

I winced. "Yeah, that was a pretty sticky situation. My first guests at the inn, and someone dies during the haunted swamp walk. Can you imagine?"

"That was bad luck." Renee shook her head. "It didn't seem to hurt your business any, did it?"

I shook my head. "Strangely, no. We were swamped over Christmas and New Year's, and honestly, this is the first week since then that I haven't had any guests. We do have a couple that's coming this weekend, though. They'll be here tomorrow."

"Well, that's wonderful," Renee said. "The Crescent Moon building is one of the most beautiful in town. I'm glad you were able to save it. We all worried when Shirley passed. You know how those developers can be."

I was about to launch into my laundry list of planned renovations when Julia cleared her throat and her expression turned serious. "Marigold Wentworth's case has troubled us for years. She would have been our coven's first leader, if she hadn't vanished."

Three

I leaned in, now even more invested. "Tell me all about it. I'd love to help with whatever you need."

Renee picked up where Julia left off, her tone dripping with sadness. "Marigold was an incredibly promising witch. She grew up here in Cypress Grove, and in 1993, was in the midst of forming this very coven for Gen X women and girls. Then one day, she vanished. Like, poof. The whole town looked for her, and everyone was devastated. She's never been seen since."

"Were you two here then?"

Renee and Julia shook their heads. "Sadly, no," Julia said. "I was in Michigan in college at that time, and Renee was in Vermont. I didn't even know I had powers back in 1993. That's what was so remarkable about Marigold. She knew from an early age, unlike many of us who come into our abilities at midlife."

I felt a chill run through my body. This wasn't just any puzzle. It was a deep dive into the coven's history.

"What about the police? Surely, they investigated."

Julia curled her lip and snorted. "The police back then, well, they weren't as thorough as they are now. Or as accommodating to witches. They treated Marigold's case as if she were an adult who simply decided to skip town. But everyone we've talked to who was here back then said Marigold wouldn't have up and left, especially not in the middle of founding the coven. She was only twenty-three."

I knew nothing about this poor young woman, but this definitely seemed odd. Had she really vanished without a trace? Or was something more sinister involved?

Renee added, "Here are some other details that tell us she didn't intend to leave. One, she was in college. Two, she had many friends, including a co-founder of the coven. And three, she left her dog behind. She was an animal lover, so that last one always seemed super hinky."

I sucked in a breath. "I can imagine."

"There aren't many people left in town who were around when she was here. Florida's so transient, you know..." Julia said apologetically, her words trailing off as she stared into her mug. "And her poor parents, they moved a year or so after her disappearance. All the way to Australia."

Wow. This sounded like a tough mystery to crack. It felt monumental, honestly, and I didn't know where, or how, to even begin. "And you think I might be able to help? I've been in Cypress Grove for all of five minutes."

"Yes, Amelia, we absolutely think you can help," Julia's gaze was steely. "Your gift of psychometry is powerful. More than you might realize. We've all tried, in our own ways, to uncover the truth about Marigold, but we've never had someone with your particular talent."

"Yeah, even my astral projection abilities didn't yield much," Renee said.

Julia reached into the canvas bag and pulled out the woven basket purse.

"This," she said, placing it gently on the table, "holds some of Marigold's things. The basket was her grandmother's, we were told, a woman on Nantucket decades ago who was a witch. Julia really identified with her, so she cherished this. When she vanished, her friend, who was another witch and the co-founder of the coven, kept it as something of a talisman for the group. The few others who knew her have kept her memory alive over the decades, but eventually they too moved away or have passed."

"Where is that friend and co-founder of the coven now?" I blinked in confusion.

"Tracy? She passed two years after Marigold, in a car crash on I-4," Julia said quietly, tears forming. She reached for a fresh napkin and dabbed at the corner of one eye. "Even just talking about it makes me emotional. You see, Tracy carried on Marigold's legacy and was technically the coven's first leader. There were other early founders as well, but none are around now."

"Such a terrible shame what happened to them both," Renee said bitterly. "You can find Tracy's gravestone in the Enchanted Eternity cemetery. She's in the recipe wing — Tracy was a culinary student when she passed into the next realm. Excellent cookie recipe on her headstone, by the way. You'll appreciate it. Her name was Tracy North. Definitely check that out."

Wave after wave of awareness flowed through me. Inexplicably, I felt deeply connected to Marigold and Tracy. So much tragedy in this story, and I could almost feel the pain emanating from Julia and Renee. Could I shed light into this darkness?

"We've kept Marigold's things safe, hoping one day we'd find someone who could use them to uncover the truth,"

Renee said, running her hand over the basket. "We think that's you."

I nodded slowly. "All right. I'll do it."

Julia wagged a perfectly manicured finger. "But only if you're comfortable with it. This is a lot to ask, especially for someone new to their powers and to our community. Your coven membership isn't dependent on this, by the way. We do ask prospective members to solve a puzzle, but you can choose another if you'd like."

"Duck no," I said. "I'm in."

The two women stared at me blankly.

"Uh, *duck*, as in, phone autocorrect to the F word. It's my personal joke. Sorry," I winced, embarrassed, but then the two women dissolved into laughter and I happily joined in.

After a few more instructions about when and where to open the basket of clues, Julia and Renee handed me the tote bag and hugged me goodbye.

"I'll get on this right away," I said, already planning in my mind how I'd return to the inn this afternoon and dive into the contents of the basket.

"About that." Renee waved her arm, which held at least a dozen silver bangle bracelets. "We're not trying to rush you or anything, but..."

Julia leaned in, her voice dropping an octave. "The founding anniversary of the coven is coming up in a week. If you could find new clues or even solve it before then, it would be incredible. The membership would be so grateful. There are about a hundred of us, and we're planning a big cookout."

A week? Yikes. Clearly these two women had more faith in my ability than I did. "I'll see what I can do."

We all walked out together. On Main Street, the two women went left toward the town parking garage, and I went right — right into the Astral Attic, the new age shop owned by my friend, Liz Lopez.

She gave a little whoop of joy when she saw me, and practically skipped to fold me into a hug. I beamed as I hugged her, feeling grateful that I was surrounded by such awesome women my age. Liz's wild, curly hair nearly enveloped me, as did her signature lavender and vanilla scent.

"Girl, I was just thinking about you and your lunch with Julia. How did it go?" Liz was already a member of the Sisters of Hecate. We hadn't talked about my prospective membership much, mostly because she wanted me to decide about joining on my own. I also suspected there were some secrets that she couldn't share with non-members, and I hadn't pried.

I let out a long breath. "Well, ah. Wow. It was pretty wild."

"This needs some tea. Go sit in the command center."

That was Liz's nickname for her cozy sitting area. She'd recently added a sapphire blue velvet settee that matched the overstuffed pillows. The nook was a haven in the store, surrounded by books and an enormous agate crystal that sat on a pedestal and sparkled with the light of a thousand diamond rings.

"Oh, hang on." Liz swept past me and scooped what looked like headphones off a pillow. "Did I show you these?"

She waved the little device in the air. I shook my head.

"It's my neck fan. Perfect for hot flashes."

"Ooh. Nice. I need one of those."

"I'll send you the link," she called out as she walked toward her tea station.

I settled into my seat and thumbed through a copy of today's newspaper. There were the usual stories about the city council and the school board, and about an upcoming bake sale to benefit the town library. They needed donations for the sale, and I jotted a note on my phone, vowing to make some cookies.

An ad for "Happy Zappy Hour" aura cleansing looked interesting, too.

Liz bustled over with two mugs of tea and handed me one. "Marisol gave me this recipe."

I set the newspaper down and lifted the steaming mug to my face. Inhaling deeply, I smiled. Marisol was another friend in town, a woman who was much older and considered one of the world's most pre-eminent tea witches. "Lemon balm? Is that what I smell?"

"This is her Clarity of Sight tea."

As she listed the ingredients, my eyes widened. "Whoa. That's oddly serendipitous."

"Really?" She sank onto the settee, kicked off her Birkenstocks, and tucked her feet under her. "Why?"

I told her about the lunch and gestured to the tote bag containing the basket. "The clues are in there. I'd show you, but Julia gave me strict instructions that when I first open the basket, to do it alone, and with intention. I'm pretty keyed up now, so I'm hoping to do it this evening when I'm by myself, and calmer."

Now it was Liz's turn to be wide-eyed. "She's given you Marigold's case?"

I nodded gravely.

Liz sank back into the cushion with an exhale. "Wow. This is serious."

"I'm gathering that."

We sipped our tea in silence for a beat.

"I'm going to have a ton of questions for you, but Julia suggested I not talk to anyone in detail about the case until I've had a chance to look through the basket."

Liz nodded. "I don't know a lot beyond what I've heard around the coven, and what I remember from the local paper back in the day, but I'll help any way I can. We'll chat after you've absorbed all the clues."

Another long pause between us.

"I'm scared," I finally said.

"Of what?"

I shook my head slowly. "Not solving this. When Julia and Renee told me about Marigold, I felt this pull. Like a need to find out what happened."

A little smile formed on Liz's face. "That's an excellent sign. Oooh, I'm excited. If you can solve this, everyone in the coven will be ecstatic. It's bothered us that we haven't been able to figure it out, and the unsolved mystery has cast a shadow of sorts over the group. The other covens in town whisper about it and some of the nastier folks say our powers are shallow because we can't solve the mystery of our own leader."

I leaned in. This made me want to get to the bottom of it even more.

"But," Liz said, her voice turning businesslike, "I'll shut up now and we can talk about it more after you've looked through the clues. Let's change the subject. What have you got going on this weekend? Anything exciting?"

"Well, I also came by to talk to you about this very topic, because I'd like you to join me." I grinned. Since Liz had lived in town since birth, she was usually the one introducing me to new things. "Oliver is playing a show at The Cauldron on Saturday. His first in a long time."

"What? Really? I haven't heard about it." Liz was like a clearinghouse for gossip and events in town.

"It's kind of a stealth thing at the moment. You know how he used to be in a band, right?" Liz was about five years older than Oliver, but both were born and raised in Cypress Grove.

She squinted. "That rings a bell. That was years ago, right?" Then she laughed. "By years, I mean, decades."

"Yes. And he used to play with this one hard rock band in the early '90s. They were called Stardust Riot. Apparently, they were like Motley Crüe. Oliver ended up going to grad school, but the band got big. They're returning and doing a secret show and Oliver's going to join them for one night. They're doing one set of cover songs, and another of original music from their first album."

It was impossible to hide the excitement in my voice.

"No way, I've heard of them. They're kinda spicy, and if I recall, the drummer's from Orlando and he's still kinda hot even though he's like sixty. In a classy way, like Jon Bon Jovi."

"Mmm. AARP-era Jon Bon Jovi. Now *there's* a silver fox." Liz and I dissolved into cackles. Sometimes being around her made me feel like a teenager again.

"Stardust Riot's on a reunion tour. They apparently broke up for a while because a couple of the members went to rehab. But Oliver's so excited about playing some of the old songs and a few covers on stage. It's so cute how he's nervous. It's all he's been talking about." I paused to sip my tea. "Do you want to go?"

"Absolutely. I wouldn't miss 80s hair band music for the world. Maybe Wolfie will want to go. Unless you're organizing a girls only night."

That was her nickname for Chief Christopher Wolf. He was new in town, and a big, handsome, by-the-book cop. He was also hopelessly in love with Liz.

"Of course he can come," I said, while wondering if the chief even liked music. He was such an outdoorsy kind of guy.

She wrinkled her nose. "But, how late will it go? I need to be in bed by eleven."

Liz was on a sleep diet, where she attempted to get eight

hours a night, no matter what. She was convinced that it might help her perimenopause symptoms.

"Here's the good news: they're only doing two, forty-five minute sets. It starts at eight and should be finished by no later than ten or ten thirty. On Sunday, the drummer has to prep for his colonoscopy."

Liz's eyes widened. "Whoa. That's hardcore. Playing a rock show and having a colonoscopy in the same week? Dang."

We chatted for a bit about colonoscopy prep, then about her last date with Wolfie, and then her brief, failed experiment as a band groupie in her twenties (she got food poisoning during her first concert and that ended the adventure). We finished our tea. I set the cup on a small table and stretched.

"I guess I'd better get going. I feel a little antsy because I want to open this basket of clues."

"I can imagine. You're going to knock this out of the park. I can tell."

My eyebrows shot up as I stood. "You seem to have more confidence in my abilities than I do."

"And that, my friend, is why the coven asks everyone to solve a mystery or puzzle before membership."

"What? Why?"

"To show everyone what they're inherently capable of." Liz winked.

Four

I didn't go straight home. Instead, I stopped at the Enchanted Eternity Park, the town's cemetery.

As one did, when looking for answers in Cypress Grove. Today, I was searching for Tracy North, and hoped her headstone would yield a clue or two to Marigold's case.

The Enchanted Eternity Park was an oasis of calm, a stark contrast to downtown. As I stepped through the wrought iron gates, the chatter of the town fell away, replaced by a hush only occasionally interrupted by the distant call of a bird or the gentle rustle of leaves.

Since this was a draw for tourists because it was such an unusual cemetery, the town had recently installed a visitor's center. It was a small, white clapboard booth near the entrance. I parked and walked over, looking for Phuong Le. She was a graduate student at a local college studying gastronomy who'd been hired to work the center part time.

Thankfully, she was here today, and her brown eyes lit up when she saw me since I was a regular here.

"Hey, Amelia, how's it going?"

"Not bad, not bad. Gorgeous day, isn't it?"

"This is why people move to Florida, for this kind of weather. Not what we get in August." She made a face. "You looking for a recipe?"

This was the real reason why tourists flocked to this grave-yard: the recipes. There was an entire wing filled with hundreds of gravestones. All of the dearly departed in that section had arranged to engrave recipes in the marble. The place was a huge draw for all sorts of folks, from home cooks to celebrity chefs to curious onlookers.

Liz had taken me here on my first day in town, probably correctly surmising that a woman who used to own a cookie delivery business would enjoy the dishes created by the dearly departed. I quickly learned that the culinary instructions on the headstones were something of a town competition — while alive, people pondered for years about what to engrave on the granite.

"Yes," I smiled at Phuong. "I'm here for a recipe."

Phuong pulled a large, black binder from under her desk. "Sweet or savory?"

I shook my head. Usually, I came here and searched by course, not by name. "Pretty sure it's sweet. But today I'm looking for a person: Tracy North."

"Okay, let's see here..." she flipped to a section in the middle of the book. "North... North... ah! Here we go. Okay, she's in the wing close to the woods, at the southwest perime-ter. Here, let me show you on the map because it gets kind of tricky back there."

She tore off a page from a pad of pre-printed maps and grabbed a blue highlighter, then used to mark how I could either walk or drive. "It's about a ten-minute walk, I'd say. That particular section is near a massive oak tree here," she circled a spot on the map, "and the town founder's crypt here. But you can take this."

"I think you've given me a dozen of these. Thanks."

I took the map and we said goodbye — but not before I promised to bring her whatever I ended up baking.

I set out on the path, my shoes crunching softly against the shell gravel.

The air here always felt a touch cooler than the rest of town. It was either because of the dense canopy of ancient oak trees or it was some kind of weather magic — a possibility that I didn't dare discount. The Spanish moss that draped from the oaks' sprawling limbs hung like delicate, ethereal curtains, swaying slightly in the soft breeze.

The paths that wound through the cemetery were lined with weathered tombstones and elaborate mausoleums. It was one of the most peaceful places I'd ever been, and the fact that I could visit it anytime for a mental cleanse was a blessing.

Following Phuong's map, I strolled through the cemetery. The further I ventured, the more the traffic noise from the main road faded from earshot. I found the giant oak she'd mentioned, and realized I hadn't been in this part before.

The tree's branches stretched out like open arms, as if welcoming me.

Tracy North's grave was the closest headstone to the tree. It was modest compared to some of the more grandiose monuments. The dark gray granite gleamed in the afternoon sun, the little flecks in the stone sparkling like crystals.

Tracy North
Beloved Daughter, Baker, and Witch
May 12, 1971 - September 23, 1995

In life, she mixed sweetness with spice,
A dash of laughter in every memory.
Here lies the recipe of her legacy:
Love, seasoned with a pinch of truth.

My heart felt like it surged into my throat as I read the inscription. Something about Tracy's death, so soon after Marigold's, made my entire mission that much more meaningful.

I moved around to the back of the headstone. That was where most of the recipes were, although a few folks had separate granite stones dedicated for that purpose. Usually, those sat nearby, as if the deceased wanted to gaze lovingly upon their final recipe for eternity.

"Whoa," I murmured aloud when I saw Tracy's recipe. My voice was swallowed by the silence, but I read the title aloud anyway.

"*Chocolate Dipped Candied Pecan Orange Shortbread Cookies.* Well, yum."

I scanned the ingredients, which were simple. The cookies sounded so delicious that for a couple of seconds I almost forgot I was here to search for clues about a long-vanished woman. I was too busy imagining myself rolling out dough and cutting the cookies into perfect rounds.

I pulled my phone out so I could take a picture of the recipe. It would be perfect for that library bake sale I saw in the newspaper.

"Okay, now focus," I whispered to myself once I'd gotten a clear photo. Sometimes the carvings were difficult to read, which is why one of Phuong's projects was to launch tombstone rubbing classes for the older, faded recipes.

We both shared a worry that the recipes would be eventually lost to the elements and time.

After slipping the phone back into my bag, I walked around the headstone a few more times, trying to absorb it all. What was I missing? I read every word on the front and back twice more. I ran my hand over the top of the cool stone, then the grooves where Tracy's name had been carved.

I closed my eyes, trying to harness the power of my psychometry. Nothing.

Raking in a deep breath, I leaned over and traced the words of the poem, attempting to still my mind. Sometimes, I'd discovered, the psychometric visions were faint or jumbled if my mind wasn't clear, or if the external world around me was in chaos.

But I was standing in the optimal condition for a vision here in the serene cemetery, and I didn't feel as much as a tingle in my pinky. My eyelids snapped open and I softly huffed with frustration.

I moved to the back, to the recipe, and did the same, closing my eyes and skimming my fingers over the smooth stone. A tingle bloomed.

Okay, here we go...

The world around me fell away. I was in a garage. No, a workshop. It was dusty, as if chalk was in the air, and my nose tickled. I held back a sneeze. What was this place? The form of a hunched-over man came into view, and a knot formed in my stomach. I crept closer toward the man, who was focused on something sitting on a table. A sound similar to a woodpecker filled my ears.

Tap-tap-tap-tap-tap.

In the vision, I shifted to get a better look.

Oh. It was the granite carver's workshop, and he was engraving the recipe on the stone with a metal tool. This had nothing to do with my mystery. Ugh. Not the clue I'd hoped for.

I opened my eyes, even more disappointed than before. Sometimes this happened with my visions. I'd see, feel, or hear mundane, everyday things from objects. Once I touched a figurine in my aunt's house and had a vision of it sitting on the shelf at K-Mart.

Another time at a historical society open house, I was handed a quill pen that had been used by a well-known witch decades ago. I'd hoped to soak up the vibe and feel what it was like when the witch used it to write her memoirs.

I had a vision of the pen being kicked under a chair and hitting a dust bunny.

Talk about anticlimactic. Not all metaphysical revelations were interesting, I'd come to find out.

I continued to touch, pat, and inspect the grave. "Nothing," I muttered.

At times like this, a little twinge of panic hit me. What if my psychometry had dried up like a cake left too long in the oven? While I'd initially been skeptical, then a little afraid, of the psychometry, I now welcomed it.

The soft jangle of my cell startled me, a mechanical chirp cutting through all this hushed nature. I dug the phone out of my purse, wondering if it was my daughter at college — or if there was an issue at the inn. My one employee, a man named Jimbo, was supposed to be there this afternoon.

It was neither. The name that flashed on the screen made me grin.

OLIVER

"Hello," I purred.

"Hello yourself." His voice, warm and rich, sent a jolt of both desire and happiness through me.

"How's it going today?"

I hummed while squatting all the way down. I leaned back

against the cool granite of Tracy's headstone, the soft grass cushioning my butt.

"Would you be surprised if I said that a lot of really wild things have happened this afternoon?"

"In Cypress Grove? No way," he laughed.

"I'm at the cemetery."

"In search of answers from the beyond? Or recipes?" His tone was playful, but I could hear the unmistakable curiosity, too. That's what I adored most about Oliver — he was genuinely curious about the world around him. Okay, that and his dreamy, dark eyes. And his muscular arms.

"A little of both, to be honest."

"Oh yeah? Hang on, I want to hear all about it. Let me close my office door. I'm at school." Oliver taught history at a nearby university, and that's where he spent many long days. I heard the sound of shuffling, footsteps, and the snick of a door shutting. "Okay, I'm back. What was so unusual about today?"

"Well, I'm sitting against a headstone right now. How does Chocolate Dipped Candied Pecan Orange Shortbread Cookies sound?"

"I can be at your place in two hours. That's how it sounds."

I could feel my cheeks flare with heat.

"But I'm guessing you're really there for something else. Was it related to the lunch with Julia?"

Amazing. I'd mentioned that lunch exactly twice. Once a couple of months ago, and once last week. "It is absolutely related to that. So get this..."

I launched into a recap of the meeting, the Marigold mystery, and the basket of clues that I had yet to open.

"I was on my way home and thought I'd stop here to begin my sleuthing. But now I want cookies, and I think I'm out of pecans. And the grave hasn't given me any clues."

"Hmmm." I heard the creak of Oliver's office chair in the background. "Marigold Wentworth. Interesting case."

"You were here when it happened, right?"

"Sort of. I was living at my folks' house and going to school, but back then I was in the band and touring a lot around Florida so I was gone a lot. Let's just say those were my wilder days and I wasn't, ah, paying close attention to news events."

I bit my lip, thinking of a young Oliver in his rockstar days.

"Can I help with research?" he asked.

"Only if I can pay you in cookies."

"Deal."

"Here's the thing. I'm trying to piece together clues, and something about Tracy's death, so close to Marigold's disappearance, feels significant. I can't explain why, though."

There was a pause, and I could almost hear the gears turning in Oliver's mind. "Interesting. You think there's a connection between the two?"

"Maybe. It's just a hunch right now, but I'm digging deeper."

"I have no doubt you'll crack it. You've got an excellent track record for unraveling Cypress Grove's mysteries."

Just then, a boom of thunder rolled overhead, and I yelped.

"Is it raining there?" Oliver asked. His office was in Orlando, about thirty miles away, with terrible traffic between here and there.

"No. Well, not yet. It was sunny and clear but then this thundercloud appeared out of nowhere." I eyed the sky. "I'd better start walking back to my car, because the sky's about to get pretty dark."

"Yeah, don't get struck by lightning. Florida is the lightning capital of the world, you know."

"So you've reminded me many times." I hoisted myself to

my feet, took one last glance at the gravesite, and started walking. "I'm headed home now. Can't wait to look in the basket. I wish we could do it together, but Julia gave me specific instructions that I should be alone when I first absorb the energy of the clues."

"Definitely listen to Julia," he said.

A fat raindrop fell on my cheek, and I picked up my pace. "Anyway, enough about me. How's everything with you? All ready for your big show this weekend?"

He laughed. "I've been practicing. Haven't played any of those old glam rock songs in years. I've got one special tune." His voice lowered to a husky rasp that sent tingles — and not the psychometric kind — through me. "Thought I might sing it for a certain innkeeper."

"Well, that innkeeper will be quite honored. Which might result in me baking a pie for you."

Or more. Oliver and I had met a few short months ago. I had only been divorced a couple of years, and he'd gotten out of a relationship at about the same time. Usually, I felt the sweet pace of our relationship was perfect, but other times, I wanted to climb the man like a tree.

"Sounds like a perfect exchange. Music for food. But, Amelia?" His tone shifted, a hint of seriousness mingling with our flirtation. "I'd love to see you tonight for those cookies, but unfortunately, I forgot I have a department meeting. And it sounds like you have a date with a basket of clues."

Oliver and I hadn't seen each other much since the holidays, but his news that we wouldn't hang out until the weekend was only a little disappointing, given the mystery at hand.

"We'll catch up at the show. Er, after the show. I owe you a drink."

"No, I owe you one. I really am looking forward to seeing

you at The Cauldron for Saturday's show. It's been a while since I've felt this excited about something."

His words echoed my own sentiments about, well, everything in my new life. "Me too, Oliver. There's something special about this, isn't there?"

"Yeah, there is." His agreement was simple, but it held a whole wonderful world of meaning.

Five

I arrived back at the Crescent Moon to find the inn empty. Jimbo had left a note on the front desk next to an orchid plant. I set the canvas bag and my purse on a chair and went behind the antique desk in the lobby.

"Why does he keep giving me these orchids?" I muttered aloud, sliding the potted plant aside.

> Amelia—
> I heard the hardware store was closing early today for inventory, so I left so I could buy the tool I need to fix the bathroom in room three. Holler if you need any help, otherwise, I'll see y'all tomorrow.
> Jimbo

"Good deal," I murmured, setting the note aside and quickly checking the inn's email account to see if anyone had reached out about booking a stay. One person wanted to make a reservation for March, and my fingers flew over the keyboard with a response.

As soon as I was done, a pathetic sounding meow echoed through the downstairs of the Crescent Moon. I checked my watch.

It was almost dinnertime, and Freddie was registering his displeasure at my absence. I grabbed my bags and hustled into my aunt's apartment. That's still how I thought of it, as hers.

As comfortable as I was here, the place still didn't quite feel like my own, but I wasn't sure why.

Freddie came sprinting out of the bedroom when he heard me walk in, purring and *brrrrapping* and meowing the entire way.

"You sure are vocal today, little man." I bent over to give him a scratch. He tilted his chin up so I could get that one special spot. I knew I'd never have a second of peace if I tried to open the contents of the basket without feeding him first. "Let's get you an early dinner."

In the kitchen, I quickly prepared his stinky wet food, then did a quick inventory of my cabinets. Part of my mind was still on that cookie recipe from Tracy's headstone. Oh, I did have pecans. Past me was apparently thinking ahead to this moment. Liz would probably call this "serendipity."

I called it a well-stocked pantry.

I took a deep breath to center myself. It was four in the afternoon, there were no guests coming today, Jimbo wasn't returning, and although I always had inn business to take care of, there was nothing too pressing. The rooms upstairs were all clean, in case a last-minute visitor came knocking.

I could safely spend all night pouring over the contents of the basket, unbothered and happily alone. As I opened the fridge door to reach for a bottle of pinot grigio that I'd brought back from my last visit to California, I mused at how, when my daughter Jenny was first at college, I worried that I'd hate being alone.

Sure, at first it had been scary and sad. But now? I adored my alone time.

I poured myself a glass of wine and went into the living room. I absentmindedly flicked on my aunt's old boom box. Although I'd moved many of her things into a storage room in the rambling old inn, I'd kept this, despite it having zero aesthetic value.

For some reason, the thought of listening to the radio, as my aunt did for years, made me feel closer to her. The strains of Mazzy Star's "Fade into You" soared into the air, the perfect dreamy accompaniment for what I was about to do.

I set my wine down on an end table and reached into the bag for the basket. I turned it in my hands, soaking in its heft. It sure was a beautiful lightship purse.

Carefully, I slid the scrimshaw latch aside and lifted the lid. I half expected a bright light to blind me, or for sparkles to flutter out. Instead, the contents were neatly packed, almost like a 3D puzzle.

My hand hovered over all the items inside. What to look at first? I plucked out the item that looked oldest, the most likely to be damaged if I pulled everything out at once: a photograph that was already bent into the curved shape of the basket. It was jammed along the back edge, and with my index finger and thumb, I carefully plucked it out.

I instantly recognized two things about the photo. One, was that it was probably taken in the late 80s, given the oversaturated, almost faded purplish-brown hue, and the rounded edge of the paper. I had hundreds of these kinds of photos myself, sitting in boxes that had been shipped from California. They were now stashed in a back room used as a junk repository. I hadn't looked at the pictures in years, and now that I was holding this in my hand, I realized how much nicer cell phone photos were today.

Why were pictures back then so brown?

The other familiar thing was that the building in the background was that of the Cypress Grove library.

But the girl standing in front of the library was what truly captivated my attention.

I flipped it over. In neat cursive, in blue pen, the words "Marigold, 1989. Taken by Tracy."

"Hmm. Interesting," I said aloud, taking a sip of my wine. I studied the photo more. Marigold was quite a distance from the camera, so it was difficult to discern her expression. I brought it closer to my face.

People back in the 80s sure didn't know how to pose for photos like they do today. Everyone looked so awkward back then.

I set the photo on the coffee table in front of me and turned back to the basket. I wondered if I'd experience any visions with my psychometry; I'd come to realize I needed to focus hard if I wanted to draw information from certain objects. If my mind was scattered, like it was right now, I sometimes couldn't tap into my power.

I pulled out a tattered sheet of paper next. It looked like it had been ripped from a spiral notebook. I unfolded it carefully and saw it was a diary entry, written in looping cursive:

> February 12, 1993
>
> The solstice moon holds powerful energy for new beginnings. E wants to meet at the willow grove after midnight to try a binding ritual. I have my doubts it will work, but anything is worth a shot at this point to free myself from this path I'm on...

The entry trailed off there, leaving me with more questions than answers. Who was E? What kind of ritual was Marigold going to do? And what path did she want to free herself from? I gulped more wine. Willow grove? That didn't sound like anything I'd heard of in town. Were there even willow trees in Florida? I didn't think so, but I wasn't an expert on the flora and fauna here.

I set the cryptic diary page aside and reached into the basket again. This time I pulled out a dried flower, pressed between what looked like wax paper. It was unmistakably a marigold blossom, its rusty orange petals still vibrant despite being over 30 years old. I ran my thumb lightly over the gossamer-thin paper, hoping my psychometric abilities would reveal something.

A fleeting impression came to me of warm sunshine, rich soil, and... safety? Contentment? It was a brief feeling, and I wondered what this decades-old flower meant to Marigold. The vision vanished as soon as it came.

Next, I pulled out a tarnished silver charm bracelet. Each dangling charm was different - a high-heeled shoe, a coffee cup, a tiny book, a heart, a teddy bear, and an unknown symbol. As I examined them closely, more psychic impressions came through about places Marigold frequented - a cafe, a bookstore, a clothing boutique perhaps? Each place could have held significance. I didn't recognize any, however, and I wondered if they were long-closed shops, or if they were in other cities.

I made a mental note to ask Oliver about the symbol.

I turned the bracelet over in my hands, feeling its warmth as if it still retained Marigold's body heat from when she last wore it decades ago. Holding objects that were intimately hers should make psychometric visions easier.

I closed my eyes and concentrated, but was interrupted by a soft meow from Freddie, who was kneading a blanket with his paws. Too excited to look through the rest, I decided to move on. For now, I set it on the coffee table and pulled out the next item - a small compact mirror, its silver backing tarnished.

Something about the mirror's aged appearance tingled at the back of my mind, like it could be enchanted or serve a magical purpose. I angled it to catch the light from my aunt's Tiffany lamp, but nothing interesting happened.

Deciding to move on, I looked into the basket again and saw a folded sheet of paper. I carefully pulled it out, unfolded it, and scanned the loopy, girlish writing, my eyes widening as I realized it was a recipe for some kind of potion or tonic.

It wasn't written with any specific instructions, though. It was more like a shopping list.

"Blackberry brambles from a wild patch, picked on the full moon," and, "Three feathers from a crow who has witnessed a birth." There were at least twenty items on the list. Huh. I wonder what all that was for — there was no explanation.

I set the potion recipe down, feeling stumped, and refilled my wine glass. Then I pulled out the next item - a crumpled ticket stub for the movie "Slackers" from February 1992. I chuckled aloud. I'd seen that movie when it came out.

As I laid each item on the coffee table in front of me, my mood shifted from intense curiosity to something more reverent. These weren't just clues; they were fragments of a life, pieces of a story.

Of a tale that was left untold.

I reached into the basket again, my fingers brushing against something small and hard... actually, make that a few somethings. I pulled out a set of polyhedral dice, the kind used for playing Dungeons and Dragons. They were a beautiful, marbled purple and gold, slightly dull with age.

As I held them in my palm, a vivid vision suddenly washed over me. I saw Marigold, younger and carefree, probably in her teens, sitting around a table with a group of girlfriends. They were all laughing and chatting, character sheets and rulebooks spread out before them. Bags of chips and cans of sodas littered the table.

Marigold was the Dungeon Master, weaving an intricate tale of adventure and magic. Her eyes sparkled with mischief as she described the challenges the party faced. Her friends hung on her every word, rolling dice and cheering when they succeeded.

It was a sweet, innocent scene. The kids were all clearly a little geeky and smart, kind of like my own daughter and her friends. Like me and my high school friends even, although we were more band geeks than gamers.

Marigold seemed so happy, so alive. I wondered what happened between her D&D days and the moment she disappeared.

I set the dice down and picked up the photo of Marigold again. It was odd how I felt so close to her after looking at all these clues. There were still things in the basket, but I needed a little break while I sipped my wine.

"I'm going to figure out what happened to you," I said fiercely, meaning every word.

Freddie meowed sharply, as if chiming in to say, *heck yeah, we will.* He jumped off the sofa and went to the door that connected the apartment to the inn. He pawed at it.

That's when I heard a faint knock, coming from the inn part of the house. I looked up. It was seven p.m.? Two hours had passed? Whoa.

I stood, suddenly feeling a little wobbly from the wine. Aw, crap. I hadn't eaten and now I was tipsy. Bad timing for a walk-in guest, but I'd have to power through.

While telling Freddie to stay in the apartment, I slipped into the first floor of the inn. When no one was here, I kept the lights off, and I moved through the library and into the lobby. There, I flicked on a light.

Whoever it was rang the doorbell, but not for a second or two. They laid on the thing, pressing it so the shrillness rang in my brain and gave me a slight headache.

"What the duck," I whispered, then yelled, "Coming."

I flung open the door and gasped.

There, standing on my doorstep, was my mother.

Six

"Mom?" I said weakly, then hoped I wasn't slurring my words.

She stood before me, impeccably dressed as always in a pastel yellow track suit that probably came from Lilly Pulitzer, and perfectly white Keds sneakers. Her frosted blonde bob was like a helmet of hairspray, not a hair out of place. She seemed impossibly youthful for her sixty-eight years thanks to a long-time love of makeup and likely some "enhancements" she'd never admit to.

I was certain I looked wild, untamed, and drunk. I patted my hair.

Duck. Duck duck duck. Why was she here, unannounced? She lived in *Arizona*.

"Mom? What a...surprise."

"Hal, get the suitcases later. Amelia finally opened the door, she shouted over her shoulder, then turned to me. "Well, it took you long enough to answer. We've been out here for at least fifteen minutes. Or are you busy? With someone? Come here and give your mother a hug."

As my mother folded me into her tiny, Shalimar-scented

body, I spotted her husband, Harold Davis, wrestling with an oversized suitcase and a comically small trunk.

"Mom, I think Hal needs some help." My mother tended to treat Hal *as* the help, which was an opinion I'd never shared with anyone and definitely not her.

She released me from her embrace. "Oh, leave him be. He loves fussing with the luggage. I'm thirsty. What have you got in your wine cellar?"

Mom brushed past me, into the lobby. "I can see you've tried to spiff up this old place."

"Mom, why...what's going on? Why are you..." My words trailed off, realizing logic was of no use to me now.

She set her purse on a chair and eyed Georgina, a giant taxidermied alligator. It had been part of my aunt's décor that I'd kept.

Mom visibly shuddered, then turned to me. "Hal has always wanted to attend this week-long golf tournament near Jacksonville. I believe that's an hour or two north of here. He won tickets in a raffle at the club and was beside himself with excitement. So, we thought we'd surprise you and come stay for a couple of days before the event. Have you gained a few pounds?"

I gripped the back of a chair, feeling my blood pressure rise as Mom's gaze took in the room. The walls were a pale pink, the accents black, the décor funky. Addams Family meets Hello Kitty had been the vibe I'd gone for when I painted the walls, and I could tell Mom disapproved by the sour look on her face.

Before I could say a word, the door flung open. It was Hal, overloaded with bags. I rushed — well, rushed wasn't the word, more like lurched, because I was far tipsier than I realized — to relieve him of a suitcase.

"Linda, I can't find the bag with my CPAP machine. I think we left it at the airport."

Mom clicked her tongue against the roof of her mouth. "Oh, Hal, you're always losing something. You'll be fine, because I'm sure it's somewhere. Amelia, we assumed the inn wouldn't be full, so please show Hal to a room so we can drop our bags and then go to dinner. I'm famished. Have you eaten? Clearly, you've been drinking."

She arched an eyebrow and I shuddered in a breath, trying to hold in my rising ire.

I adored Mom, admired her, and was often amused at her humor. But there was a reason I'd chosen to live in a different state than my mother, and now that we'd been in each other's orbit for less than five minutes, I was reminded why.

I shifted to look at Hal, who was panting.

He wore khaki shorts that exposed pale legs, black socks pulled up almost to the knee, and a garish Hawaiian shirt. His thinning gray hair was disheveled, and beads of sweat dotted his forehead. Hal was also about 6' 4" and had played college football back in his day. I didn't want the poor guy to have a heart attack.

"Let's get you two settled," I said, trying to mask my annoyance at their unannounced arrival. It wasn't that I didn't want to see my mother, not exactly. But I needed lots of warning and mental preparation, and right now I had neither.

I grabbed one of the larger suitcases from the pile, feeling a little unsteady either from the wine or the weird turn this night had taken. "I'll show you to the Lavender and Lace Room upstairs. It's our biggest and nicest room."

Hal gave me an apologetic look as he gathered up the remaining bags. Mom had already wandered off, probably to poke around in my things, hoping to find evidence that I'd lost my mind by coming here to Florida.

Oh, crap. I'd left the door to the apartment open.

I led Hal up the curved staircase to the second floor, my head fizzing a bit.

The Lavender and Lace room was the inn's most swanky guest space, with its four-poster bed and feminine shades of lilac, gold, and cream. I set the suitcase down with a thud and helped Hal haul in the rest of the luggage.

"I'm real sorry to drop in unexpected like this, Amelia," he said breathlessly. Hal was from Wisconsin and had an accent that I enjoyed listening to. "You know your mom, she doesn't like to be told no."

"Don't worry about it, Hal, we both know how Linda can get," I reassured him, though truthfully Mom's domineering ways always set me on edge, especially now, when I was trying to keep my psychic abilities under wraps. She had no idea about my powers, and I intended to keep it that way for at least a little while — if only for my daughter's sake. "Let me grab some water from the kitchen while you freshen up. We can head out to that new bistro on Main Street for dinner if you're up for it?"

Hal gave me a relieved smile. "That'd be just fine. Maybe they'll have some local beer on draft."

We chatted for a minute about the local brews, with me telling him about the various new offerings around town.

"It's good to see you, kiddo," he said, folding me into a hug. My parents had divorced when I was nine, and Mom had met Hal years later, at the retirement community. After a years-long friendship, they'd married early last year. I'd given my enthusiastic blessing because Hal seemed to temper Mom's rough edges.

He was a gentle giant and a retired accountant for a big firm. I thought Mom was entirely too hard on him.

"Excellent to see you too, Hal. I'm going to find Mom."

"Who knows what havoc she's causing downstairs, eh?"

We both laughed, but inside, panic began to well.

I left him unpacking and made my way back downstairs, gripping the railing tightly, steeling myself to deal with my mom's antics for the next couple days while also keeping my private life *private*. So much for my relaxing night poring over Marigold's mysterious belongings.

I found Mom in the living room, perched on the sofa, holding the Nantucket basket in her lap. She looked up in astonishment.

"Where did you get this beautiful piece?" She clutched it to her breast. "It's mine now."

"It's not mine, and it's definitely not yours." I reached for it and for a second, She actually tussled with me playfully, at least until she knew I wasn't joking. But she handed it over.

"Well, whose is it? And what's all this stuff? Looks like old garbage to me." She waved at the table.

I glanced in the basket. She'd removed the items I hadn't gotten to yet and had placed them in a little pile on the table. I wanted to scream.

"Mom, why don't you go upstairs and freshen up with Hal? You're the only ones here at the inn tonight. The room is on the second floor, all the way at the end. I told him about this hot new bistro in town. I'm sure you'll love it."

She stood while making a little huffing sound. "That sounds acceptable, I guess. But I can't imagine there's truly a good bistro here in central Florida."

The last word came out as though she was talking about an infestation of black mold. I clenched my molars so hard I could feel it in my sinuses.

My mother moved toward the fireplace and inspected a brass thermometer that had been my aunt's. It was so cute and elegant — and because when I touched it, I had a cozy vision of my aunt, doing needlepoint here in this room, I'd kept it where I'd found it.

"I thought you'd get rid of more of Shirley's things," Mom said, picking it up. "Like that alligator in the lobby. So odd."

"I moved some things around. But mostly, I like all of the stuff. It's fun. It's home."

"I still don't understand all this, Amelia."

I clutched the basket to my midsection as if it were a protective shield. "Understand all of what?"

"You, blowing up your life in California for... this place." She cast a glance at the old boom box radio, which was still on. A song by the Cranberries was far too soothing and cozy for this conversation. Her nose wrinkled.

"Mom, I didn't have a life in California. I was divorced, jobless, and going broke. And I wanted to be closer to my brother."

"Mike's still three states away." Mom tilted her head to look at me, as if she were laying eyes on me for the first time. "I thought you were supposed to get half of that house sale in California. That place closed so quickly. I knew it would, a gorgeous home like that in Wine Country. What memories I had of all of you, when Jenny was small. But you could've bought a nice condo or mobile home in Sonoma with the proceeds."

I sighed, not wanting to relive those bittersweet times. "I did get half of the house sale. I'm no longer broke. And I didn't want to live in a condo in Sonoma. It was more financially prudent to move here and save money."

"Well. You can pay for dinner then. Hal and I are on a fixed income."

Yeah, right, I wanted to say, and refrained from rolling my eyes. Hal squirreled enough money away that they took three long cruises every year. "Well, I'd like to change before we go out."

Mom looked me up and down. "Yes, you look a little rumpled. A little hef—"

"No. Don't say it." Mom's opinion of my weight was something I'd worked long and hard to overcome. What was it about Boomer women and their obsession with being thin? "I'm not hefty. I'm not a garbage bag. I'm a perfectly healthy middle-aged woman who has put on a bit of weight."

Mom shook her head and walked out.

I heaved a long sigh. I loved Mom, really and truly. But she could be so difficult. Body shaming. Prickly, yet meddling. Was I like that with Jenny? I cringed at the thought.

As quickly and carefully as I could, I put Marigold's things back into the basket and toted it into my room. Freddie was under the bed, concealed except for his tail.

"I know you think you're invisible, but you're not," I whispered to him, nestling the basket deep into my jeans drawer in case my mother got any more ideas about claiming the thing.

Freddie's tail swooshed in response. If only I could join him down there under the bed.

Maison de Lumiere had opened on New Year's Day, and I'd been excited to try their French-meets-Southern cuisine sometime soon.

With Oliver.

We'd talked about coming here for a couple of weeks and had promised each other a Saturday night date when we were both free. Now I was here with Hal and Linda, the latter of which was scowling at the menu.

"This is a real cute place, kiddo," Hal said, looking around.

"And you sure called it with the beer. This lager is something else."

I clinked my glass of water to his mug of beer. I'd decided to not drink for the rest of the evening, figuring I needed food and a clear head to deal with this slow-motion disaster.

The place was incredibly cozy and charming with exposed brick walls on two sides, mismatched antique wood chairs, and candle-lit tables draped in white linen. The air was filled with the aroma of fresh-baked baguettes and the soothing sounds of Carla Bruni crooned in the background.

I could totally imagine Oliver and I at one of these tables, holding hands and laughing softly.

But here I was, with a pasted-on smile. It wasn't that I didn't want to see my mother and Hal, but a bit of warning would have been nice. Much to Mom's dismay, I'd ordered the tater tot nachos for dinner.

I gnawed on a baguette and privately stewed over how Mom mentally calculated the calories of everything on the menu. Another fear struck deep within: could I get through this meal without any additional surprises?

Someone spotting me and chatting about my psychometric powers was high. That was my true concern.

Good thing we'd gotten a table far into the depths of the restaurant. I slouched down, hoping to blend into the brick wall at my back.

Our appetizers arrived, yummy-looking fried green tomatoes topped with herbed goat cheese and drizzled with lavender honey. Mom grumbled something about lavender being a flower, not a food, while Hal — to his credit — dove in. Probably because Mom had him on a diet and he hadn't eaten all day.

I was about to dig in when I spotted a familiar face walk through the door.

Holy craparoni. It was Liz. And Police Chief Christopher Wolf. Liz was dressed in a pretty, sparkly silver dress and a fluffy stole. Dang, she was even in heels. Wolf was in a slightly too-small suit, looking like he stepped out of a Jack Reacher novel. They made a gorgeous pair.

I froze, a forkful of green tomato halfway to my mouth. Which was open.

I did the only thing I could think of: shove the food in my mouth, chew, and swallow. "I'll be right back. Need to use the ladies' room."

Fortunately, we were seated on the side of the restaurant closest to the hallway that led to the restrooms. Another stroke of luck in my favor: it was a single stall, and it was empty. I quickly texted Liz. It was so dire that I dispensed with punctuation, like a millennial.

> I saw you walk into the restaurant I'm here too meet me in the bathroom URGENT

I tried to add a "please" emoji but my finger slipped and sent a zombie instead. Oh well. I stared at my reflection in the mirror. I looked rough. What was it about middle-age that one could start the day fresh, and by seven at night you looked like you hadn't slept for a week?

Zombie, indeed.

A minute later, there was a knock on the door. "Amelia?" Liz called out softly in a confused tone.

I opened the door and waved her in, then shut and locked it, slumping against the wall.

"Oh, honey, what's wrong? What's going on?" Liz's face pinched with worry. "Are you feeling okay? Do you need a tampon?"

"No. Nothing like that. I'm sorry to interrupt your date, but my mom showed up. Unannounced." I scrubbed my face with my hands. "Already she's called me hefty, she hates the décor at the inn, and has criticized my fashion choices. And she doesn't know about my psychometry, so I didn't want to run into you out there in the dining room and have you accidentally spill the beans. Oh, and I'm half-drunk."

Liz stared at me in horror, then the corner of her mouth quirked up. Then she let out a little laugh snort. I did, too. Within a few seconds, we were both doubled over in hysterics.

"I'm sorry, but the look on your face..." she said, then chuckled again. "Really, I'm not trying to make light of your situation. Mothers are difficult. My mom used to both call me fat and make me feel guilty if I didn't eat her food. It's a no-win situation."

"I love Mom, but wow. It's so hard sometimes. Usually, I can prepare myself mentally but this was an ambush."

We both shook our heads.

"Seriously, thanks for calling me in here. I probably would've said something to you because I'd been thinking about you opening the basket all night." Liz took a tube of lipstick out of her purse and angled herself in front of the mirror. "How did that go, anyway?"

"I was only halfway through when Mom showed up. She already tried to claim the basket as hers. I have no idea when I'm going to have time to investigate Marigold's case. Julia said she'd love it if I brought her new info in a week for the coven's founding anniversary."

"Mothers and their boundary issues." She rubbed her lips together then leaned back to assess. "Is this color feathering into the wrinkles above my top lip?"

"Ahh, come here. I need a better look since I don't have my reading glasses." We stood about six inches apart and I squinted at her mouth. "Nah, I think you're good. No feathering."

"Thanks. Okay, I won't mention anything metaphysical or strange. I can be normal, you know."

I snickered. "Can anyone be normal in this town?"

"We sometimes try. Hang in there. How long is she here for?"

"I dunno. My stepfather won tickets to some golf tournament thing in Jacksonville. I need to find out."

"You'll be fine. Take her downtown tomorrow so she can wander the shops like all the tourists. She'll love it, and it's supposed to be gorgeous weather. I think there's a craft fair on Saturday, too."

I nodded. "She might like that. And thanks. Sorry for being so weird."

"Never apologize, honey. I'm here for all your neurosis and weirdness." She gave me a quick hug.

"I also want to hear all about your date with Wolf."

Her hand was on the door and she wagged her eyebrows. "He's had quite a fascinating life. Grew up in Alaska."

"Oh-ho. Is this more evidence that our chief of police is a werewolf?"

"I'm determined to find out." With a saucy waggle of her eyebrows, she swept out of the bathroom.

Seven

Later that night, after we'd eaten dinner (the tater tot nachos were incredible, and as we walked out, we said a quick hello to Liz and Wolf without incident), I got Mom and Hal settled with fresh towels and a new bottle of expensive body wash that I'd bought for myself but hadn't yet opened.

At least she'd loved the room, declaring it "top-notch décor, like something out of Southern Living."

Wait, now that I thought about it, was that a backhanded compliment? I could never be too sure with Mom.

I was now downstairs in my bedroom, in my cozy pajamas. Freddie was on the bed, purring and staring in the direction of my feet, which were carefully wrapped into a blanket because I knew my cat's weakness when it came to attacking toes.

Marigold's basket was on my lap, and I was about to dive back in to check out the rest of the items, even though my nerves were frayed. My mind was racing, too tired to sleep, so I carefully opened the lid and pulled out one of the items: a weathered card, like the kind that used to be in library books pre-internet.

Marigold's name was printed neatly on the front, along with an address here in Cypress Grove. Probably her parents' place, but I'd definitely check.

The card had several date stamps on the back, the most recent from February 1993, right before she vanished.

Studying the card more closely under the light of my bedside lamp, I noticed something odd. In the margin next to each date stamp was a series of numbers, written in pencil. They looked like Dewey Decimal System call numbers. Perhaps these were titles of books?

A tingle of excitement ran through me - this could be a major clue.

I grabbed a notepad and jotted down the numbers, my mind already racing ahead to a trip to the library first thing tomorrow. Mom and Hal would have to entertain themselves for a bit. This was more important. I'd drop her off downtown and tell her I had some business to take care of.

I yawned, and sleep tugged at my lids. One more item, I figured, then I'd turn out the light.

My fingers reached for a cassette tape. "Songs From the Edge of Forever" was scrawled in jet black ink on a sticker affixed to the spine of the cassette case.

I turned the cassette over in my hands, then held it at a distance so I could examine the track listing that had been carefully handwritten onto a sticker affixed to the front of the cassette. I still wasn't used to reading glasses enough to have several pairs stashed around the house, like my friend Marisol did.

The tape was an eclectic, ethereal mix of 80s and early 90s songs, from The Cranberries to The Cure. I recognized every title and smiled when I saw Every Breath You Take by The Police. A staple of middle school dances.

I thought about my aunt's vintage boom box sitting on a shelf in the living room. That could definitely play tapes. For a moment, I considered getting up and popping the cassette in, letting the music transport me back to Marigold's world.

But Freddie was purring contentedly at my side, and the warmth of the bed was too comforting to leave after such a hectic, weird evening. Besides, I didn't want to risk waking Mom and Hal with any late-night noise. The mixtape's secrets would have to wait until morning.

As I studied the playlist, my mind drifted to my own teenage years and how I'd spend hours making tapes for friends and crushes. Agonizing over song choices, striking the perfect balance between revealing too much and not enough. The first song was always important because it set the mood. The deep tracks on the second side were the hidden keys to one's real feelings, if you were making it for a crush.

If you were making it for a friend, then you'd try to capture a vibe, or a memory, or a shared joke.

There was a boy — Jake whatshisface, my mom used to call him — who slipped a tape into my locker freshman year. It was filled with cheesy hair metal ballads, but to 14-year-old me, Guns N Roses "November Rain" was the height of romance.

What had happened to Jake? Did he hear that song on the radio and think of me, like I did with him? I could barely recall what he looked like, but I remember what it felt like to listen to his musical selection that was meant only for me.

And then there was the tape I made for my best friend Krissy before I moved away on one of my family's many zigzags across the country. It was a bittersweet mix of our favorite songs, inside jokes set to music. I can still picture us belting out Bon Jovi's "Livin' On A Prayer" in her bedroom, hairbrushes standing in for microphones.

I carefully put the tape back into the basket, then set the entire thing on my nightstand. Once I shut out the light, I continued to think about mixtapes, and what I'd put on one if I was describing my life now. I drifted off, the new wave songs of my past softly playing in my mind.

My eyes peeled open at five-thirty the next morning. Until I moved to Florida, I wasn't much of a morning person, but for some reason, I'd shifted, and now I couldn't stay in bed past six.

Plus, I wanted to get a jump on the day. I had guests arriving at five tonight — they were coming from the airport in a rental car — and I wanted to make a list of things I needed to buy at the grocery store. Plus, I had to whip up a batch of cookies that would both wow Hal and the guests coming this evening.

Somehow, I wanted to work in some sleuthing, too.

While mentally adding all this to my to-do list, I rolled over to find Freddie lying on his back, belly up, next to me. He looked like a fluffy orange football, and I simply couldn't help myself. I gently rested my hand on his tummy.

He began purring, the volume rising.

We stayed like this for a solid thirty seconds, then I eased my hand away. Sometimes the murder mittens came out when he got overstimulated.

I quickly changed from my pajamas to yoga pants and a light hoodie, and padded out of the bedroom. I wasn't about to wake Mom and Hal, of course, but I also didn't want them wandering downstairs to find the door to my apartment closed, so I swung that open. It was a bit confusing, the entrance to the apartment — my aunt had installed a hidden bookshelf door — and I often kept it open as a welcoming gesture, and a conversation piece.

After a quick check of the lobby to make sure nothing was amiss, I returned to my kitchen in the apartment. While the coffee brewed, I scanned the inn's email inbox and social media. Mercifully, there were no surprises.

As I drank my first cup at the sunny breakfast nook, I studied the recipe from Tracy's gravestone. I had all the ingredients. I'd been planning something simpler, like a chocolate chunk cookie — guests always loved those upon check-in — but now I had an urge to make the shortbread cookies instead, while listening to Marigold's tape and thinking about her case.

I gathered the ingredients, setting them on the counter, then moved the boom box into the kitchen and popped the cassette tape into the little slot. I smiled when it made that familiar click.

The first song was one that I loved: *Running Up That Hill* by Kate Bush. I'd thought it amusing when it became popular again recently because of the *Stranger Things* TV show, but the song always made me feel a longing. Had for decades, ever since I heard it one night when I was fifteen and walking into a teen club with my then-best friend.

A longing for what, I wasn't sure. Even now, my heart seemed to clench when I heard Kate Bush's voice. Now at forty-seven, that feeling was even stronger. I suspected this meant I was on the right path with Marigold and Tracy.

As I mixed the butter and sugar together, I found myself swaying to the smooth melody.

I carefully measured out the orange extract, and a faint vision came to me. I'd noticed that this had been happening more and more and wasn't sure if it was connected to my psychometry or if I was simply getting more acquainted with the magic that infused the very air in Cypress Grove.

The liquid shimmered in the measuring spoon, catching the morning light. For a brief moment, I swore I saw a flicker of golden energy swirling within the amber substance. A whispered word echoed in my mind.

"Clarity."

I shook my head, the vision vanishing as soon as it appeared. If only it had lasted longer! Still, I was grateful for the message — whoever had sent it, wherever it came from.

The orange extract filled the kitchen with a bright, citrusy aroma, mingling with the warm scent of the candied pecans I'd roughly chopped. Yum. These were going to be excellent cookies.

I snapped my fingers. This reminded me: I wanted to see if my aunt had written anything in her recipe book about orange extract. My aunt had been a witch, and although I hadn't known her well while she was alive, she'd not only left me her inn, but had sprinkled a roadmap of letters, notes, and notebooks all around the house meant for me. Call it foresight, call it magic, call it estate planning, but Shirley had clearly thought things through.

I reached for her recipe book, which was on a shelf above the counter, between The Joy of Cooking and The Practical Witch's Almanac 2017. Shirley's recipe book was well-organized into sections, and I flipped to the tab that said ELIXIRS, thinking it might be there.

"Aha," I whispered, when I saw the entry, written in her formal cursive.

> Orange extract is associated with friendship.
> Healing Benefits:
> Energizes & Uplifts for a positive outlook
> Cleanses & Purifies, natural air freshener

Boosts Immunity: antioxidants and also prevents scurvy!

Shirley had doodled a little smiley face after the last sentence, which made me giggle. I so enjoyed getting to know her sense of humor through the little notes and journals she'd left behind.

"A positive outlook is always a plus," I murmured aloud. Especially when my mother was around.

I sifted the flour and salt together, the repetitive motion allowing my mind to wander. This was the part of baking I loved best: the meditative state it inspired.

What had Marigold been like? Had she made this song mix? I imagined her carefully selecting each track, pouring her heart and soul into the playlist.

Had Tracy made this cookie recipe for her friend?

As I kneaded the dough, I wondered if Tracy's recipe and Marigold's mixtape were somehow connected. Were they pieces of a puzzle, clues left behind by two young women whose lives had been cut short?

I rolled out the dough atop floured parchment paper. With each cut of the cookie cutter, I felt a renewed sense of purpose. I would solve this mystery, for Tracy and Marigold, and for the coven that had placed their trust in me. I slid the sheet of cookies into the warm oven.

I got out the bag chocolate melting wafers then shook my head. I wanted to taste the cookies before I dipped them in chocolate. I put the chocolate away.

Minutes later, I was swaying along to Enya — goodness, I hadn't heard her in years — and sliding the sheet of cookies out the warm oven when a voice ripped me out of my reverie.

"What are *you* doing up so early?"

I looked over to see my mother, looking perfect in jeans and a lime green sweater twin set. I spotted pearls, which seemed a little formal for a Friday morning in Florida, but that was Linda. "Good morning to you, too. Coffee?"

"Of course."

Silently, I poured my mother a cup. Black, with a half teaspoon of sugar, as she'd taken it for my entire life. I handed her the mug then snapped the STOP button on the tape player. "What are you doing up this early?"

She shook her head. "Jetlag, it always disrupts my internal clock. Plus, Hal was tossing and turning. He had some indigestion after those green tomatoes last night. We don't usually eat that late. Aging is not for the weak, Amelia."

"Don't I know it." I took a sip, swallowed, then gestured to the breakfast nook. "Want to sit over there? I'll be right there once I pop another sheet of cookies in the oven."

"Sure."

I attended to the cookies then joined Mom in the nook, which was next to a large window. The sill was wide and long enough to hold several orchid plants, all of which Jimbo had given me as gifts in recent months.

"What are you baking, anyway? It smells wonderful."

Mom's question took me by surprise. She hadn't been in favor of me opening the cookie delivery service back in California, and only warmed to it when it started making me and my ex serious money. Probably because she'd watched her weight since the Nixon administration, she never seemed to care about what I was baking.

I explained the recipe to her. She nodded while sipping her coffee.

"Is that one of those cemetery recipes?"

I stilled. "Uhhh..."

"I read about that in the tourist brochure that's up in the

room. Hal's quite intrigued, mostly because he's been getting into cooking lately. He actually got online last night and booked a tour for us this morning."

"Oh! Well, yes, the recipe is from there." I was eager to steer her from this topic because it was perilously close to the one thing I didn't want to discuss with her. "What kind of tour?"

"It's one of those Segway tours. Apparently, they go all over Cypress Grove and spend an hour with the graveyard recipes. Breakfast is included. It's called Sunrise Segway. Apparently, we go all over town for hours while stopping at various breakfast places. Hal's excited."

"Oh, I've seen those around." I tried to picture Mom zipping along a sidewalk on a Segway, but my mind simply couldn't go there, and I squelched a grin. "That sounds fun. And it works out well, because I need to go to the grocery store and do some other, ah, errands. I have guests coming tonight."

"Well, that's settled. I know we surprised you by coming here unannounced, and I don't want to interfere with your business."

I nodded. This was the closest Mom would get to any sort of acknowledgement that it might not have been the best thing to bust in on me like she did last night.

"I meant to ask you about those orchids," Mom continued, gesturing to the windowsill. "They're lovely. I didn't know you had such a green thumb."

I laughed. "Oh, I don't. Those are all from Jimbo, my employee here at the inn. Aunt Shirley hired him years ago, and he works the front desk and is the handyman, too. He keeps bringing them to me, and I have no idea why."

Mom raised an eyebrow. "Well, maybe he's sweet on you."

I nearly choked on my coffee, thinking of Sage, his girlfriend. Mom would probably freak out if she met Sage, who was a cowgirl-witch with a knack for hilarity. "Jimbo? No way. He's like a brother to me. Plus, he's got a serious girlfriend."

"If you say so," Mom said with a shrug. "But a man doesn't give a woman that many orchids unless he's trying to tell her something."

I rolled my eyes. "Trust me, Mom, it's not like that. Jimbo's a really nice guy who happens to have a thing for plants."

"Well, they certainly brighten up the place," Mom said. "You should ask him what his secret is. I can never keep those things alive back home."

Just then, Hal came bounding into the kitchen, a grin plastered on his face. "Good morning, ladies! Who's ready for an adventure on wheels?"

Mom and I exchanged an amused glance. "Someone's excited about the Segway tour," I teased.

Hal rubbed his hands together. "You bet I am! I've always wanted to try one of those things. And to combine it with a culinary tour? It's like a dream come true! Would you like to go with us?"

I couldn't help but laugh at his enthusiasm. "I'm sorry. I can't, because I have to prepare for guests coming tonight. But, you two have fun. And please, take pictures. I want to see you both zipping around town on those things."

"You got it, kiddo. We'll make sure to document every thrilling moment. Linda, honey, we better get a move on if we want to make it to the tour on time. Although, I think we have thirty or so minutes to try whatever it is you're baking." Hal winked. "It smells incredible."

For the next half hour, I served Hal and Mom shortbread cookies and coffee while making pleasant small talk about the town.

"I'll be dipping these in chocolate when they're cooled, but we can have them warm with coffee," I said, sliding a plate of them toward Hal, whose eyes grew wide.

Mom even tried one and proclaimed it "nice," which was more than I'd ever gotten out of her before. She was being unusually chatty and kind today, and I wondered why the change of heart from last night.

Then they set off, leaving me in the silence of the inn with more than one mystery unfolding.

Eight

After baking the rest of the cookies, showering, and changing into a cute and comfy sky-blue dress that resembled a knee-length polo shirt, and locating all of my reusable shopping bags, I left the apartment at eight a.m. on the dot. I was armed with a shopping list and my new leopard-print fanny pack. (Although my Gen Z daughter had recently informed me that they were now called 'belt bags', which was certainly a less embarrassing name).

My white Keds sneakers reminded me of Mom's, but I didn't have the time or the will to change. My purse was stuffed full of three notebooks, pens, a shopping list, Marigold's mixtape, and a small Tupperware filled with the cookies.

I figured that if I needed help with my sleuthing efforts today, offering cookies was an acceptable bribe.

Jimbo was scheduled to arrive at nine, so I wasn't worried about the place being unattended when there were no guests. The phone was forwarded to my cell, and I tended to obsessively check the inn's email account when I was away.

My first stop was the Mirror Lake Library, the town's main

branch. It was an adorable yellow wood building and nestled next to a lake. Sometimes I enjoyed coming here, then strolling around the water to check out all the wading birds. Florida sure had some impressive feathered friends, I'd discovered.

As I jogged up the steps, I said a silent prayer to the universe that Martha Johnstone, one of the librarians, would be working. Martha was eighty-eight, ornery, and knew every nook and cranny of the place.

She also adored my cookies.

Oliver had introduced me to Martha during our first investigation together, when we researched a pesky, Elvis-loving ghost that was haunting the inn. He'd known her since he was a kid, which meant she'd worked for the library for decades. Privately, I wondered if she was some sort of immortal being. I was too intimidated to ask, though.

When we'd first met, Martha had been prickly, but she'd warmed to me (especially after I'd dropped by with a few batches of my baked goods). She also seemed charmed that I'd asked about her Crossfit hobby (but also disappointed when I declined her offer of a free class).

I grinned when I walked in and spotted her at the desk. Her eyes smiled, but her mouth didn't.

"You," she said, pursing her lips. Not exactly welcoming, but I knew the drill now.

"Morning, Martha." I strode up to her desk and whipped out the cookies. "Brought you a little gift."

Martha eyed the container, a glimmer of interest in her gaze. "What kind are they this time?"

"Chocolate Dipped Candied Pecan Orange Shortbread," I said, pausing for dramatic effect. "Fresh out of the oven this morning."

Her eyebrows shot up. "Sounds fancy. What's the occasion?"

I leaned in, lowering my voice. "I'm working on a case. An old one. And I could really use your help, if you've got a few minutes."

Martha glanced around the quiet library, then back at me. "I suppose I could spare a moment. Especially for those cookies. Come into the back and let's see what you've got."

I followed her to a small, dimly lit room in the rear of the library, lined with stacks of used books, a broken-down printer, and filing cabinets. The air smelled of dusty toner cartridges. I sneezed twice and leaned against a worn wooden desk.

Martha shut the door behind us and turned to face me, arms crossed. "This is my office. Alright, what's this old case you're working on? And why? Do you fancy yourself some sort of paranormal investigator now?"

I took a deep breath. "It's for the Sisters of Hecate. You know, the coven?"

"Ah, they've asked you to join. Go on."

"The case is about Marigold Wentworth. The young woman who disappeared back in 1993, right before she was supposed to start a coven here in town. I've been asked to find out what happened to her."

Martha nodded slowly. "Marigold Wentworth. Now there's a name I haven't heard in a long time. Such a tragedy, what happened to that poor girl. Or rather, what might have happened. No one really knows, do they? But we all have our suspicions."

"Which are?"

She regarded me sourly. "What I think is of no importance. What do you need?"

I reached into my purse and pulled out the library card with what appeared to be Dewey Decimal numbers scribbled in the margins. I held it out and she took the card from me.

Somehow, she didn't need reading glasses, and I wasn't sure why.

"We don't use these cards anymore. Everything's all electronic."

"I figured, but is there any way to look up these titles? I want to know if they mean something or provide further clues?"

"Hmm. The numbering shouldn't have changed much. I can track them down." She looked back up at me, a sly smile playing at her lips. "Especially if fueled by baked goods."

I laughed and handed over the cookie container.

"I'll be right back." She took the plastic tub and left me in the small room alone.

While waiting, I busied myself with my phone, texting Liz to see how her date went, and Oliver to see how his morning was going.

Before I got a response from either, Martha came bustling back in, a stack of books in her muscular, wrinkled arms.

She set them down on the table and I scanned the titles, my heart racing with anticipation.

"V for Vendetta, the graphic novel. I saw the movie," I murmured, running my finger along the spine. "Jurassic Park by Michael Crichton, The Witching Hour by Anne Rice, and Generation X by Douglas Coupland. Quite an eclectic mix."

Martha nodded. "These were all fairly popular titles back in the early '90s when Marigold disappeared."

I flipped through the pages of each book, hoping for any clues or marginalia that might shed light on Marigold's disappearance. But the books appeared untouched, their pages crisp and unmarked, like no one had opened them in years. Did these have any significance? Or was Marigold simply a fan of bestsellers?

"There's one book not in regular circulation." Martha

handed back the card. "But I hate to break it to ya, but there's a school tour group of rugrats out there and I need to help the other librarian with that. But I can show you to the special collection."

"Great." I shuffled the books into a pile and stood.

Martha eyed me suspiciously. "You don't have any food, drink, or gum, do you? Let me see the inside of your bag."

"Uh, no. Why?" I set the book stack down and opened my purse to show her the contents.

"I won't allow you in the special collection if you have any of those things. The books in there are rare, mostly one-of-a-kind books on psychics, witchcraft, and other metaphysical topics. Oh, and the early town zoning maps. People rarely go in there, and I'm taking a big risk trusting you."

"I swear on my KitchenAid mixer I won't damage anything."

"Fine. Let's go. Hurry up, I don't have all day."

Feeling both chastised and special that Martha was letting me into the inner sanctum of the library, I followed her through the stacks, the excited din of a class tour in the lobby bouncing off the walls.

We went through a door that led to a corridor. Brooms, mops, and boxes of cleaning supplies were stacked haphazardly along one wall. We walked a few steps and came to a door. Martha took a key ring out of her jeans pocket and fiddled with the lock.

"Haven't been in here in months. Hardly anyone comes in here anymore." She shook her head. "Dang lock."

Finally, she jimmied it open, snaked her hand inside and flicked on a nearby light switch, then she stepped aside. "There ya go. Oh, and here."

She reached into her back pocket and pulled out a pair of

white cloth gloves, placing them atop my stack of books. "Wear these when you touch anything. Please."

She seemed like she was about to take off and I panicked, exclaiming, "Wait, what am I looking for in there?"

"Oh, right. You're trying to find a book with the title "The Early Covens of Cypress Grove. Thes books in there are quite old. You'll have to go through every shelf. Personally, I've never heard of that volume, so you might be on a wild goose chase. Good luck. And remember: don't tear, damage, or mark any of the items in this room. You'll have me to answer to if you do."

To emphasize her point, she gestured to her chest with a wizened thumb.

I watched her power walk off, grumbling about how she "had to do everything around here."

Oh dear. The last thing I wanted was to tick off Martha. I stepped into the room and the door swung shut behind me with a dull click.

As my eyes adjusted to the dim lighting, I took in my surroundings. The space was larger than I expected, with a low ceiling and dark wood paneling. Totally incongruous to the familiar, bureaucratic efficiency of the public library humming on the other side of these walls.

Antique brass lamps with green glass shades cast a muted glow over the bookshelves that lined three walls of the room. I ran a finger across a wooden map table, noting the dust on top, then pulled open one of the drawers. Something that looked like parchment was inside, but I didn't dare touch the paper for fear it would disintegrate. I gently shut the drawer.

The air felt thick and heavy, infused with the musty scent of aging paper and something else, something ominous. My heart began to beat faster.

What town secrets were hiding in here? I'd been here long enough to know there were many. I wished Oliver was with me, because I'd give anything to see the look of excitement on his face — an expression that was infectious.

For a split second, I thought about taking a selfie and sending it to him. But that seemed almost vulgar in such a serious, heavy room that held probably centuries of history. I set my stack of books and the purse on the table.

"Okay, okay, let's focus," I whispered, moving to the tall shelf closest to me. "The Early Covens of Cypress Grove. Oh, crap. The gloves."

I shoved my hands in them, and somehow, they fit snugly like, well, gloves. I flexed and curled my fingers, feeling a little silly, like a mime. I quickly checked my watch. It was time to get down to business, since I still had errands to run.

I ran my gloved index finger over the spines of the books, scanning for the title that matched what I was searching for.

The tomes were all old, their covers faded and worn. Some contained languages I didn't recognize, while others were so decrepit that the lettering had faded from the ravages of time. For those books, I carefully pulled them off the shelf to check the title page.

I moved methodically, my anticipation and anxiety growing with each passing second. Nothing on the first bookcase. Or the second. By the time I reached the third wall of shelves, I was starting to panic. Maybe the book was lost, or perhaps it had never existed at all.

I felt my neck getting hot. That was my latest foray into perimenopause: a hot flash that only erupted on my neck and nowhere else. Perfect timing.

But then, on the very top shelf, I spotted it. *The Early Covens of Cypress Grove.* The silver embossed letters gleamed in the lamplight, the intricate scrollwork on the spine as delicate as lace. My heart leapt. How had I not seen that before? The title was almost like a flashing neon sign.

I reached for the book, but my fingertips barely grazed the bottom edge. I grunted, feeling a twinge in my lower back. Even on my tiptoes, it was barely out of reach. I looked around, hoping to spot a step stool, but instead my eyes fell on an old wooden library ladder propped against the far wall.

With sweat forming on my neck, I rolled the ladder over, wincing as its wheels squeaked in protest. I tested its stability, then slowly climbed, one creaky rung at a time until I was eye-level with the book.

I was perspiring all over. Full-on hot flash. Was there no A/C in here? Now I was glad Oliver wasn't around, because I knew my face was beet red.

Paranormal sleuthing and perimenopause: two things I never dreamed I'd have to deal with. The former never entered my mind prior to moving to Cypress Grove, and the latter, well...

It wasn't as though society was open to talking about what really happens to women at midlife, so I was bumbling along like everyone else.

As I slid the heavy tome from its resting place, a tingle ran through me that had nothing to do with the exertion of climbing or my hot flash. The leather binding felt warm beneath my gloved hands, almost as if the book were alive.

Magical.

Even through the gloves, I could feel my psychometric powers activating. It was thrilling.

I descended the ladder, more cautiously than I normally would. Goodness only knew what would happen if I slipped and fell, and how long it would take someone to find me — although I imagined Martha would eventually haul me out. I hugged the book to my chest. It felt like the tome was pouring pure energy into my body.

Back on solid ground again, I carried it to the wide map

table and set it down. For a moment, I stared at the cover, tracing the silver letters with a gloved finger. Then, with a deep breath, I opened it. I had the overwhelming feeling I was treading on hallowed ground.

The pages were yellowed and brittle with age, the ink faded in places. I turned them delicately, scanning the contents for any clues. According to the copyright page, the book was printed not long after the town's founding. The first few pages contained old, sepia-toned photos of serious-looking women.

To my surprise, they weren't dressed in black. They were in formal gowns with high necks, looking stern and regal against a studio backdrop. The caption gave their names and then two words: founding witches.

Hunh. Interesting. I could see why Marigold would find this interesting if she was starting a coven. She was doing her research.

As I neared the middle of the book, I noticed something peculiar. A soft spot in the middle. I flipped a page and another. I touched the spot and my finger almost went through the paper. I turned another page.

A large square had been cut out of the middle, forming a compartment. My stomach plummeted. I needed to tell Martha about this right away, otherwise she'd blame me for defacing this beautiful old book.

But I couldn't tear myself away now. I wanted a closer peek, so I leaned in. Nestled inside the makeshift hiding spot was a small object of approximately three inches long, wrapped in what looked like gauze.

"What's this?" I murmured, plucking it out.

With trembling hands, I carefully unwrapped the gauze. As the layers fell away in one long ribbon, I gasped, nearly dropping it in shock.

There, nestled in the thin fabric, was a bone. Possibly a toe, or a finger, if I had to guess based on my limited anatomy knowledge. Unlike the latch on Marigold's basket, this was most definitely not scrimshaw.

As I stared at the macabre discovery, a wave of psychometric energy crashed into me. Suddenly, I was no longer in the quiet library room, but whisked to a scene of violence and chaos. The vision was hazy and disjointed, filled with impressions and emotions and thankfully not clear images.

An overwhelming sense of fear and desperation was palpable.

I couldn't make out specific details, but I felt the echoes of a struggle, of pain and terror. The bone in my hand seemed to hum with the dark energy of its owner's final moments.

I wanted to drop it, to fling it away from me, but I was frozen, consumed by the intensity of the scene. Somehow, probably because of my trembling, the bone slipped from my hand and landed a few inches below on the table.

The vision dissipated as quickly as it appeared. I gasped and cried out as if I was waking from a nightmare. A split second later, I realized I was sobbing aloud.

I leaned against the map table, knees weak and my stomach churning as if I was going to throw up. I buried my head in my hands. I couldn't bring myself to touch that bone again, not after what I'd experienced.

And definitely not after what I'd seen in the vision.

The bone was Marigold's, and she hadn't vanished.

She was dead.

Nine

Next, I did the most reasonable thing: I had a panic attack. And a hot flash. Also, I had to pee something fierce. It was like a trifecta of terrible. I wasn't sure whether to run to the bathroom, call for help, or whimper in the corner until someone decided to search for me.

After a few more strangled cries, I used a brochure from my purse to scoop up the bone and put it back into the book hiding place, slammed the cover shut, then fled the room. My first stop was the bathroom, which thankfully was in the hallway leading to the main library. That's where I not only relieved myself but stripped off the gloves and splashed water on my red, sweaty face.

I hauled in a breath while wiping my face with a paper towel. At least I wasn't sweating as much anymore, and my bladder was empty. Small victories.

With shaking hands, I found my phone and dialed Julia. She barely said hello when the words poured out of me in one long sentence.

"I came to the library to research Marigold and found a

bunch of books and then an old book with a secret compartment there was something wrapped in gauze and it was a bone maybe from a foot or a finger I'm not sure and oh duck I had a vision and it was so scary and I think she's most likely dead and—"

Julia cut me off. "I'll be right there."

Then she hung up.

For the next fifteen minutes, I paced the hallway outside the archive room. I tried the door, but it had locked behind me. Then the door to the main library swung open.

Julia, Renee, and Liz marched in, all wearing worried, serious expressions. It was like the midlife Avengers, only in comfy shoes and stretchy jersey clothing.

"Marigold's dead," I whimpered loudly. "There's a bone in the book, and I saw how her finger was cut off...I can't even put it into words. Oh, my word. Oh duck. It was so intense."

I gulped in a few breaths and tried to wipe the wetness from my cheeks.

Liz reached me first and opened her arms for a hug. "Oh, honey."

I shuddered in a breath, then broke apart from her and mustered a smile. She was wearing her neck fan and it hummed softly, an oddly soothing sound. "I'm better now that you're all here."

Julia squeezed my arm and Renee rubbed little circles in my back. "Can you tell us everything?"

I nodded, and tried to explain as best I could.

When I was finished, Julia jangled a keyring. "Martha gave us the keys to the room. Amelia, you can stay out here if you'd like."

"No," I said, feeling a little braver now that this trio was with me. Something about these women's support gave me a jolt of bravery. "I'll go with you."

My heart hammered as Julia unlocked the door. The four of us filed in. The temperature in the room seemed to have dropped at least ten degrees, and I shivered, wrapping my arms around my midsection.

"Where's the bone?" Julia asked.

"It's right here, inside the book where I found it." I stepped around Liz and moved toward the map table. The awful book was still there, sitting calmly as if it was simply a book of fairy tales waiting to be read. The unwrapped gauze and the brochure I'd used to scoop up the bone sat nearby.

When looking at the book's cover, I could feel my chest tightening, my breath coming in short gasps.

"I think you should sit," Liz said. She pulled a nearby chair away from the wall and I sank into it. While Julia and Renee inspected the book, Liz stood behind me and started kneading my shoulders and neck.

"Yeah, you're stressed," she said. "I can feel those knots."

"That feels so good," I groaned. "Sorry I'm sweaty."

"Oh. Here." There was a pause, and I was about to turn around, but she slipped something cool and plastic around my neck. It was the neck fan.

"Whoa, this feels great." The thing chugged cool air onto my fever-hot skin.

"It's saved my sanity, that's for sure," she said, returning to my shoulders and squeezing as though she was working with dough.

I shut my eyes, focused on listening to the conversation happening by the book.

"I've never heard of this book. Hmm." That was Julia.

"I don't get a good vibe from this book. Don't feel good energy from this room at all," said Renee.

Liz kept rubbing my shoulders.

"Amelia," said Renee, "Who knew you were in here looking at this book?"

"No one. Just Martha." I didn't open my eyes. "She let me in and gave me the gloves to handle the books."

"Interesting," one of the women said.

Then, Julia spoke. "Martha has powers of her own. And she knows Amelia is here on coven business. She wouldn't mess with our investigation."

Snippets of their conversation floated into my brain as I tried to calm myself with slow, deep breaths. I wondered if they should be using gloves to handle the book, but I figured that if the book was strong enough to withstand holding that cursed bone, it could handle the touch of a couple of women.

"Oh, there's the compartment," Renee muttered. "And there's the bone."

"Let's take photos," Julia said.

My eyes flew open. Despite not wanting to, I had to watch their reaction.

"Yep, that looks like one of the proximal phalanges."

Renee studied Julia for a moment. "That's oddly specific. How do you know that?"

"I was a pre-med student."

Renee took out her phone and used the cell flashlight to inspect the bone. "Is that what I think it is?"

Julia slipped on a pair of reading glasses that were atop her head. She bent over. "Yeah, I think so."

"What? What is it?" I started to rise from the chair, but Liz gently kept me in place.

Julia picked up the bone and brought it to me, holding it in the palm of her hand. "There's an inscription on the bone. Do you see it?"

I shook my head. "I don't have my glasses with me. Sorry.

I'm in denial about needing them and keep them next to my bed for reading only."

Liz stopped her massage and went to her purse, which she'd slung on the back of the doorknob. "Here. You can keep these. I have a million pairs."

They were wild, leopard print frames, with a chain attached to them. I stood up, slipped them on, and the four of us clustered around Julia's open palm while Renee shone the light on the bone. It looked so innocuous and innocent now, I could barely believe it had inspired such a frightening vision.

Now that I had donned the glasses, I leaned in and spotted small carvings in the bone. It appeared to be etched with intricate symbols that seemed to writhe and shift like a kaleidoscope. It would have been trippy and cool had I not been so frightened.

"What the heck? What are those?" The panic was evident in my voice. Even I knew that carvings didn't belong on bones.

Renee blew out a breath, her cheeks puffing. "That's a moon curse charm. They're used in some of the darkest hexing rituals."

I could feel my chest tightening, my breath coming in short gasps. "What...does that mean? Was some sort of curse put on me when I had the vision?"

Julia shook her head. "No. Definitely not. It takes a lot more than that to hex someone with your level of ability. But the fact that you had such a powerful vision, well, that's a strong indicator of something far more complex going on. Something more sinister. We'd always speculated whether Marigold was murdered, but we had no indication of it. Until now."

Silence overtook the room. Julia and Renee exchanged glances. I was left wondering about my ability. Was it really that strong?

"Wait," Renee said, her voice low and uncertain. "Do you feel that? There's definitely something off about the energy in this room and I'm pretty sure it has to do with this bone. Or the book. Or both."

Liz nodded, her face pale. "I feel it too. It's like a dark presence, watching us."

All of us glanced around the room, as if we were expecting something horrible to pop out of the shelves.

Julia flipped the book shut and began carefully wrapping the bone in the gauze. "I think we need to discuss over coffee. This is a serious situation and we need to do it with a clear head, away from all these bad vibes in here."

The four of us took over the coziest nook at Ice Ice Baby, the nearby café that served iced coffee, iced tea, and delicious pastries. The place had been renovated recently and the nook had a pale pink, curved velvet sofa around a low-slung plexiglass table that had an aquarium in its base. Two other matching pink chairs were on the other side of the table.

Still wearing Liz's fan, I sank into the plush sofa cushion with my iced Coconut and Macadamia nut coffee and studied the goldfish swimming inside the table. Finally, I was feeling a little more normal.

"Do you want this back?" I asked Liz while pointing at the little device around my neck. "It feels great."

She waved me away. "I'll order another one. Honestly, I think I should buy a case and hand them out to everyone I know."

Renee and Julia joined us with their coffees. We all turned to Julia, who blew out a breath.

"Things just got extremely complicated with Marigold's

case." She sipped her coffee. "Amelia, if you don't want to investigate, I totally understand."

I paused. Given that Mom was here, and that a guest was arriving, I should agree and take a pass.

But I shook my head, still unable to get the images from my vision out of my head. "I want to see this through."

"We won't think less of you if you decline," Renee said gently. "The coven encourages women to learn to say no, since it's usually so difficult for us."

"I can't *not* look into this. Once I've had a vision, it's difficult to forget. And this one," I shuddered, thinking of how I'd seen Marigold's finger severed in my vision, "makes me want justice."

"All right," Julia said softly.

"But I do have questions," I said.

Renee nodded. "We can try to answer, but I'm afraid we might be confused, as well."

I took another long gulp of my drink, then swallowed. "You all have looked at this book before, right? Was the bone inside that compartment? Did anyone else have a vision when they touched it?"

Julia and Renee shook their heads in tandem, but only Julia spoke. "Lots of us have inspected the book over the years. All the books listed on the card, in fact. We've never seen the bone. Not sure how, or when, that got there."

Renee nodded. "A few of us from the coven tried to review the clues of the case about six months ago. The bone wasn't there then."

"What does that mean?" I said, slightly panicked.

Julia shrugged. "It means that the person we're dealing with is pretty powerful, and anticipated someone was going to poke around so they planted the bone. Or they were hiding the bone for some reason. Or your powers conjured it somehow. I meant to ask you; did you see the carvings when you first picked up the bone?"

I shook my head.

"It's possible that you unlocked something powerful. You're the only one with psychometry, and the only one who has had this vision. Even Renee, whose astral projection abilities are quite strong, wasn't able to learn anything, but..."

Renee easily finished her sentence. "...but vibes. I felt extremely awful energy from the book and the bone."

"Wow," I muttered. It seemed difficult to believe that I had such strong powers. I was about to say something else but my gaze was drawn out the window. "Oh no."

The three women all twisted to look. We watched as people zoomed by on Segways. Bringing up the rear were my mother and Hal. Mom looked oddly gleeful, a detail that I thought endearing and a bit puzzling. I wouldn't have pegged her to enjoy that sort of thing.

Fortunately, they didn't stop, whizzing past in one long parade.

"Those things are dangerous. I swear, someone's going to get run over," Julia said, shaking her head.

I let out a nervous giggle.

"What?" Liz asked.

"Mom and her husband. They're on that tour." My hands nervously folded a napkin into a fan then figured I should clue in Julia and Renee. "My mother showed up unannounced last night. We have a bit of a difficult relationship, so this was a bit of a shock."

Collectively they murmured "ohhh," and wore faint expressions of alarm.

"It'll be okay, though," I said quickly. "She looks like she's having fun."

"Moms can be difficult," Renee said, in a tone that told me

she knew exactly what I was going through. The other two women nodded vigorously.

"I love her. But yeah, she's difficult. She's so, I don't know. Stiff upper lip. Won't talk about feelings. Thinks I'm being soft because I talk about my hot flashes. Refuses to discuss how angry or emotional I am while going through perimenopause." Somehow revealing these details to the group was almost as difficult as talking about the vision I'd just had.

Julia inhaled while nodding. "Those boomers and older women, they don't like to talk about anything involving midlife. It was something shameful. Something to be hidden."

"*The change of life*," Liz said. "That's what my mother called it. I remember she brought home a brochure with a butterfly on the cover. Then threw it in the trash."

"What are we changing into? I don't want to be a butterfly." I said, then shook my head. "Anyway. Back to business. Do we have any idea of who hurt Marigold? Do we think it had something to do with her starting the coven, or was it something more personal, like a boyfriend?"

Julia again shook her head. "Your guess is as good as ours. Since none of the current members were around when it was founded, it's difficult to say. It's Florida, so the population has been quite transient. We've only had a relatively stable membership these past five years or so."

I nodded, my mind already racing ahead to the next steps — and my next stop, which was the grocery store. Would I really have time for all this?

At that moment, the door to the café jingled, and a familiar figure walked in. My heart leapt. It was Oliver looking as handsome as ever in a fitted, oatmeal-colored Henley and jeans. Goodness, his shoulders looked muscular in that shirt. He was also growing a goatee, which made him look extra foxy.

His face lit up when he spotted me, and he made his way

over to our table. "Amelia, fancy meeting you here." His warm gaze took in the other women, and he gave a little wave. "Hey, everyone."

I stood, feeling a blush creep into my cheeks. "Oliver, hi. I wasn't expecting to run into you."

He grinned. "Needed a caffeine fix. You know how it is." He glanced at the group. "Mind if I steal Amelia away for a moment?"

The women all shook their heads, smiling knowingly. Liz winked.

I followed Oliver to a quiet corner of the café, out of earshot but still visible to my friends. That's when it hit me that I was wearing not only a fan around my neck, but a leopard print fanny pack around my waist and leopard print reading glasses on my head.

Despite being the biggest middle-aged dork on the planet, I summoned all of my confidence and grinned saucily at him.

"Cool headphones," Oliver said, pointing to my fan. "Are those Beats by Dre?"

Fan for perimenopause, I wanted to say, but decided not to get into it. "They're Liz's."

"Oh, sweet." He grinned, and I thanked the universe that men were so clueless about, well, most things. "Are you liking the coven leaders? How's the investigation going?" he asked, his eyebrows rising with curiosity. "I'll bet you've solved it already."

"Uh, no. Far from it." I took a deep breath and gave him a quick rundown of the morning's events: the library, the hidden bone, the terrifying vision. His expression grew serious as he listened.

"Whoa, Amelia. That's intense. Are you okay?" He reached out and squeezed my hand, his touch comforting. "Any headaches?"

I shook my head. Oliver had been with me during many of my first visions when I came to town. He knew that sometimes I'd had splitting headaches afterward.

"Oddly, no headache. I'm a little shaken, but I'll be okay. I can't stop thinking about poor Marigold and what might have happened to her. I need to figure this out. Probably that's stupid of me, but I can't shake that feeling. It's like when we were looking into Billy's case."

Billy had been the ghost who haunted the inn when I bought it — and once I'd had an intense vision of how he was murdered in the attic, it was difficult to forget.

Oliver nodded. "Listen, I've got some free time this morning. Why don't I check the newspaper archives to see if I can dig up any old articles about Marigold's disappearance? There might be some clues there. Those articles should be online through LexisNexis and I have an account through the university."

Gratitude washed over me. "That would be amazing, Oliver. Thank you."

He pulled me in for a quick hug, his lips brushing my cheek and his chin bumping into my fan. "Anything for you, Amelia. I'll let you know what I find."

He stepped back, a mischievous sparkle in his eyes. "And don't forget the concert tomorrow. I've got that surprise planned."

I grinned, but inside I was groaning. What was I going to do with Mom and Hal during the concert? Mom wouldn't pass up an opportunity to check out the guy I was dating. They'd have to come along with me. Hal loved jazz, so he'd probably appreciate Oliver's guitar playing. Or perhaps they'd stay at the inn, exhausted from their days of fun.

That's it: I could tire them out.

"I wouldn't miss it for the world," I said.

We said goodbye, with him going to the counter and me returning to the ladies. They all studied me with slight smiles as I sat back down.

"You know, Oliver seems like a different man in recent months." Liz tapped an index finger on her chin.

"I wonder what it is." Renee broke out into a grin.

"Hmm," Julia added.

"Hmm, indeed. Listen, I would love to stay and hang out, but I want to go through the clues in the basket again, and I have to get ready for some guests. And brace myself for Mom and Hal. Would it be okay if we—"

Renee flapped her hand at the door. "Do what you need to do! We'll be around if you need us."

"But make sure to call us if you come up with anything else," Julia said, staring at me over her reading glasses.

Ten

An hour later I was in the produce aisle of Sprout and About, the town's sprawling natural foods store. I preferred this over the large chain supermarket, mostly because it had a wide selection of herbs, spices and organic produce — and a well-stocked baking aisle, along with candles and other witchy items.

I paused at the rhubarb. The greenish-pink stalks looked lovely, and I imagined making strawberry-rhubarb French toast for the guests tomorrow. I'd no sooner stuffed some into an eco-friendly paper bag when my phone buzzed.

It was Oliver. He didn't even say hello.

"Are you sitting down?"

"Uh, no, I'm in the produce aisle of Sprout and About."

"Okay, well, hold onto your celery. You're not going to believe what I've found. I'll email everything but let me give you a recap."

Holding the phone between my ear and shoulder, I pushed the cart to a secluded corner, in between the potato and onion displays. "Lay it on me."

"I found an article in the student paper archives." He

sounded excited, almost out of breath. "It was written by two students back in 1993. Tracy North and Marigold Wentworth. A couple of months before Marigold went missing."

"Really?" A zing of adrenaline went through me at the mention of their names.

"According to what they wrote, the two women were in the early stages of founding a coven for young witches in Cypress Grove, and this article was something of a call to arms for Gen X witches. A manifesto."

"That checks out with what Julia and Renee told me."

"As part of their research, they were looking into the life and death of a woman named Tiffany Ferndale, who apparently died in 1986. In Cypress Grove. Drowned in a lake."

I gasped. "Wait. Could that be—"

"Tiffany who lives in the lake?"

"My favorite ghost?" I'd met Tiffany while investigating the murder of my bridesmaid guest. She somehow resided in a lake here in town and was able to come ashore only via my psychometric powers. She also sported the most fabulous 80s outfits. None of it made sense to me, but I visited her every week or so to chat about old music. I considered her a friend, one that couldn't leave the small beach.

Interestingly, the lake was located in Marigold Wentworth park. "The plot is definitely boiling, if not thickening."

"Sure seems like it. Here, I'm emailing you the article. And a few others, too. They're mostly crime stories about Marigold's disappearance and Tracy's death in 1995 from the car crash."

"Wow." I stretched the word out in a long exhale. "I'm now wondering if all of their deaths are connected."

Oliver sucked in a breath. "Might be a bit early to say, but it sure seems like more than coincidence. Three young women, either missing or dead."

"Thanks for all this."

"Anytime. Let me know if you need anything else. Oh, hey, I have a Zoom call. Crap. You've distracted me again, Amelia." His rich chuckle was so wonderful to hear. "Gotta run."

"Bye."

After I hung up, I let out a grunt of annoyance. I should've told him about Mom and Hal coming to the concert. I checked the time. It was only noon. I still had time for a little more sleuthing before I had to return to the inn to prepare for the weekend guests.

Since I didn't have any perishables — and because I always carried a cooler in the back of my car — I stashed the groceries in there and drove to Marigold Wentworth Park. I'd gotten to know the place well during my investigation last October.

It had become one of my favorite places in town, mostly because of Tiffany. I visited her enough to keep a small, 80s-era boom box in my car, since she enjoyed music and could only listen on devices from her era. It was a quirk of people like her who resided in the In Between.

I'd come to think of it as sort of a way-station between the living and the dead, one where the ghosts desperately wanted to listen to tunes from their era.

What I didn't know, however, was how Tiffany died. I knew nothing about her arrival in the lake or the In Between. She'd seemed hesitant about telling me any personal details, and I hadn't pried, instead deciding to enjoy her company and bonding over the music of my (our) youth.

By now, the neck fan had run out of juice, so when I arrived at the park, I pulled the car to a stop and removed the device. I then attempted to read the email from Oliver with the newspaper article, but since it was a PDF and my eyesight was failing in mid-age, I quickly abandoned that effort.

The small, round boom box fit discreetly into a backpack, and I strapped that on, stuffing my fanny pack and the mixtape inside as well. Then I set off, down the wooden boardwalk.

Truthfully, I was thankful for this interlude. I needed exercise, and being in nature cleared my head from all the swirling thoughts about the investigation and Mom.

Something about the wind rustling the leaves of the cypress trees lulled me into a Zen-like state. It was difficult to be anxious out here, under cloudless blue skies and a warm Florida winter sun.

The only sounds were the creak of the boards under my sneakers, the distant call of a mockingbird, and the gentle lapping of water against the cypress knees that rose from the dark, tea-colored swamp. It was as if the grove existed in a world apart, untouched by the passage of time. Maybe this was the real In Between, the place between old and new Florida, the checkpoint between the living and the dead.

Within fifteen minutes I reached the lake. It was a small body of water with a crescent of sand. Today, a couple of families dotted the beach with umbrellas, buckets, and coolers. I toe-heeled my sneakers off and left them where the boardwalk met the sand, then marched down to the water's edge.

The only way to get Tiffany out of the lake was to touch the water. Somehow, my psychometry summoned her. I skimmed my hand across the surface, as if I was testing whether to swim. Of course, I never would, since there were almost surely gators in the lake. But this part was safe enough, and I didn't see any nearby critters.

Within a few seconds, I watched as a sparkling, iridescent Tiffany emerged. Today she wore a hot pink, off-the-shoulder sweatshirt with a neon aqua triangle on the front, and what looked like electric blue parachute pants.

"Hey, what's up?" she said while walking out of the water.

"Hey. Let's step into our office," I whispered. "Love the pants."

She knew that was her cue to be quiet and not engage me in conversation. I was most likely the only one here who could see and hear Tiffany. And while Cypress Grove was known for its paranormal and metaphysical practitioners, that didn't mean I wanted to be seen talking to myself at the park.

Tiffany glided next to me as we made our way over to a semi-secluded picnic bench under a couple of palm trees. It was out of earshot of the families, and shady, which was a bonus. I'd come to realize I could see Tiffany better in the shade.

"What's new with you?" Tiffany asked. "Did you watch the MTV video music awards?"

"Sadly, I didn't." I unzipped the bag and took out the boom box, and the tape. "I don't think I would recognize any of the singers these days anyway."

Tiffany sighed impatiently. It must be difficult to be a young adult for eternity.

"How about you? How are things in the water?"

"Oh, you know. Chad's being a total grody jerk." Chad was one of the newer ghosts who lived in the lake, and Tiffany sure seemed to talk about him a lot. Our friendship wasn't so solid that I felt as though I could joke about their relationship yet. Instead, I treated her as I did my own, twenty-year-old daughter: with amused interest and a firm-yet-gentle Mom attitude.

"What tape have you got today?"

I popped Marigold's cassette into the boom box, pressed play, then slid the plastic holder across the picnic table. She bent over it.

"I know some of these songs. The others, not so much.

Songs From the Edge of Forever. That's an awesome title. Wish I'd thought of it."

The deep bass of The Police's Every Breath You Take started.

"I used to love this song," she said, sighing dramatically like only a young person could.

"Yeah? I did too. Still really like it."

We listened to Sting croon.

"I don't like it anymore. It's creepy. The lyrics are creepy. You ever think about how this is sung from a stalker's point of view?"

Her words sent fear fizzing through me, similar to when I'd had the vision earlier. "That's an interesting take."

"Where'd you get this tape, anyway?" She scowled at the plastic case.

"That's an interesting story. It's the mixtape of a young woman who went missing in 1993."

"Oh, really? Another investigation?" Tiffany had helped me piece together clues in the bridesmaid murder.

"Yep. Another one. But this one, it's a real puzzle. I'm not sure if I'll be able to figure it out."

"Oh yeah? How come?"

"Because the woman who disappeared, and who I think was murdered, died while she was trying to start a coven here in town. And she and her friend were researching *your* case when she vanished. Her friend died in a car crash later. I'm trying to figure out if all this is connected, so I was hoping you could tell me about your life, and maybe if you are up for it, your death. There are too many coincidences here."

The song faded out and I pressed the pause button. An uncomfortable silence settled between us.

Tiffany stared at me, her glowing gray eyes wide with shock.

"They were researching *me*?" Her usual bubbly demeanor had evaporated. "Why would anyone look into my death?"

I leaned forward, sensing I struck a nerve. We'd never had a conversation about her demise, and never one this tense. "I'm not sure. That's what I'm trying to figure out. I think Marigold's disappearance, her friend Tracy's death, and your, ah, situation, might all be connected somehow."

"Marigold." Tiffany's voice had gone low and flat.

"Yes. Marigold Wentworth. The woman the park is named after. If you could tell me more about what happened to you, it could help me put the pieces together."

Tiffany abruptly stood up from the picnic table, her expression a mixture of fear and anger. I'd never seen her look so alarmed. Usually, her demeanor was a cross between a saucy Valley Girl at the mall and a bubbly cheerleader.

"No way. I can't go down that road again. You have no idea what you're getting yourself into."

"But Tiffany, if there's a chance your death is linked to the others, don't you want the truth to come out? Don't you want justice?" I pleaded, also rising so I could look her in the eye. "Please. I can help you if you help me."

She shook her head. "You totally think I haven't tried to help myself? That I haven't spent years wondering why, haunted by my own questions and mistakes?" Her voice trembled. "Some secrets are better left buried. I won't drag you into my mess. I like you too much for that. I don't know what happened to those other girls. But if it's anything to do with me, then I'm sorry for them. They should've left everything alone."

Before I could respond, Tiffany turned and floated towards the water's edge. "Forget about me, Amelia. Forget all of this. Trust me, you'll be better off," she called over her shoulder.

"Tiffany, wait!" I called out, not caring about the people on the beach, who had turned and were staring at me. But it was too late.

Her shimmering form hit the lake's surface and instantly dissolved into a million molecules, blending into the gentle current until no trace of her remained. I stood, stunned, staring at the spot where she evaporated into the water.

Tiffany's extreme reaction only reinforced my hunch that her death was the key to unraveling this whole mystery. But her refusal to confide in me, her insistence that I abandon the investigation for my own good left me reeling.

Now I had even more questions.

Frustrated, I ejected Marigold's mixtape from the boom box and carefully slid it into the case. The 80s tunes now felt like a mocking soundtrack to my 21st century crime-solving dilemma.

As I slowly packed up my things to leave, my mind raced to make sense of Tiffany's warning. What dark secret was she so afraid of unearthing? How much danger was I really in by pursuing the truth? And what had Marigold and Tracy discovered about Tiffany that had put their lives in danger?

Eleven

The Sisters of Hecate:
A Coven for the Totally Bitchin' Witch
By Tracy North and Marigold Wentworth
Central Florida College Daily Beacon

I paused to snicker at the headline then looked down. Freddie was rubbing against my ankles. I was now home and slumped over my phone at the kitchen counter, reading everything that Oliver had sent. The article in the school paper seemed like a good place to start.

> *As young witches coming of age at the end of the twentieth century, the two of us often felt like we didn't quite fit in, either in the mainstream education system or in the established Wiccan circles frequented mainly by our parents' generation.*
>
> *We yearned for a spiritual home that spoke directly to our experiences, our pop culture touchstones, and the challenges of practicing the Craft as Gen X women.*
>
> *That's why we decided to create our own coven: the Sisters of*

Hecate. Named for the ancient goddess of magic, sorcery, and necromancy, our vision is an inclusive sisterhood for Wiccans, Pagans, and metaphysical practitioners in their teens and twenties. This will be a haven where we can honor the Old Ways while boldly reinventing modern witchcraft.

A little shiver went through me as I squinted at the plain text PDF. Probably I should get out my laptop but I was already too engrossed. This was the true origin of the coven.

Central to our approach is the belief that magic is all around us, woven into the fabric of our everyday lives. The Sisters of Hecate find enchantment in urban cityscapes and natural landscapes. We draw power from pop songs and ancient chants. For us, an MTV music video can be a potent magical experience, and our Book of Shadows might be scrawled in a Lisa Frank notebook.

Marigold and Tracy covered a lot of ground: the environment, technology, addiction. It was a lot to absorb, but I was impressed how two young women had identified so many women's issues at such a young age. I think in my early twenties I was still trying to balance my checkbook without having a mini panic attack every month, while trying to afford the Banana Republic sale rack and crappy box wine.

Ours is a path of both mysticism and resistance, of shadow work and social justice, of dance parties and direct action.

In a world that calls our generation apathetic slackers, we want to harness the revolutionary power of connection and community. In a culture that commodifies and co-opts the sacred, we are fiercely protecting the one true thing we can do for free: form female friendships.

"Awww," I whispered, pressing my hand to my heart. The entire piece was filled with youthful fire and idealism. I could easily see my daughter writing something like this in a journal. Or me, back in the day. Although I was never bold enough to try to get anything published, I'd been far too unfocused in my early twenties for that.

I had to admire Marigold and Tracy for putting themselves out there in the school paper. I read it twice more and was stuck on one part:

One such story that haunts me is that of Tiffany Ferndale, a young woman whose body was found in a lake under myste-rious circumstances in Cypress Grove back in 1986. Her death was ruled an accident, but we believe something more sinister was at play. We've discovered whispers and rumors that suggest Tiffany may have been targeted for her witchy interests and independent spirit.

"Wow," I whispered aloud. Seeing Tiffany mentioned, learning her last name, and finding out she'd been into witch-craft had come as a shock. "Goodness, that letter's something else."

"Howdy? Anyone here?" The male voice cut through my thoughts.

"Jimbo? I'm in the kitchen."

Heavy footsteps echoed and a few seconds later, my lanky employee stood in the doorway. Today he wore jeans, a Crescent Moon Inn T-shirt and a trucker cap embroidered with a tarpon fish.

"I wanted to check in before I left. Everything okay with you, Miss Amelia?" He took off his cap and ran his fingers through his thinning, sandy brown hair.

"I'm great, just trying to put together some hors d'oeuvres

for the guests coming soon." I wiped my hands, briefly studying the deviled eggs loaded with bacon, chives, steak seasoning and pickled jalapenos. "You want one?"

"I never turn down food from you, ma'am." Jimbo was a native Floridian. It had taken me a while to get used to his polite speech, but now I loved listening to his genteel accent.

I slid a couple of eggs on a small plate and handed it to him. "I meant to tell you when I came in, but you were on the phone. My mom and stepfather are staying in the Lavender and Lace room this weekend. It was an unannounced visit."

"Well, that's nice. Sometimes family surprises are the thing you need." He popped an entire egg into his mouth and chewed.

"I don't know about that, but it's good to see them, I suppose." I placed another egg on his plate, since I'd made a few dozen. "Mom and Hal don't know about my, er, powers. Let's keep it that way, okay?"

Jimbo swallowed, winked, cocked his thumb and forefinger at me, and clicked his tongue. "Got it, partner."

Recently, he'd started dating Oliver's sister Sage. She considered herself a "cowgirl witch," and Jimbo had picked up a lot of her lingo. I smiled. "How are the eggs?"

"Real good. Real good." He popped another one in and I noticed his eyes go to the window, where the orchids sat. "Those are growing great with the light in here."

"My mother loved them. She thinks you're interested in me because you're giving me plants."

We shared a chuckle. "I guess I probably shouldn't tell her about *my* secret power, either."

I tilted my head. Was he joking? "Hunh?"

He tilted his head, too, but in the opposite direction of me. "Wait. You don't know? Sage didn't tell you?"

"Know what?"

"Why I've been giving you all the orchids."

"Uhh...no."

He tipped his head back and chuckled. "I thought someone had told you."

I shook my head and turned to the eggs, sprinkling some chives on top. "Told me what?"

"I'm a plant shaman." He wolfed down another egg.

I stopped with the chives. "I'm sorry. What's a plant shaman?"

"I hear the call of the plants. I believe plants can heal us, if we listen. And I talk to them, too, say some real tender and kind things so they grow. That's why I bring you the orchids, I don't have much room at my place. And Sage kills all the plants I give her." He let out a sigh.

"So you talk to...plants grow...when did you...what?" I stammered, shaking my head.

"Yeah, it surprised me when I first moved to town. I got a job as a landscaper and randomly started talking to some sad-looking bromeliads at one lady's house. The next day they'd not only healed, but they'd multiplied. My boss at the time was into plant magic, and that's when I discovered my ability."

This wasn't the strangest thing I'd heard in Cypress Grove, but it was definitely in the top five. "Well, that explains a lot, Jimbo. That's cool, actually. But yeah, let's not tell my mom that. Say you have some special fertilizer or something."

He laughed. "Will do. And if you ever need a plant revived, or information about a plant, you let me know, okay?"

I narrowed my eyes and wiped my hands on my apron. "You know, that reminds me of something. Come here."

Passing Jimbo, I walked into the living room where the basket of clues sat on the coffee table. I flipped open the top and reached in for the delicate flower pressed between two pieces of wax paper. I held it out to him.

"I'm trying to investigate the disappearance of Marigold Wentworth. She left this behind. Do you think you could gather any information from it with your shamanic powers? Is that the right term?"

He took it from me as if it were a sacred text, holding it in his big, rough hands. "I'll try, Miss Amelia. I'll try real hard when I get home."

"Thank you," I said. "Now, let me pack you some cookies to go."

The guests arrived, right on time. They were a lovely couple from Wisconsin, a fact that I suspected would make Hal giddy with joy. He seemed to miss the upper Midwest while living in Arizona with Mom and had once mentioned to her that he'd like to return.

Mom had adamantly said no, she wasn't living anywhere with snow.

The guests, who were about Mom and Hal's age and whose names were Maude and Steve, were in town to visit psychics and reiki masters. After that, they were headed to meet the grandkids at Disney. They also adored my eggs and the expensive bottle of Napa cabernet I'd uncorked.

They snacked, stashed their suitcases in their room, and left for some psychic banquet happening at the community center. I cleaned up and poured myself a second glass of sparkling water, wondering why Mom and Hal hadn't returned yet.

I'd texted them earlier but had only gotten a quick response back from Mom.

Having fun, see you later.

I hoped "later" meant "soon," because I was getting hungry. Eh, duck it. I broke into the eggs, my cheese stash, and some Triscuits. I added a few baby carrots to the plate so I could claim I'd eaten a vegetable.

Girl dinner, my daughter would call it.

I was making serious headway on the plate when Mom and Hal strolled in, looking surprisingly fresh.

"What a wonderful town," Mom gushed.

"There's a lot happening here," Hal chimed in.

I washed down a cracker with a quick sip of bubbly water. "Glad you had fun. I saw you two out on the Segways, but you were moving too fast for me to catch up."

"I think Linda and I will be buying a pair of those so we can cruise around our community," Hal mused while eyeing my plate.

"Oh! Let me get you some snacks. I've been busy entertaining the guests." I babbled for a moment about the couple from Wisconsin.

"We've already eaten," Mom said, snapping back to her normally frosty self. She poured herself a splash of the wine and scowled into the glass.

"We did the early bird at some pub," Hal offered.

Mom pointed at me. "And you need to get ready."

"For what?" I offered Hal my plate, which had one lone egg. He snarfed it down before Mom could say anything, but she shot him a dirty look anyway.

"We met a wonderful man who opened an art gallery downtown. Tonight's the launch party. He's heard of you and I want you to meet him. I think he's just your—"

I held up a hand. "Mom, don't try to play matchmaker. I'm serious. I'm not in the market for a man."

Because I already have one, I wanted to say. But I didn't, because I didn't feel like launching into that particular conversation right now. I figured I'd let her see how talented and wonderful Oliver was first, then spring the news on her.

"As a local business owner, you should get to know others in the community. Now go get ready. It's going to be quite the party. With heavy appetizers and wine."

I perked up like Freddie sometimes does when he rises on his hind legs. "Heavy apps?"

Hal met my gaze with a pleading look.

"Give me ten minutes," I said, hauling myself to my feet. I scooped up the clue basket for fear Mom would try to snag it again and took it with me into my room.

"Wear something feminine," Mom called out. "And put on some blush. You'll look more alive."

Heavy apps, I repeated to myself like a mantra.

Twelve

Once again, I found myself shuffling into the unknown with Mom and Hal. Fortunately, I wasn't tipsy tonight since I hadn't been drinking. Yet.

"How did you guys find this place, anyway?" I asked as Hal parked the rental car. I was in the rear seat and poked my head into the front. We were a couple of miles from Main Street, in a small village area with a neighborhood park ringed by small shops. I'd driven past here but hadn't yet stopped to check it out.

"We came all the way here on the Segways," Hal said. He'd raved about the scooters for the entire drive over. "Cypress Grove has a bike path from downtown to here. Have you been on it?"

"Not yet. I need to get a bike. That's on my list."

"Dear, you really must get out more. You can't stay in that stuffy old house all the time with your cat. What's his name again?"

"Freddie. And I don't stay inside all the time. I've met a

wonderful group of friends and have an active social life. More so than in California."

"Hmph. Then how did you not know about this event tonight?" Mom said in an accusatory tone while Hal expertly parallel parked on a side street.

"Mom. I'm forty-seven, going through perimenopause, just moved cross country a few months ago, and started a new business. I also try to keep up with Jenny. Geez. There are only so many hours in the day." I wanted to add that usually I tried to be in bed by nine because midlife exhaustion was kicking my butt.

But Mom never displayed any sort of weakness when she was my age, so I sucked it up. We all climbed out of the car. Mom did a quick, head-to-toe appraisal of my outfit. "Well, we're out now, and we're going to have fun. I can't wait for you to meet Dominic."

The three of us set out on the sidewalk. "Already on a first name basis, hmm?"

Hal chuckled. "Your mom talked his ear off today. That's how we finagled an invite to this shindig."

I fought back a grimace. The promise of the *heavy apps* was starting to be in question. I started mentally going through the cheese drawer in my fridge, trying to remember if I'd eaten all of the Brie.

We turned a corner onto a busy block. A café with sidewalk tables and hanging plants, along with what looked like two open galleries, a bar, and a bookstore were positively bubbling with activity. It was a cozy neighborhood hub, and I imagined living nearby, walking to meet friends for a drink.

"Cute," I murmured aloud while stuffing my hands into the pockets of my dress. I'd changed into a flowy, long, batik print dress I'd gotten at Liz's shop.

The gallery was in the middle of the block, and probably

the busiest place with the exception of the café. Mom marched in, weaving her way around clusters of people, while Hal and I brought up the rear.

The gallery was packed with people, their chatter and laughter mixing with soft jazz music playing in the background. The walls were adorned with vibrant abstract paintings, and servers wove through the crowd with trays of appetizers and glasses of wine.

I had to admit, the place was quite swanky. Strains of Chet Baker wafted through the air, instantly elevating the party with a sophisticated, city vibe.

But I couldn't pause to soak it all in, because Mom was on a mission. She clamped her hand around my wrist, her eyes scanning the room like a hawk searching for its prey.

Suddenly her manicured nails dug into my skin. "There he is! Yoohoo! Dominic, darling!"

A tall, handsome man in his early fifties turned at the sound of his name. He had salt-and-pepper hair, a well-trimmed beard, and was dressed in a stylish suit. His eyes widened slightly as he saw my mother barreling towards him, dragging me along and flapping her other hand in a wave.

I detected a hint of panic in his expression.

"Linda, so lovely to see you again so soon," he said smoothly, his gaze flickering to me. "And this must be your daughter, Amelia. The motel manager."

"Innkeeper." I reminded myself to give the man a chance and not dislike him in the first five seconds of meeting him.

"Yes, yes, this is my beautiful, single daughter," Mom gushed, practically shoving me into Dominic's personal space. "Amelia, meet Dominic Harper, the owner of this fabulous gallery. He's new in town."

I extended my hand, trying to ignore the heat of embarrassment rising in my cheeks. "Nice to meet you, Dominic. Welcome to Cypress Grove. I'm also a newcomer."

He shook my hand firmly, his eyes crinkling at the corners as he smiled. "The pleasure is all mine. Your mother has told me so much about you."

I shot a hard stare at Mom, who was wearing the same expression Freddie did when he caught a lizard the other week. "Oh, I'm sure she has."

A stunning young woman in a form-fitting red dress sauntered by, catching Dominic's eye. She couldn't have been more than twenty-five, and she was absolutely gorgeous.

"If you'll excuse me," Dominic said, his attention drifting, "I need to attend to some other guests."

Without waiting for a response, he made a beeline for the young woman, leaving me and Mom standing there awkwardly.

"Of course," I muttered under my breath, rolling my eyes. Mom sure could pick them. But what did I expect? She'd also adored my philandering ex-husband.

Mom huffed, clearly disappointed by the turn of events. "Well, that was rude. He could have at least finished the conversation."

I couldn't help but laugh. "Mom, it's pretty clear that Dominic isn't interested in being set up with your middle-aged daughter. He's got his sights set on a younger model. And once again, I have to remind you: I'm not interested."

Mom opened her mouth to argue, but then thought better of it. "Fine. Let's enjoy the party, okay?"

I nodded, grabbing a glass of wine from a passing tray. As I sipped my drink, I scanned the room, hoping to avoid any familiar faces. The last thing I needed was for someone to approach me and start gushing about my psychic abilities in front of Mom.

I caught sight of a woman with long, frizzy gray hair and a loose sapphire-colored caftan. It was Corinne, a friendly acquaintance I'd met at Liz's shop. She was a psychic who frequented the store for crystals and herbs. Corrine spotted me and waved enthusiastically, making her way through the crowd.

I panicked, quickly downing the rest of my drink and grabbing Hal's arm while pretending not to see Corrine. "Hey, let's go check out the snack buffet over there."

Hal, who was likely starving, didn't question my suggestion. We left Mom to chat up a young couple and swarmed the food table, piling our small plates high with cheese cubes, crackers, and mini quiches, the adorable and tasty kind that seem to always disappear first at parties.

"Mmm, bacon," Hal said in between mouthfuls.

"Is Mom starving you?" I joked, reaching for a cheese cube.

Hal responded with a chuckle. "You know Linda. Always the health nut."

As we wolfed down our snacks, I couldn't help but scan the room again, keeping an eye out for Corrine.

To my horror, I spotted her across the gallery, chatting animatedly with none other than my mother. They were smiling and laughing, and I could feel my stomach drop as Corrine gestured in my direction, waving at me with such enthusiasm that she looked like an air traffic controller.

I knew in my bones that she was telling Mom all about me. I'd only met her a couple of times, but she was a chatty sort. She was also about eighty, and from my few dealings with her, got the distinct impression that she didn't have an internal filter.

Something Liz had said echoed in my brain: *Corrine's lovely but she can't keep a secret to save her life.*

I grunted aloud, stuffing my plate into a nearby garbage

can. Hal shot me a questioning look, but I shook my head. "I'll be right back. Duty calls."

Reluctantly, I made my way over to Mom and Corrine. I passed by Dominic, who was still seemingly captivated with the young woman. I caught a snippet of his conversation.

"When I owned a gallery in New York..."

The young woman looked bored. He didn't acknowledge my presence, nor I his. I had far bigger fish to fry.

As I approached Mom, I plastered on my best fake smile despite the churn in my guts.

"Amelia, darling!" Corrine exclaimed, pulling me into a hug. "I was telling your mother about how incredible you are with your psychometric gifts. She claims to have no idea, but I found that hard to believe! I told her all about how you solved the mystery of Billy, that ghost in your inn."

Oh duck. Duckity duck. My worst fears had turned to reality. Mom stared at me, unblinking. This was exactly the way I didn't want to tell Mom about my new life. She wasn't going to understand, and now I was decidedly on the defensive.

I shot Mom a panicked look, but she raised an eyebrow, her expression unreadable. "Is that so?" she said, her tone neutral. "How interesting. At midlife, no less."

"Oh yes," Corrine gushed, oblivious to both my discomfort and Mom's steely gaze. "Amelia is one of the most talented practitioners in Cypress Grove. Her abilities are truly remarkable. She's getting a real reputation around town."

I cleared my throat, trying to find the right words while my chest squeezed with anxiety. Was I having a heart attack? I pressed my hand to my chest and rubbed in a circle.

"Corrine, I appreciate the kind words, but I don't think that's exactly true or even interest—"

"Nonsense," Mom cut me off, her voice sharp. "I think it's

fascinating. Please, Corrine, tell me more about these...abilities."

Corrine beamed, clearly thrilled to have a captive audience. "Well, Amelia has this gift called psychometry. She can touch an object and get all sorts of information. Emotions, memories, even facts. It's quite extraordinary. We have many run-of-the-mill psychics and witches here in town, but Amelia's abilities are on another level."

Mom turned to me, her eyes narrowing. "I see. And what else have you been up to here? Seances? Ghost hunting?"

"Erm..." I cleared my throat, hoping this would be the moment that a sinkhole opened below my feet and swallowed me whole. This was exactly what I'd hoped to avoid with my mother. I knew she'd somehow turn this around and make it my fault.

"Actually, yes," Corrine chimed in unhelpfully. "Remember that séance we went to a couple of weekends ago?"

It was true, and a night I'd almost forgotten, what with Mom's visit and Marigold's case and the coven. Liz had hosted a séance to connect with a deceased business owner in town. She'd owned the old movie theater, and Liz thought it would be a fun idea to ask her for Oscar picks.

I shot Corrine a pleading look, silently begging her to stop talking. For a psychic, she wasn't that perceptive, at least not tonight.

But it was too late. The cat was not only out of the bag, but was roaming around the room looking for a meal. I massaged my collarbone. The fleeting chest pain had subsided, but the anxiety hadn't. Mom hated when other people knew juicy details and she didn't.

"Well," Mom said finally, her tone icy. "It seems there's a lot you haven't been telling me, Amelia. I thought we were close, but apparently, you've been keeping quite a few secrets. I'd really like—"

Before she could say more, I interrupted. "It's not really a big deal, so let's discuss this later, in private."

Corrine had finally dialed into my discomfort and turned to my mother. "Linda, that's your name, right? I think the second bar recently opened. Why don't you join me for a gin and tonic?"

"Wonderful idea." I clapped my hands together, still feeling a mixture of guilt and shame. "And oh, look! It's the police chief. Excuse me, I need to chat with him about something important."

I quickly extricated myself from Mom's stare and power-walked over to Christopher Wolf, who was standing alone in front of a large painting of a crystal ball. At least that's what I thought it was. Upon further inspection, I think it was a snow globe.

But I wasn't here for an art appreciation class. "Hey there, Chief! How's it going?"

Being a tall man, he looked down. "Oh, hey. Are you here with Liz?"

He had it bad for my friend. I cracked the first grin of the night. "No, I think she has theater tonight. She didn't mention this so maybe she didn't know about it? Usually she's so plugged in."

He snapped his fingers. "That's right. The Shakespeare thing. She's so busy I can't keep up."

Liz, whose grandparents came from Cuba, was doing the costumes for an all-Latino youth theater group. I nodded. "Enjoying the art?"

We stood next to each other and studied the painting. He took a sip from his drink and pulverized an ice cube with his teeth. "What is it?"

"I think it's a snow globe."

We both tilted our heads. "Or maybe it's a globe," he said.

"The more I stare at it, I think it's more like the universe." I shook my head and turned to face him. "Hey, I have a question for you about missing persons."

"And why is that?"

"I've been watching a lot of those true crime shows." It struck me that I wasn't a great liar, but I pressed on. "Do police keep records of missing persons?"

A frown darkened his face. "Of course. We don't throw things away, it's all on a computer. You copy?"

That was the other thing about Chief Wolf. He spoke in cop lingo, like he was perpetually on a police radio. Liz thought it was adorable, but I secretly wondered if he said things like "10-4" after they kissed.

"Even a case, from, say, the mid-eighties or early nineties?"

"Amelia, stop beating around the bush. What's going on?"

"Well." I cleared my throat, then coughed.

"Do you want something to drink?" Wolf asked. "Water?"

"Wine. Please. White."

He nodded once, and being a southern gentleman, hustled off. I remained in place, trying to gather my thoughts while eyeing the crystal ball-snow-globe-universe painting.

Maybe it was a womb?

Wolf returned within a few minutes, holding two glasses of wine. He offered one to me. "Are you in trouble?"

I was about to take a sip when I huffed in protest. "No, why would you think that?"

He shook his head. "Something tells me you're poking around."

I rolled my eyes. "Fine. Yes. I'm part of a civic group," I paused, hoping that sounded plausible, "That is doing some research into the founder. She disappeared in the early 90s. That's all. It's information for the organization."

He narrowed his eyes. "Is Liz involved in this?"

"Ummm," I took another sip so I could stall. "Not exactly, no."

"What do you need from me? Police reports are public record."

I studied his face. Usually, Wolf looked like something out of an action movie. Totally not my type — I liked the more studious, nerdy guys — but something about Wolf's earnest expression made me nod.

"I'd love to see any reports about Marigold Wentworth. From 1993." I gave him the salient details about her case, including the date.

He handed me his drink while he took a notebook and pen out of his back jeans pocket. He clicked the pen in my direction. "I'm always ready to investigate."

He jotted a few things, then slipped everything back into his pocket. I handed him his wine.

"I'll try to check this out tomorrow when I'm in the office."

"On a Saturday?" Inside I was doing a fist pump. It would be incredible if he could find reports for me that soon.

"A chief's work is never done. Anyway, I'll be happy to look up that case. Since you're friends with Liz and all." He grinned. "She talks about you all the time."

We chatted about her for a while, and I was grateful to get a few minutes break from thinking about Mom, murder, and mayhem. A waiter strolled by with a tray of pigs-in-a-blanket, and Wolf and I piled two plates high.

"So, let me ask your opinion," he said, brandishing a cocktail wiener on a toothpick. "Since you're new in town like me."

"Okay." I braced myself for a question about Liz.

"Do you really believe all this stuff in town? All the," he popped the hot dog in his mouth. "Psychic stuff?"

"It's a smart question. But, yes. I do. Before coming here, I would've laughed at the idea of psychic powers. And I've stayed awake many nights since moving here, wondering how I developed certain abilities since moving to Cypress Grove. But Liz always tells me that it's best not to think about it too much, to let the vibes take over."

He nodded. "She's told me that as well."

"Do you think you might have some abilities?" There had been a rumor around town that he was a werewolf. Some signs had pointed to this, specifically the fact that he owned a rather large Husky. Both Liz and I didn't feel like this was quite enough evidence. Still, I wasn't going to be the one to ask him if he turned into a canine.

I'd leave that to Liz.

His thick brow furrowed. "I'm not sure. And that uncertainty is possibly more unsettling than the truth."

It sure sounded like he was grappling with something. "Maybe Liz can suggest a men's group. Or something."

"Good idea." He turned to stare at the painting. "You know, now that I look at this again, I think it's a toilet bowl."

I squinted at the painting while closing one eye. "You might be onto something there."

We drank in silence for a few minutes and then I saw Hal approaching me with an apologetic expression.

"Hey, Hal. Let me introduce you to our police chief."

Hal and Wolf chatted briefly, then Hal glanced at me. "I think your mom's ready to leave."

"Oh! Oh." I sensed tension in the air. "Of course. Well, have a good night, Chief."

"You too, Amelia. I'll be in touch about that thing. 10-4."

Hal and I weaved through the clusters of people, back to

the bar. That was where Mom was downing her gin and tonic. She tossed the empty cup in a nearby trash can.

"I'm ready," she said, her head held high and stiff.

We walked out, silent the entire way to the car. My stomach was in knots as we drove back to the Crescent Moon.

The tension was palpable, with Mom's frosty demeanor and my own unease about the confrontation that awaited me. As Hal pulled into the inn's driveway, I mustered the courage to break the silence.

"Mom, do you want to talk about what happened at the gallery?" I asked tentatively.

Mom's reply was curt and dismissive. "No, Amelia. We'll discuss it tomorrow." Without another word, she exited the car and marched upstairs. Hal shot me an apologetic smile and a whispered good night, then followed her.

Deflated and exhausted, I retreated to my apartment on the ground floor of the inn. My phone pinged and I lunged for it, hoping it would be a distracting text from Oliver.

Instead, it was Jimbo.

> Hey there. After studying this flower, I've determined that it almost certainly came from Vine Street here in town. The plants whispered to me something cryptic: "The shadows have eyes on Vine Street." I'm not sure what it means, but I thought you should know. Let me know if you need anything else. Be careful, Amelia.

After thanking him, I reread the text five times. What did that mean? Anything? I was no closer to solving Marigold's case. Jimbo's text shed no light on anything, which was a bummer.

I curled up in bed with Freddie, seeking comfort in his soft fur and gentle purrs. As I lay there, my mind raced with doubts and insecurities.

Was I handling everything the right way? Mom always seemed so composed and in control, while I felt scattered and unsure of myself. It was this very reason that made it so difficult for me to open up to her: I never felt like I measured up or had a voice in our relationship.

Guilt settled in, heavy and confusing. I heaved a sigh, and Freddie snuggled closer to me. At least he understood.

As I fell asleep, I wondered, once again, if I'd made the right choice by coming to Florida. Maybe if I'd stayed on the West Coast, I could've strengthened my relationship with Mom — and not fractured it more, like I'd obviously done this evening.

Thirteen

The next morning, I didn't have time to sit and marinate in my feelings. I woke up a little late — at six-thirty — and threw on some yoga pants and a long-sleeved T-shirt. Starting breakfast early was the key to guests' happiness, I'd come to discover.

Today, I had planned a simple, yet delicious spread: apple omelet (it was supposed to resemble a puffy pancake), savory apple-chicken sausage, sourdough toast, and homemade chai. Also coffee, fresh squeezed juice, and some mini poppyseed lemon muffins that I'd taken out of the freezer and popped into the oven.

It seemed like a lot for four guests, but a delicious, giant spread was what folks expected. Plus, I knew Hal would appreciate every bite — Mom wasn't much of a cook and had a phobia about carbs.

My stomach was still in knots about Mom learning about my psychometric powers from a random stranger. Because of this, I made herbal tea instead of coffee for myself, thinking it would be gentler on my digestion. My friend Marisol was a tea witch, and she'd given me a blend called "Tummy Tranquil-tea." I detected hints of chamomile, ginger, peppermint, and something else.

I took another sip. Lemon balm. *Nice.*

Then I poured myself into cooking and baking, falling into a familiar rhythm of chopping, mixing and stirring.

The scent of cinnamon and apples filled the kitchen. The sizzle of the sausages was soothing, almost meditative. As I whisked the eggs for the omelets, the yellow mixture frothed and bubbled, and I found a strange comfort in the repetitive motion. Baking was my solace, a way to quiet my mind when life got too confusing. It had gotten me through rough times in my marriage, teenage years with Jenny, and my divorce.

Freddie, who was parked on the floor near the kitchen door, meowed. The sound of footsteps in the living room made me stop whisking. I turned to see Hal coming in with a suitcase in his hand.

My heart sank. Were they leaving already? Had Mom been so upset by last night's revelations that she couldn't stand to stay another minute? Crap. I was a terrible daughter.

"Morning, Hal! What's up? Where are you headed?" I asked, trying to keep a smile on my face.

Hal set the suitcase down and offered me a sheepish smile. "Well, kiddo, your mother strongly suggested that I head up to the golf tournament a couple of days early. She wants to stay here in Cypress Grove for a bit. Spend some quality time with you."

My smile faded. Mom wanted to stay. Here? With me? After the bombshell Corrine had dropped about my psychic abilities? I found that difficult to believe and wondered about her ulterior motive.

Probably she wanted to give me a piece of her mind without Hal around. This was not good.

"I see. Well, I hope you have time for breakfast first."

Hal's eyes roamed over the counter, where various breakfast items were in stages of completion. His gaze landed on the muffins.

"I'm in no rush. I'm going to put this in the car, and I'll be back. Your mom's coming down soon, she was finishing up in the bathroom." He paused and picked up the suitcase. "You've got a nice place here, Amelia. I'm glad you finally found your calling."

With that, he turned and walked out. I stood, whisk in hand, frozen. Hunh. I lifted my eyebrows and returned to the omelet.

I carefully arranged the apple slices and poured the egg mixture over them, making sure everything was nice and coated. The familiar creak of the wood floor hit my ears and I tensed.

My mother appeared in the kitchen door, looking preppy and jaunty as always. She wore white capri pants and a swirly, blue-and-white Lilly Pulitzer sweatshirt, her hair straight as always. Her expression was unreadable as she surveyed the scene. Mom had always thought of cooking as a necessary evil, and it wasn't until college that I was drawn to the kitchen.

"Good morning, Amelia," she said, her tone even.

"Morning, Mom. Sleep well?" I tried to keep my voice light, but the tension between us was palpable.

She nodded, then her gaze fell on Freddie, who was now rubbing against her ankles. To my surprise, Mom bent down and scooped him up, cradling him against her chest. "And how's this handsome boy today?"

I blinked. Mom had never been much of a cat person, let alone affectionate towards Freddie. She hadn't even known his name until yesterday, despite the fact that I'd sent her and Jenny photos of him over the last year since adopting him as a kitten back in California.

Was this her way of extending an olive branch? Or was she trying to butter me up before the inevitable confrontation?

Before I could say anything to her, Hal lumbered back into the kitchen, a grin on his face.

"Whew! It's gonna be a scorcher today. Good thing I packed my sunscreen and my special hat for the golf course. It says 'Let's Par Tee.' Get it? Par? Tee? Don't you love that?"

Despite the awkwardness with Mom, I couldn't help but snicker at Hal's corny joke. That was one thing I loved about the guy: he always knew how to lighten the mood. Mom's mouth puckered, like she'd eaten something sour, then quirked upward into a smile.

Apparently, this was a morning for miracles.

Voices interrupted us. It was Maude and Steve calling out from the main part of the inn. "Hellooo?" Maude had a creaky voice.

"Good morning, everyone," I called out brightly, then wiped my hands and walked through the secret bookcase door — which was open — and into the inn's library. I found Maude and Steve inspecting the hidden bookcase door to my apartment.

"This is something else," Steve said, moving the door back and forth. "How much did this cost to install, anyway?

"I'm not sure. I inherited this place from my aunt. She had a taste for the quirky." Mom and Hal joined us in the library, with Mom still carrying Freddie, whose eyes were round and confused. "Why don't you all head to the dining room? I'll bring out breakfast in a few minutes."

They agreed and filed out, chatting amiably. I bustled back into the kitchen. To my shock, Mom followed. She set Freddie down and he scampered off. "Can I help with anything, dear?"

I nearly dropped my dish towel. Mom, offering to help? In the kitchen? Had I woken up in an alternate universe? Had

Cypress Grove's magic seeped into Mom's subconscious and turned her into a kind granny? This was a woman who begrudgingly made me buttered toast and instant coffee the last time I stayed at her house.

"Ah, sure," I stammered. "Could you maybe pour the coffee and juice? The mugs and glasses are in the cabinet to your left."

She nodded and set to work. From the corner of my eye, I watched her while I plated the omelets and sausages, half-expecting her to criticize my technique or choice of ingredients. But she remained silent while filling mugs and glasses.

Together, we carried the plates and beverages out to the dining room. Hal was already deep in conversation with Steve, laughing about some shared boyhood experience in the upper Midwest. As I set down the plates, I couldn't help but smile.

This was why I loved running the inn. Seeing people connect and relax, while savoring a delicious meal.

"Everything looks wonderful, Amelia," Maude said.

"Absolutely," Steve agreed. "You've outdone yourself. This is a far better spread than when we stayed at a BnB in Savannah."

I beamed. "Thank you. It's my pleasure. Now, please, dig in while it's hot! Oh, and I have muffins."

Mom took her seat. She seemed to be holding her head a little higher. "My daughter's always been wonderful in the kitchen. When she was in college, she rented an apartment with another girl, and that's when she taught herself how to cook and bake. Goodness knows she didn't get it from me."

"I guess that it's her magical ability," Maude said. "A true gift."

"One of many." I swear Mom looked oddly proud in that moment. I went back into the kitchen, wondering what was going on in her mind.

After breakfast, Hal said goodbye to Mom and me with bear hugs. He seemed genuinely excited for his golf adventure, and I was thrilled for him. He whispered something to me about stopping at a strawberry stand for shortcake, and I gave him a thumbs up.

Maude and Steve also took off, eager to attend their seminar on astral projection that was being held at the town's community center.

"Look for a woman named Renee," I said, no longer trying to hide my link to the town's witchy vibe.

But once everyone was gone, the inn felt deathly quiet with only me and Mom. We worked in silence, clearing the dishes and wiping down the dining room table. The only sounds were the clink of plates and the scraping of food into the compost bin. I kept sneaking glances at her, trying to gauge her mood, but her expression revealed nothing.

Mom missed her calling at a career in poker.

Finally, as we finished arranging the last of the utensils in the dishwasher, I couldn't stand the suspense any longer. I turned to face her, my hands nervously twisting a towel.

"Mom," I began, my voice soft but determined. "Can I ask you something?"

She looked up at me, one perfect eyebrow arched. "Of course, dear."

I took a deep breath. "Why did you decide to stay? Here in Cypress Grove, I mean. With me. Especially after last night's..."

I trailed off, unsure how to finish that thought. *After last night's revelations about my psychic abilities? After realizing I'd been keeping secrets from you? After seeing how different my life is from anything you could have imagined?*

Mom was silent for a long beat, her gaze drifting to Freddie, who was on the floor licking his butt.

When she finally spoke, her tone was thoughtful. She even furrowed her brow a little, something she normally didn't do because it caused wrinkles.

"Amelia, I know we haven't always seen eye to eye. And the news last night, well, it was a lot to take in. I didn't sleep much, thinking about you being a...witch. Or whatever you call yourself."

I nodded, my throat tight. Here it comes. The lecture. The disapproval. The same old same old, how I should've stayed in California and sucked up all my ex's crap because we lived a picture perfect life on the surface. How I should've stayed married and remained in that big house because Sonoma had *cache* (her word, not mine).

But what Mom did next shocked me to my core.

She reached out and took my hand, her perfectly manicured fingers warm against my own. "But seeing you here, in this place, I can tell you've found something special. Something that makes you happy. And that's all I've ever wanted for you, even if I haven't always shown that with my words."

My jaw dropped. I looked around. Even Freddie glanced up with round, green eyes, his legs still splayed in the air.

I'm as shocked as you are, buddy, I wanted to say to him.

"Um," was my snappy comeback.

"Why don't we refill our coffee and sit somewhere comfortable? You can tell me all about..." she waved a hand at a foot-high pink quartz crystal that had been my aunt's, which was sitting on a shelf near a stack of cookbooks. "About your mystic powers."

"Okay, sure. Let's get the coffee and we can go sit out back in the garden." With shaking hands, I bustled around, pouring the java into two fresh mugs. So much for a calm tummy today — I needed caffeine for this conversation.

Mom followed me out the back door and into the garden.

We stepped into the lush backyard, and I heard her gasp. "This is absolutely breathtaking," she murmured, her eyes wide.

It was a tropical oasis and a riot of color. Squat palm trees swayed gently in the warm breeze, their fronds casting dappled shadows on a stone pathway. Bright hibiscus flowers in shades of red, pink, and orange ringed the entire garden. Fragrant jasmine vines twined up a wooden trellis, their star-shaped blossoms perfuming the air. Plants with leaves as large as pillowcases flanked one side, a dense green barrier from the property next door.

In the center of the garden stood a tranquil koi pond, the water lilies floating serenely on the surface while the fish darted beneath. A wrought iron table and chairs sat nestled amidst the greenery, inviting us to sit and admire the natural beauty. The table was shaded by a pergola sporting more jasmine.

"I never took you for a tropical foliage lover," I said to Mom. "You always seemed to enjoy desert landscapes."

Mom smirked as we settled at the table. "I can appreciate beauty when I see it. Did you do all this? When did you have the time?"

"Oh, no." I let out a laugh. "Aunt Shirley and Jimbo started this garden years ago. And according to what he recently told me, he has a, um, special gift with plants. He's a plant whisperer. Plant magician. Yeah."

Mom nodded thoughtfully, her fingers wrapping around her mug. "That explains all the orchids he's been giving you. I thought he was a potential date, but it's more than that, isn't it? It's his way of sharing his magic with you."

"Well, that and the fact that his place is overrun with flowers, apparently." I took a sip. "And I probably should tell you something else. I'm seeing someone."

"Well, you are full of surprises, aren't you?"

"I guess I am." I sighed softly. "I'm sorry for not telling you everything. I was planning to, when I got more settled. When I—"

"Start at the beginning, Amelia. I want to hear all about this new life of yours. Then I think I'll be able to fill in some gaps for you."

What did that mean? Goodness. This morning was getting weirder by the minute. Still, I launched into my story, starting from the moment I stepped out of the rental car in Cypress Grove four months ago.

I told her about the visions I had upon setting foot in the inn. How I'd seen things that had happened during my one visit to town as a child, when she and Dad had brought me and my brother here. How I'd investigated the death of a ghost who haunted the inn, how I'd helped solve a murder of a guest, how I'd met a spirit at the lake named Tiffany who wore leg warmers.

Mom looked a bit startled at that detail, but I plowed on.

I added in several more details, about DJ Ghostwave who broadcast to the undead, about the coven invite, and the current investigation into Marigold's disappearance.

"So, Tiffany didn't want to talk about Marigold?" Mom said, probably trying to keep up.

I shook my head. "She vanished into the lake."

There was a flicker of disbelief on Mom's face. I recognized it immediately because of how she pursed her lips, making the wrinkles around her mouth apparent. Mom never intentionally made an expression that would court a dreaded wrinkle.

But I continued, listing my new friends: Liz, the budding

witch who was taking grimoire classes. Marisol the tea witch. Sage the cowgirl witch.

Then I paused and blew out a breath.

"That's a lot," I said, feeling slightly exhausted by it all. "It's been a busy few months. Plus, the renovations inside, and you know, running a new business."

"And what about the person you're seeing? Wait. Are you about to tell me you're lesbian? Is Sage your new partner? The cowgirl? That sounds lesbian to me. Which is fine! We have lesbian neighbors now. Did I tell you? Lovely ladies, they're great at bingo."

"What? After all that, you ask me who I'm dating? Not about my ability to communicate with the dead or the visions or the fact that I've been invited to a coven?" I squinted at Mom, worried she didn't grasp the significance of anything I'd said. "I'm seeing Sage's brother, Oliver Everhart."

"Oh." She nodded, still seeming slightly confused. "When can I meet him?"

"Tonight, I guess. He's playing guitar at a place here in town."

"Hmm. What kind of guitar? Classical? Flamenco? We had someone in our community come to play a Flamenco concert and it was so fascinating." Her gaze momentarily drifted to a Monarch butterfly that flapped lazily around the hibiscus flowers. *Fascinating* was her word for something she didn't quite understand, but knew it was probably cultured.

"Um, rock-n-roll, I guess?"

"Oh. Too bad." Her eyes snapped back to me. "None of this surprises me, you know. When you said Shirley had left you the inn in her will, I suspected something like this would happen."

"What do you mean?" Despite the warm morning sun, a chill went through me.

"When we came to visit here when you were small, your father and I were scared out of our minds when you had that vision in front of the old mirror."

I blinked. That had been the first indication something had been weird when I arrived in town a few months ago. The mirror. I'd seen it in an antique store and thought a demon was coming for me. "Really?"

"Shirley immediately knew what happened to you. After you and your brother went to bed that night, she explained to us that she had certain powers, and that her mother — your father's mother — also had similar powers. She said the abilities were often passed down to the women in her family, and she wasn't at all shocked when you saw the demon. Or had the conversation with a ghost. Whatever it was. It certainly scared you, and because of that, it scared me. I hated seeing you that frightened, Amelia."

I shook my head. This was all news to me. "That's understandable. But you never thought to tell me this?"

She sighed. "Your father didn't want me to, and I honored his request because it was his family. He'd always been a little frightened of his mother and her magic. And truthfully, she was a frightening woman. She was a real witch to me, and not the magic kind."

"Wild." I wrinkled my nose. "I only remember Grandma visiting in the seventies with those amazing cookies. She seemed pretty fun, from what little I remember. I'm only now getting back some of my childhood memories, though, since coming to Florida."

Now that I thought about it, was she the origin of my cookie obsession? My grandmother, who I barely knew? My grandmother, *the witch*? How had I existed nearly a half century not knowing my own grandma was a witch?

"She was wonderful to you, probably because you shared

her power. Your father forbade her from talking to you about it, but then she passed when you were what, ten?"

I nodded. That sounded about right, although that was part of my spotty childhood memory, why I couldn't recall when Grandma died.

"Is this why Dad was always standoffish with Shirley? I thought they had a fight or something."

"He didn't want you involved. She visited a few times, and wrote, but eventually he asked her to stay away. She desperately wanted to tell you. They fought so much about whether to tell you. Have you let Mike in on your secret? Your daughter?"

I shook my head, chastised. "I'm waiting. For what, I'm not sure. I guess for them to come here and see me in, er, my new element. Somehow this seems like an easier place to tell them."

"Fair." She took a sip from her mug. "Once your father passed, I assume that's when Shirley reached out to you. You know, she didn't even come to the funeral. That's how deep their rift was."

"How terribly sad." I did some quick math in my mind. When Dad died, and when I heard from Aunt Shirley after years of no contact. "That fits the timeline, yeah."

We drank coffee in silence for a few minutes while I absorbed this news. I couldn't be angry at Mom. As a mother, I wouldn't have encouraged my daughter to have psychic visions if they terrified her. And Dad, well, he was gone. I couldn't ask him his thoughts on the matter.

Or could I? For a few seconds I mused about doing a séance to try to connect with my father while my mother was here. Then I recalled my parents' divorce. The two of them insisted they'd grown apart and Dad wanted to "sow his wild oats."

For mom, that meant being a sour and bitter single parent, then moving to an "active senior community" in Arizona the minute she turned 55. She'd seemed to thrive there, and had a full social schedule of bingo, bunco, and bocce ball. Dad sowed his oats for years, and died single.

No, trying to contact Dad would probably bring up a lot of old memories and grievances that were best left buried. Especially since Mom seemed so happy with her life.

"What's on the agenda for today?" Mom asked, ripping me out of my thoughts.

"Well, I thought perhaps we could visit the small botanic garden in town, and maybe grab lunch, and then check out an antique—"

"No, I meant with the investigation. The girl who disappeared. Marigold."

"Oh, uh, well, if you weren't here, I'd probably poke around town. Do some interviews, look over the clues again."

Mom slapped her knees. "Well, that's what we'll do, then. Since I'm here, I'll help. Two heads are better than one, right? And I can see what it's like to be an amateur sleuth in the Psychic Capital of the World. Then I can try to understand why you want to stay here instead of moving to Arizona to be with your family. Or perhaps you'll come around to my point of view and realize that you'd live a much better life away from all this chaos."

Her wink sent a ripple of tension through my muscles. Could her new, helpful attitude be a ploy, a simple act of appeasement, before she intensified her efforts to persuade me to move?

Fourteen

Mom and I settled onto the couch in my living room, the basket of clues on the coffee table in front of us, and Freddie sitting in a chair across the room, as if supervising.

I carefully removed each item, laying them out like pieces of a puzzle. She donned a pair of cat-eye, electric blue reading glasses and scrutinized everything.

"I have to admit, this is pretty exciting," Mom said, leaning forward to examine the dice. "It's like we're in one of those true crime documentaries."

I couldn't help but smile. "You watch those?"

"All the time. Hal jokes I'm learning how to kill people."

I snickered. This was a side of her I rarely, if ever, saw. "Okay, so here's what we have."

I walked her through each clue. I explained the significance of the library book with the hidden bone and my vision of Marigold's final moments.

Mom's eyes widened in horror as I recounted the details. "Oh, honey. That must have been so frightening for you."

I nodded, swallowing hard. "It was. But it also made me really want to figure out what happened to her. That's the thing about these cases. I feel this sense of justice, like I might be the only one who can right some wrongs. Is that bad?"

Mom shook her head. "A little dangerous, perhaps, and maybe not best for your mental health, but not bad."

As we pored over the items, Mom picked up the mixtape case and studied the writing on the sticker pasted to the front. "Songs From the Edge of Forever," she read aloud. "You used to name your cassettes, too."

She fiddled with the case, opening it and taking out the flimsy, folded insert. That was blank, and Mom unfolded the heavy paper.

"What's this?" Mom said. "Did you see this? There's something inside here."

She picked at it with her fingernail. Suddenly, a slip of paper fluttered from the case.

I picked it up. The paper was square, about two inches high. It was a newspaper clipping, yellowed with age and only two paragraphs. The number *1992* was written in tiny handwriting, in blue ink, at the top.

The headline read: "Cypress Grove Woman Stirs Controversy."

Esmerelda "Esmee" Blackthorn, a self-proclaimed witch and prominent figure in Cypress Grove's magical community, has once again found herself at the center of a heated debate. Known for her unconventional practices and outspoken nature, Blackthorn has often clashed with the town's more traditional covens.

"Esmeralda's methods are unorthodox and dangerous," said an anonymous source within the Wiccan community. "She's pushing the boundaries of what's acceptable, and it's only a matter of time before someone gets hurt." Blackthorn, however, remains defiant in the face of criticism. "I refuse to be bound by

the narrow-minded views of the past," she declared in a recent interview. "Magic is about embracing change and pushing limits. If that makes some people uncomfortable, so be it."

"Huh." I reread the little article, wondering if there was more to it. Then I closed my eyes and held it in my palm, hoping to inspire a vision. I breathed deeply for a few seconds, and Mom stayed silent.

But nothing came. I'd noticed that nearly-weightless objects like paper sometimes didn't jive with my psychometric power.

"What are you doing?" Mom asked.

I opened my eyes. "I was trying to see if I could glean any information from this. Have a vision. Whatever you want to call it."

Mom tilted her head and studied me. Probably trying to decide if I'd gone completely off the rails. "Did you see anything?"

I shook my head. "It often doesn't work if it's text only, and a single sheet of paper. It's all very random."

"Hmm. Do you know this Esmerelda woman?" Mom asked.

"Never heard of her. But I know people who might. Let me text Marisol."

I handed Mom the little slip of paper and inspected the folded cassette insert. It appeared that whoever wrote the track list on the sticker had also tried to list the songs on the insert, but had messed up the handwriting. One song was crossed out with a scribble.

I felt bad for Marigold, or whoever messed up the handwriting. That was always the worst, a sloppy-looking cassette track list. No wonder someone had put a sticker on the front plastic cover.

While Mom looked over the article, I went to find my

phone, which was in the kitchen. Of course, Freddie followed, hoping for a snack. I obliged him with a stinky fish treat.

When I grabbed my phone off the counter, I realized I had a voicemail from Chief Wolf. I pressed play and walked back toward the living room while listening to his deep baritone.

"Amelia, hello. It's Chief Chris Wolf. I found a report on the woman we were discussing, and I've sent it to your email. I hope this illuminates some things for you. Copy that."

"Oh, cool," I murmured.

"Well, he sounds foxy," Mom said. "Is that the police chief?"

I looked up from my phone. "Yeah, the guy I was talking to at the party last night. He might be a werewolf. And he's dating my friend Liz. Totally head over heels for her."

There was no solid reason to keep any of the town's eccentricities from Mom now.

"Oh." She clutched some invisible pearls around her neck.

"Okay, let me open this ..." I sank onto the sofa next to Mom, checking my email. "Aha. Here it is."

I zoomed and squinted to read the old police report, finally giving up on my phone's tiny screen and going for my laptop, which was on a desk in the corner. "My eyes aren't what they used to be," I muttered.

"Whose are?" Mom responded. "Wait until you need a hip replacement. Did I tell you about Doris? She got one and now she's back to playing Bocce."

"Hang on, this is interesting." I angled the laptop so we could both read.

Mom scooted close to me and stared at the screen. "I can't see the darned thing. Do you have the brightness turned all the way up?"

I magnified the screen, adjusted the levels, and chuckled. "We're like the Scooby Doo gang, but with AARP cards."

I skimmed the police report, reading key sections aloud to Mom.

"Marigold Wentworth, age 23, was reported missing on April 3, 1993 by her mother, Eliza Wentworth. Marigold was last seen by her roommate, Tracy North, on the evening of April 1st. North stated that Wentworth left their shared apartment around 8:00 PM, saying she was meeting a friend, but did not specify who. Wentworth did not return home that night and failed to show up for her shift at the Shop-n-Save the following morning."

I scrolled further, my voice growing louder as I took in the following details.

"During the investigation, a witness came forward claiming to have seen Wentworth in a heated argument with an unidentified woman on the night of her disappearance. The witness, who wished to remain anonymous, described the woman as being older than Wentworth by at least two decades. The argument took place in the alley behind the Cypress Grove Apothecary around 9:30 PM. The witness overheard raised voices and glimpsed the women through a gap in the fence but could not make out what was being said."

Mom pointed at the screen. "Who was she arguing with? Who was the witness?"

"That's what we need to find out. Esmerelda, maybe."

I clicked to a page that said SUPPLEMENTAL REPORT at the top. It was dated a year after her disappearance.

The first lines of the report left me chilled to the bone. "As no further leads have been uncovered despite extensive searches, the case is no longer considered an active investigation."

Mom sat back and blew out a breath. "This is a tough one, isn't it?"

Was she patronizing me? Or was she serious? It was difficult to tell with her sometimes. Deciding to take her at face value, I snapped the laptop shut. "I know exactly who we need to visit first."

Fifteen

Mom and I pulled up to Marisol's cozy bungalow, nestled on a quiet, tree-lined street about two miles from the inn.

The house itself was like its owner: it seemed to radiate warmth and magic, with its vibrant purple door (she'd recently painted it), the wind chimes tinkling softly in the breeze, and a garden overflowing with rosemary and mint. The heady aroma surrounded us and I inhaled deeply.

Since Marisol was a tea witch, she grew a lot of her own herbs right here in her yard.

As we walked up the path, the door swung open before we even had a chance to knock. Marisol was there, grinning. She wore a flowing, turquoise caftan that made her skin glow. Her silver hair was piled atop her head in a messy bun. Oversized glasses were perched on her nose, and a dozen beaded necklaces adorned her neck.

"Amelia, my dear! And this must be…" she paused to hug me. "Your mother. The two of you look alike."

"Yes, this is Linda, my mom. Mom, meet Marisol, one of my new friends, and something of a mentor to many in town."

She went to embrace Mom. This didn't surprise me, since Marisol was one of the kindest, most accommodating people I'd ever met.

I assumed Mom would return the hug stiffly with a puckered expression. But she greeted Marisol as if they'd known each other for decades.

"Come in, come in!" Marisol motioned for us to come inside.

The interior was as inviting as the outside. Plush, colorful furnishings were accented by tons of plants, crystals, and eclectic artwork. Shelves lined the walls, overflowing with books on every magical subject imaginable, plus popular fiction. Marisol ran one of the most popular book clubs in town.

"Please, make yourselves at home," Marisol said, gesturing to the overstuffed sofa. "I'll put the kettle on and bring out some tea and cookies."

As she bustled off to the kitchen, Mom leaned over and whispered, "She's like a magical fairy godmother. I half expect woodland creatures to come help her with the tea."

I giggled, picturing Marisol with an army of cute bluebirds and bunnies. In Cypress Grove, it wasn't entirely out of the question.

Moments later, Marisol returned carrying a tray laden with a steaming teapot, mismatched cups, and a plate of what looked like homemade Oreos. As the former owner of a cookie delivery company, I was often skeptical of others' baking abilities. Liz, for example, couldn't even master a basic chocolate chip recipe.

I had no such concern with Marisol and reached for a cookie. It was delicious, with a creamy center — and mint chocolate wafers.

"Yessss," I whispered between mouthfuls. "That's a twist on an old favorite."

"Thanks. The mint's from the garden." As she poured the tea, she said, "This is a special blend I created for you two. It's designed to open the heart, ease tension, and encourage understanding between loved ones."

I raised an eyebrow, wondering how much Marisol had intuited about the often-strained relationship between Mom and me. Her tea magic never ceased to amaze me.

I thought Mom might be miffed by her words, but instead, she smiled and sipped, exclaiming that it was the best tea she'd tried in years, since her trip to London for the Queen's jubilee.

We sipped the brew, a delicate balance of floral and spice dancing on my tongue, as I filled Marisol in Marigold and my assignment from the coven.

"I guess it's okay I'm telling you this. Even though it's for the Sisters of Hecate coven." I tilted my head. "Is it okay?"

"Is Marisol not in the coven?" Mom asked.

Marisol shook her head. "The coven Amelia's in, or about to join, is for Generation X only. I run my own coven, one that's statewide. It's for people in the Caribbean diaspora, since my family's from the Dominican Republic. We have members from all across the islands."

"Fascinating," Mom said. "So you all have your own groups?"

"There are some general covens, and some that accept men, and warlocks. It depends. Some people caucus with different covens. And I think it's fine if you need outside help on your investigation. Julia and I have helped each other over the years. What are you searching for?"

Although Mom's eyes were getting wider by the second, I explained the lead we'd uncovered earlier, about Esmeralda Blackthorn.

Marisol's expression sobered. She let out a sigh. "Ah, yes. Esmeralda. She was quite something back in the early '90s."

"What can you tell us about her?" I asked, leaning forward while gripping my teacup. Marisol was normally so sunny and gentle, so the serious expression on her face gave me pause.

"She was always interested in pushing the boundaries of magic, especially when it came to harnessing its power for youth and beauty. She was about my age, maybe a few years older. She was obsessed with looking younger, turning back time. She spent most of her time with younger folks."

Mom's eyes widened. "Turn back time? Wouldn't we all love to do that at our age!"

Marisol clicked her tongue. "It's a tempting thought, but other than some Oil of Olay, I've always welcomed becoming a crone."

"I'm working on that too," I chimed in. "I can't wait for my crone era."

Mom's face contorted in horror, as if growing visibly old was the worst fate possible.

Marisol grinned. "Your time will come soon enough, dear. Esmeralda took things to an extreme. She was in her forties and midlife hit her hard. She was convinced that Cher had the key to eternal youth and was trying to replicate that in her own way."

"Like, the singer, Cher?" I asked, trying to wrap my mind around this detail. A song of hers wafted into my brain.

"The very same."

"Hunh," I grunted, perplexed.

"I loved Moonstruck," Mom said.

"What a great movie," Marisol added.

I nodded. "I could watch it over and over. Also, the Witches of Eastwick."

We all agreed that that was a classic.

"Apparently, Esmeralda saw her as the ultimate symbol of ageless beauty. She even started dressing like her, all leather and lace and big hair. It was quite the sight. But it was the 80s and 90s, so we all made fashion mistakes back then."

We all exchanged smiles. I tried to picture a Cher-worshiping witch in Hot Topic garb. It sounded like Esmeralda had been even more eccentric than the article let on. I handed Marisol the small newspaper clipping.

"So, what happened to her?" Mom asked, dunking a cookie into her tea. "Is she still around?"

Marisol shrugged. "She moved away to start a new coven in Las Vegas in the mid-nineties, but I heard she's back and living in Willow Oaks. You know, that 55-plus community?"

"The one near the Wal-Mart?" I asked.

She nodded. "Someone I know ran into her at the market a few weeks ago. Apparently, she missed small-town life. And she's no longer actively practicing witchcraft anymore, but I can't see her ever giving up her quest for youth. My friend said Esmee, that's what we called her, was quite bitter. You know, I think I might have some old photos of her. Sit tight."

Mom and I sipped our tea. Every sip seemed to be tastier than the last. I munched on another cookie.

"I like this," Mom piped up.

"What, the tea?"

"No, us working together on a mystery."

Wow, this heart opening blend was working wonders. Maybe I needed to ask Marisol for some to go, so Mom and I could work through our differences about weight, makeup, and appropriate clothing choices for grocery shopping (I felt that sweatpants and T-shirts were fine, she thought I was being a slob). Maybe Marisol could give Mom some empathy tea while she was at it.

Then again, I knew I had to be wary of Mom's true intention: to get me to leave Florida and move to Arizona, to be closer to her and Jenny. Perhaps she was merely buttering me up and going with the flow. I smiled and nodded, still on guard.

Marisol returned a few minutes later, carrying a boot-sized shoebox held together with duct tape. She set it on the coffee table and carefully removed the lid, revealing a jumble of yellowed newspaper clippings, photographs, and handwritten notes.

"I knew I had some stuff from back then. I'm kind of a pack rat," she said, sifting through the contents. "Over the years, I've kept things that have to do with witchcraft in town. Someday I'd like to donate everything to the library or put it together as a history of practitioners in town. Ah, here we go."

She found a photo album, the small plastic kind that held a handful of photos, the kind Fotomats used to hand out when you got pictures developed.

I flipped the cover open.

"There. Look closely. It was a group of young women interested in witchcraft."

She tapped on a photograph featuring a group of girls in their late teens, all dressed in '80s fashion. In the center of the group was someone who looked familiar: Tiffany. She was in her '80s glory, complete with teased hair worthy of a metal band, and a denim jacket covered in pins. In fact, the photo was taken at the lake. I recognized the spot immediately.

"That's my friend. Tiffany."

"The ghost?" Mom said, skepticism lacing her voice.

"Mmm-hmm."

Marisol leaned in and squinted at the photo. "We used to meet at the park. Back then it was called Grove Park, but in the 90s, a couple of years after Marigold disappeared, the town named it after her."

"Interesting," I murmured. "And who's this?"

Standing next to Tiffany, with an arm draped over her shoulder, was an older woman. She had wild, dark hair and a mischievous glint in her eye. Even in the faded photo, I could sense her charisma and intensity. She wore lace gloves, like Madonna. Or maybe Cher had worn them, too.

"That's Esmee," Marisol said, taking the photo out of the plastic sleeve and handing it to me. "This is what I wanted to show you."

As my fingers brushed against the thick photo paper, a jolt of energy surged through me. Suddenly, I was no longer in Marisol's cozy living room, but transported back in time to the moment the picture was taken.

I found myself standing in a park, surrounded by the same group of girls from the photo. Adorably, one of them wore a long, white T-shirt that said, SWEET DREAMS ARE MADE OF THIS.

Aww. I'd loved that song.

The air was filled with their laughter and chatter, a sense of camaraderie and excitement palpable. It had all the vibe of a really excellent school field trip. Tiffany was there, her smile bright and her eyes sparkling with innocence — so different than when I saw her yesterday.

And there was Esmeralda, looking as vibrant and magnetic as she did in the photo. She was holding court, her tone animated, her hands gesturing as she talked.

I strained to hear what she was saying, but the words were muffled, like a radio station just out of range. I could only catch snippets here and there. "...power in numbers...sisterhood...secret rituals..."

As I was leaning in closer, trying to make out more, the vision began to fade. The colors blurred and the sounds grew distant, until I was blinking back to reality in Marisol's living room.

"Amelia? Are you alright?" Mom's concerned voice cut through the haze. Her arm slipped around my shoulders and gave me a squeeze.

I shook my head, trying to clear the fuzz. "I saw something. A vision. From the photo."

Marisol's eyebrows shot up. "What? You did? What was it?"

I described the scene in the park, the gathering of young witches, and Esmeralda's presence among them. "I couldn't quite make out what she was saying, but it seemed important. Like she was teaching them something."

Mom sucked in a breath. I glanced at her and for once she didn't look smug or amused. She seemed a little alarmed. Perhaps she was beginning to understand the seriousness of it all.

Marisol nodded thoughtfully. "Esmeralda always did consider herself a guru of sorts. She loved being around young people, molding their minds. She seemed to feed off their youth. Personally, I thought she seemed a little cult-like, so I steered clear."

"Smart." Mom frowned. "But why do you have all these photos?"

"People in town die, and their families give me boxes of witch-related things. Or I find it in junk shops around town. If I recall correctly, this album came from one of the women who was on the fringes of Esmerelda's group. The woman was leaving town and didn't want to bring her wicca-related things. Said she wanted distance from Esmerelda. I assumed she was merely being a fickle young woman. But now I suspect otherwise."

"Esmerelda sounds a bit weird. Why didn't anyone investigate her back then? A grown woman, hanging around kids. That's perverse, if you ask me."

"It was a different time. We were all more naïve in those years." Marisol shook her head. "But I can see why it might raise some red flags now."

I looked down at the photograph again, tracing my finger over Tiffany's face. She looked so happy, so full of life. What had happened to her? And what role did Esmeralda play in her story? And why didn't Tiffany want to talk about it?

"I think I need to visit Tiffany again," I said slowly. "Marisol, can I borrow this photo for a few hours?"

"Sure," Marisol replied while pawing through the box. "I'll keep going through my stuff to see if I can find anything else. Oh, look. Here's a brochure with Esmee's old contact info. Here's where she used to work."

She pulled out a faded, tattered brochure that said COLOR ME BEAUTIFUL.

"I was a winter," Marisol said, smiling. She looked at Mom. "Remember this company?"

"Oh, so do I! I was a summer," Mom said, clapping her hands together. "I still use some of those tips."

"I do as well," Marisol said.

The two of them started chatting about color theory and then Merle Norman cosmetics. While they were deep into discussing how they'd never found makeup as good as Merle's, I inspected the brochure.

Stapled to it was a card with Esmerelda's name, phone number, and address.

488 Vine Street
Cypress Grove, FL

"The shadows have eyes on Vine Street."

Jimbo's text! My heart rate kicked up. I needed to visit this place.

Next to it was the handwritten word "home" on the card in tight cursive, with an arrow. I quickly took a photo of the card. I recognized the neighborhood as one not far from the inn, a brick lined street with smaller, older homes.

I knew Esmee didn't live there and hadn't in years. But what about her neighbors? It was worth a shot. A number of people in Cypress Grove had lived in town for decades. I began to feel antsy.

Mom and Marisol were still chatting. The two of them were about the same age and had found common ground in various cultural touchstones, apparently.

"Don't you think Amelia would look wonderful with a little more rouge?" Mom asked Marisol.

"Actually, I do. Sometimes she seems pale," my friend responded with a wink.

"Okay, cut it out, you two boomers. Keep your rouge to yourself. I need to get a move on here and do some sleuthing, then get ready for tonight."

"What's ton...oh," Marisol grinned. "Oliver's concert. Linda, you're going to love Oliver. Listen, why don't we have lunch together and let Amelia do some investigating on her own. I'll take you to a lovely place for lunch. It's next to the cutest boutique, too."

Mom looked at me, then Marisol. She couldn't resist the word *boutique*. "Well, if Amelia doesn't mind..."

I very much did *not* mind, not in the least. In fact, I was thrilled and thankful that Marisol offered. "You go have fun, Mom. I'll meet you back at the inn in a few hours."

Before either one could change their minds, I scooped up the photo album and stood up.

"I'll walk you out," Marisol said, following me out as I waved goodbye to Mom.

At the door, we paused. "Thanks for that," I said.

She folded me into a hug. "Sometimes a tea witch uses brewed leaves in their magic, and sometimes she uses some good old fashioned hospitality, too."

"She wants me to leave Florida and move to Arizona," I murmured into her patchouli-scented hair.

Marisol pulled back but kept hold on my upper arms. She peered into my face. "Oh no, no, no. We're not giving *you* up that easy. I'll have a talk with your mother. I sense that she doesn't quite understand what's going on with you, and I'll talk to her as a friend and a peer. I think she'll come around, so don't worry. Go do what you need to do. Good luck with the investigation."

"You're a gem," I said, giving her one last squeeze before I left.

Sixteen

As I drove away from Marisol's house, my mind swirled with thoughts about Esmerelda and her possible connection to Marigold's disappearance. I plugged the address from the old Color Me Beautiful brochure into my phone's GPS and headed across town.

Vine Street was lined with modest, older homes, most of them small and well-maintained. This part of town didn't have the towering old oaks, but many houses were painted in colorful hues, and I even spotted a few murals on garage doors. I vaguely recalled that Oliver said this neighborhood attracted artists because of its affordability.

But as I pulled up to Esmerelda's former residence, I noticed the little ranch home stood out like a weed in a vibrant garden.

The yard was overgrown, the grass nearly knee-high, and the bushes wild and untrimmed. The house itself looked rundown, with peeling paint and a dingy white door. It was clear no one had lived here for quite some time. There were no flowers of any kind, which made it even more impressive that Jimbo had identified the street.

After making a mental note to someday discuss Jimbo's powers with him, I parked at the curb and stepped out, shielding my eyes from the bright afternoon sun. As I made my way up the cracked sidewalk, I couldn't shake the feeling that I was being watched.

I glanced around and noticed an elderly woman sitting on the porch of the cute, pale-yellow house across the street, a glass of iced tea in her hand. She was watching me with undisguised curiosity.

Figuring it was worth a shot, I changed course and approached her instead, walking across the brick street with a smile. "Hello, ma'am," I said with a friendly wave, trying to conjure my best southern drawl. "I'm sorry to bother you, but I was wondering if you might be able to help me with something."

The woman set down her glass on a small table and leaned forward in her rocking chair. She wore a 1960s-style housecoat, the color of coral and with white flowers splashed on the front. My grandmother — the one who had been a witch — had something similar, I recalled.

"What's that, dear? You might want to talk with my daughter, but she's not home."

"Hmm." I pondered this for a second. "How long have you lived here?"

"Come closer. I can't hear well."

I did, and repeated myself.

The woman beamed and to my surprise, her teeth were perfect. Dentures, I guessed. "My family built this little house in the forties. I've lived here almost my entire life, except for a few years in the sixties."

Okay, she might actually know something important. "I'm

looking for someone. She hasn't lived here in a while, though." I gestured to Esmerelda's old place. "Did you by any chance know the woman who used to live there in the 80s and 90s? Esmerelda?"

At the mention of Esmerelda's name, the woman's eyes widened. She nodded slowly. "Oh, I remember Esmee all right. Hard to forget a piece of work like that."

I tried to keep my excitement to myself. "Really? What can you tell me about her?"

The woman shrugged. "She was a weird one, even by Cypress Grove standards. During the day she worked as a cosmetologist. But always coming and going at odd hours, wearing those outrageous outfits, looking like a rock star. And the people she had over! Mostly young folks, college students and such. They'd traipse in and out of that house at all hours of the night. It was odd, since she was in her forties and didn't have kids herself. She called herself a witch and those kinds were different back then. Not like today. The witches now are all about tourism and that darned Facebook."

She shook her head, like she longed for the old days.

I inhaled sharply. This aligned with what Marisol had said about Esmerelda being drawn to younger people. "Do you remember anything specific about the people who visited? Or what they might have been doing there?"

"Well, I never saw anything outright scandalous, mind you. But there was something off about the whole thing. You could feel it in the air, like a bad energy coming from that place. I didn't have much to do with her, because I was busy with my own family. I had a son who was in and out of jail, so that kept me busy."

She paused, lost in thought for a moment, then continued. "I remember one girl in particular. Pretty little thing, with big hair. Always wore those things on her legs. That dancers wear."

"Leg warmers?" I offered.

The woman waved a wrinkled hand in the air. "That's it. Leg warmers. In neon colors. She was there a lot, more than the others. Sometimes I'd hear them chanting or singing through the open windows. Gave me the heebie jeebies, to be honest. But I'm not a witchy type. No, I stay away from that stuff."

"That girl... did she look like this?" I asked, walking up the porch steps while pulling out the photo album from my bag. I flipped to the photo of Tiffany and Esmerelda.

The woman squinted at the picture, then nodded emphatically. "Yes, that's her! I'm sure of it. And that's Esmee, looking as wild as ever. Thinking she was the Cher of Cypress Grove. Good gravy, that woman played Cher all the time, full blast. I like Cher as much as the next gal, but it was extreme back then. She also had a young lover. Esmee, not Cher. Well, maybe Cher, too. A guy in his early twenties. I thought it was a little perverse."

I felt a chill run down my spine. This was a major piece of the puzzle.

"Do you remember when all this was going on? What years, roughly?" I asked, hoping to establish a timeline.

The woman thought for a moment. "The mid 80s. Around the time of the Challenger explosion. That's the only way I remember things anymore, by tying them to news events. I watch a lot of news, you know. It's all I can do these days, being ninety-five. Esmerelda moved out in the mid-nineties, around the OJ Simpson trial. The place has been empty ever since. And her boy toy moved away, too. Heard he was some motivational speaker in Chicago now."

This tale was getting weirder and weirder. "The girl, Tiffany. Did you ever see her again after Esmerelda left?"

The woman shook her head sadly. "That girl's body was found some years later in the lake."

"The lake in the park? The one with the boardwalks?" I knew the answer before I even asked the questions.

"That's the one. It was called Grove Park, but the name changed and I can't remember it now. I always wondered whether Esmee knew anything about her death. Gave me the creeps, the whole thing."

I swallowed hard, my heart racing with this new information. Tiffany, Esmerelda, and Marigold had to be all connected. And two of them were dead. Wait, no. Three women were dead, if I included Tracy. At this point, I wasn't convinced her death was an accident, either.

"Well, thanks, ma'am," I said, unsure of where to go from here.

"You some sort of police officer? FBI? Investigating those X-files?"

I blinked, trying to determine if she was joking. "Um, no. Well, sort of. I am investigating, but I'm not law enforcement. It's complicated."

The woman shook her head and sighed. "The people in this town. I swear. They get weirder every year."

I couldn't argue with that, so I thanked the lady for her time and made my way back to my car. I definitely needed to take another run at Tiffany in hopes that she'd talk. Maybe the photo of her would make her open up.

Probably I should pay a visit to Esmerelda, too, but that didn't seem like something I should do alone. A call to Julia was needed for that.

I was about to climb into the driver's seat and take off, but something made me hesitate. I turned and stared at Esmerelda's abandoned house, curiosity gnawing at me. Before I could talk myself out of it, I crossed the street and stepped into the overgrown yard. As I picked my way through the knee-high grass on the side of the house, away from the old woman's prying eyes, a child's voice startled me.

"Hey lady, whatcha doing?"

I spun around to see a scrawny kid, maybe ten years old, straddling a bike on the sidewalk. He wore a faded t-shirt that said "Gators" and had a mop of unruly brown hair. He looked like Jimbo, my employee at the inn — if Jimbo was ten and rode a BMX bike.

"Hey there," I stammered, caught off guard. "I was only looking around."

The kid raised an eyebrow. "You wanna see inside? I can show ya, for five bucks. It's way cool."

I hesitated. Breaking into an abandoned house with a random kid didn't exactly scream "good idea." But my desire for answers overrode my common sense, a frequent occurrence here in Florida.

"Okay, deal," I said, fishing a crumpled bill from my purse.

The kid grinned, pocketing the money into his jean shorts. "Follow me. Oh, I'm Chase, by the way."

"Amelia. Nice to meet you."

With the swagger of Steve Irwin, Chase led me through the weeds, around the back of the house, to a drained, cracked swimming pool that looked like it hadn't held water in decades. We carefully stepped over broken concrete patio pavers.

Chase moved a broken chair aside. We were at a sliding glass door.

"You come here often?" I asked.

"Yeah, I live in the neighborhood. I keep a lookout on the place, and let some teenagers use it. For money, though. I charge them ten bucks a pop. You got the friends and family discount."

"I'm honored, Chase. Truly."

The kid reached through a shattered pane and fiddled with the lock until the door slid open with a high-pitched squeal.

"Ladies first," he said with a cheeky grin.

"You sure this is safe?" I asked.

"No problemo," he said.

I stepped gingerly into the musty darkness, my heart pounding. The air smelled of mildew and decay. Dust swirled in the thin shafts of light that peeked through the boarded-up windows.

This seemed to be all problemo in my opinion.

"This place is a little creepy," the kid whispered, his bravado slipping a notch. "They say it's haunted."

I swallowed hard and pulled out my phone, activating the flashlight. "Haunted by what? And who's they?"

He shrugged. "Ghosts, I guess. Or demons. Some girl died here, I think. That's the rumor in the neighborhood."

A chill crept up my spine. Could he be talking about Tiffany? Or Marigold? Or someone else? I stepped further into the gloom, my eyes adjusting to the dimness. No, I didn't get a good vibe in here at all.

I flashed my cell light around, revealing busted furniture, a spot on the linoleum where someone had obviously tried to start a fire, and liquor bottles in a corner. It could be merely a party place for teens and a crash pad for the homeless. Maybe this was a bust.

"Oh yeah? What rumors have you heard?"

Chase kicked at a balled-up newspaper, his voice dropping to a whisper. "Well, they say this scary witch lady used to live here, back in the day. She was into some really dark stuff. Black magic, human sacrifices, that kinda thing."

I felt my blood run cold. Human sacrifices? Surely that couldn't be true. The cops would've done something about that, right? But after what I'd seen in my vision...

"And the girl who died?" I prompted, my mouth dry.

"Yeah, so the story goes, this witch was, like, obsessed with staying young forever. And she thought she needed to steal the youth from pretty young girls to do it. So she lured this one chick here and tried to do some kinda ritual on her. But something went wrong, and the girl ended up dead. They found her body in the woods or something. I'm not sure."

Yikes. It sounded like Esmerelda's twisted attempt at immortality had claimed at least one life. But was it Tiffany? Or had there been other victims? Was Esmerelda a serial killer?

"And you said this all happened... when? The 80s?"

Chase shrugged. "I dunno, I wasn't even born then. That's ancient, like the Romans and the Greeks. But the '80s sounds about right."

I rolled my eyes. History apparently wasn't a priority in school anymore. "Ancient, huh?"

"Yeah, a long time ago. My dad told me about it, said his older brother knew the dead girl. Messed my uncle up real bad."

"Where's he now, your uncle? He in town?"

"No, he's in New York."

"I see."

We fell silent while Chase inspected a tattered album cover: Cher's *Heart of Stone*.

"This looks like something from your era," he said, holding up the album. Cher stared at me with her toned arms and unlined face from 1989. "Have you listened to this?"

This made me feel old as dirt. "Yeah, a few times."

The living room was a time capsule from the 80s, with a sagging floral couch and a bulky TV set coated in cobwebs. Faded, framed art posters of Patrick Nagel seemed to rot into the walls. An open can of Tab sat on a coffee table, alongside an overflowing ashtray.

It was as if Esmerelda had walked out one day and never returned.

I moved down a narrow hallway, the floorboards groaning from our footsteps. Bedrooms done up in 80s cream and mint green branched off either side. Some rooms were sparse, while others were filled with jumbled old furniture and piles of moldering clothes. But it was the room at the end of the hall that drew me like a magnet.

As I pushed open the door, my breath caught in my throat. It was some sort of altar space, with shelves of long-burned out candles, the still-colorful red wax dripping in long, frozen strings. Jars of mysterious herbs that had turned mostly to dust sat on one table, and strange symbols were painted crudely on the walls.

Oddly, there was also a framed portrait of Elvira. Esmerelda sure had some questionable taste, but who didn't back then?

"Creepy," Chase whispered. "I'll bet that woman in the poster on the wall is a grandma now."

I grimaced. "Teenagers didn't do this?"

The décor in here had the crude and amateurish look of kids, if it were mixed with my grandma's place in the 1980s.

"Nope. My dad and uncle came in once with me and said it was always like this in here."

In the center of the room stood a round table draped in a tattered blue velvet cloth that had been a snack for moths.

And on that table, glinting in the wan light coming from the gaps in the boards on the windows, was a dagger. An antique-looking dagger with a bone handle and a curved blade etched with the same symbols that were on the walls.

"I'm surprised no one has taken this," I said to Chase.

"No one dares to. They're worried the witch will return and kick their butts."

"A reasonable assumption, I suppose."

I couldn't help but reach for the knife. I had to know what it had seen, what it had felt, what it had done. The symbols reminded me of the ones on the bone, but in my current state, I wasn't a hundred percent certain.

As I touched the weapon, a scream echoed through my mind and images flashed behind my eyes. A dark ritual. Chanting figures in robes. And Esmee, presiding over all of it.

"Tiffany, this is for the best," she said, her voice a seductive purr. "You'll always be young, and you'll help me stay young. And if my spell works, you'll remain alive, forever beautiful. We'll both benefit."

The scene flickered and warped, like a corrupted video tape. A new scene came into focus. I watched in horror as Esmerelda wrapped a limp body in a faded, oriental rug. Was that Tiffany? Or some other poor soul who had fallen victim to Esmerelda's dark obsession?

I reeled back, gasping, my heart racing. I was back in the present. The kid stared at me with wide, frightened eyes.

"What's wrong with you, lady? You're not having a heart attack, are you?"

"No. We need to get out of here." I tried and failed to catch my breath. "Now."

We ran out of the house, past all the moldering trash, my mind reeling from the horrible vision. Whatever dark magic Esmerelda had been practicing, it was far more sinister than I could have imagined. Something had gone wrong with her spell, and someone, perhaps many people, had suffered. I needed to persuade Tiffany to tell me everything.

When we were outside on the sidewalk, the kid's confidence had returned. He folded his thin arms and stared at me with hard eyes. Then he held out his palm.

"You'd better not tell the cops about this. I'll deny we were ever here, lady."

I eyed him, then took out twenty and slapped it in his outstretched hand. "We've never met, Chase."

Seventeen

I drove like a madwoman to Marigold Wentworth Park, my mind still reeling from the horrific vision at Esmeralda's abandoned house. The dagger, the dark ritual, the limp body wrapped in a rug, the weathered Cher album — it all swirled in my head, a sickening kaleidoscope of images.

I needed to talk to Tiffany. I had to know what really happened to her, and how it all tied into Marigold's disappearance. The pieces were falling into place, but I was still missing many crucial connections.

I pulled into the park's lot, barely taking the time to turn off the engine before I leapt out and started jogging down the boardwalk. Thank goodness I'd worn comfy footwear today. My sneakers slapped against the weathered wood as I weaved between families out for a stroll and couples walking hand-in-hand.

"Excuse me, pardon me," I muttered, dodging a toddler dawdling in the middle of the path. The mother shot me a dirty look but I barely noticed. I had tunnel vision, my mind focused on one thing and one thing only: confronting Tiffany.

When I reached the lake, I was dismayed to see the beach packed with people. Families lounged on colorful towels, kids splashed in the shallows, and a group of teens played a rowdy game of volleyball. Sometimes Tiffany was reluctant to come out when there were lots of families, in case some kid or random person had psychometry. That was the only way she could be seen by people who were fully alive. Since so few people had psychometric ability, usually she could come out of the water, undetected.

I hesitated at the water's edge, trying to look casual as I slipped off my sandals. I stepped into the cool water, letting it lap at my ankles as I scanned the shore for a more secluded spot.

There. A little further down, partially obscured by a stand of cypress trees, was a small inlet. I sloshed through the water, dodging a Frisbee that sailed over my head, and made my way to the quiet cove.

Once I was sure no one was paying attention to me, I knelt down and skimmed my hand through the sun-warmed water, focusing all my psychic energy on Tiffany. "Please," I whispered. "I need to talk to you. It's important."

I waited, my heart pounding, but nothing happened. *Come on.* The water remained still and undisturbed. No shimmering form rose from the depths. Had I lost my connection to Tiffany? Or was she simply refusing to appear because of our last meeting?

"Hey, Tiffany," I muttered through gritted teeth, trying to conjure my best Valley Girl lingo in hopes of appeasing her. "Dude. I totally know about Esmeralda. Way uncool. I know what she did to you. Please, talk to me."

Still nothing. I was about to give up and wade back to shore when the water in front of me began to churn and bubble. Slowly, like a figure emerging from fog, Tiffany's form took shape. But instead of her usual bubbly demeanor, her expression was stormy, her translucent brow furrowed. She wore all black, like a punk rocker from the '80s.

"What do you want, Amelia?" she snapped, every inch the petulant teenager. "I thought I made myself clear last time. I don't want to talk about the past. You're harshing my buzz."

I held up my hands in a placating gesture. "I know, and I'm sorry for pushing. But Tiffany, I saw something. At Esmeralda's old house on Vine Street. Something horrible. And someone else gave me a photo."

Her eyes widened and she seemed to flicker. "What...what did you see?"

"Look. A friend had it." I dug around in my purse for the photo album and flipped to the first picture, flashing it to Tiffany. I wasn't sure how it was possible, but her transparent skin seemed to grow more gray and pale.

She let out a groan. "That was such a fun day. The last good day we had. She'd taken a group of us out in the woods, in the Ocala National Forest, to show us about herbs and stuff. I was so happy then. It was rad, the things she taught us."

"I know," I said softly. "I had a vision that showed me the good part of your day. Then I had another vision, and that wasn't so pleasant."

Tiffany's form flickered again, and I worried I was losing her. I took a deep breath. "When I was at her old house on Vine Street, I saw a ritual. You were there, and Esmeralda. She said something about making you young forever, about a spell. And then," I swallowed hard. "I saw her wrapping a body in a rug. Tiffany, was that you? Did she kill you?"

Tiffany's face crumpled and she let out a choked sob. It was a strange sight, seeing a ghost cry. No tears fell, but her anguish was palpable. It was something I could feel in the air, like humidity.

"It was an accident," she whispered. "The spell. It went wrong. Esmeralda, she didn't mean to. She loved me, in her own twisted way. She thought she was helping me. Helping us both."

I reached out instinctively to comfort her, but my hand passed through her shimmering form. "I'm so sorry, Tiffany. You didn't deserve that. No one does. What she did was wrong, and misguided, and criminal. Why wasn't she ever brought to justice?"

"Her dad was a cop back then. And I trusted her. We all did." She hugged her midsection, her gaze distant. "I was so young, so naive. I thought Esmeralda had all the answers. That she could make me special, make me immortal. I didn't realize the price. It sounded totally awesome at the time. And I guess, in a way, she did make me immortal."

She let out a bitter laugh that made the hair on my sweaty neck stand up.

The situation was becoming clearer. A misguided witch with a policeman dad. This was why she hadn't been held accountable for her crimes. Ugh. I let her collect herself for a moment before gently pressing on. "Tiffany, do you think Esmeralda could have done something similar to Marigold?"

Tiffany's head snapped up, her eyes wide with fear. "I do."

She trailed off, seemingly lost in thought. Then, in a small voice, she said, "There were others, you know. Other girls Esmeralda took an interest in. I was one of many. It was an accident, I think. I don't know what happened after she brought me here. Maybe there are others."

My stomach churned at the implications. How many lives had Esmeralda destroyed in her obsession with eternal youth?

"I need to find out what happened to Marigold, and anyone else Esmerelda might have hurt. Will you help me? I believe you know some key details that could benefit me when I go and talk to Esmerelda."

Tiffany hesitated, her form flickering like an old TV station about to go off-air for the night. "That's totally scary. I don't think you should do that."

"I'm not doing it today, or tonight." I wiped sweat off the back of my neck, remembering that Oliver's concert was tonight. Crap. What time was it? I needed to meet Mom back at the inn, serve happy hour to the guests, make sure Mom had her salad, then go to the show. I checked my watch. I had almost exactly an hour to spare. "And I promise I won't go alone."

"Her magic is hella powerful. I don't know if bringing someone will help. And no offense, if it's your boyfriend, I'd rethink that. From what I know about Oliver and his lack of powers, I'm not sure he's the guy you should rely on."

"I won't bring him." No, I'd never involve Oliver in something this dangerous. This was a job for the coven — I could only hope they'd want to join me. "Please? Will you tell me everything?"

She paused for what seemed like an eternity. Then, with a nod, she said, "Okay, fine. I'll tell you what I know. It's time for the truth to come out, no matter how painful. Esmeralda needs to face what she's done. I don't think she can harm me now, not here. At least I hope not."

Relief washed over me. This felt like a breakthrough. "Thank you, Tiffany. I promise, I'll do everything I can to get justice for you, and for Marigold. And I'll be safe about it. I'm a middle-aged woman who recently bought a pair of Aerosoles that I'm planning to wear to a concert tonight. Safety is my middle name."

Her face wrinkled. "What are Aerosoles?"

"Awesome shoes that are comfier than Doc Martens. Let's go to the office."

We walked — well, she floated — in silence to our usual picnic table. As Tiffany began to recount how she met Esmerelda, I settled in to listen. The sun beat down on my skin, and a disconcerting trickle found its way into my cleavage. Children's laughter echoed across the beach, a jarring contrast to Tiffany's bleak story.

Eighteen

"It all started back in 1985," she began, her voice soft and distant. Her gaze looked toward the lake. "I'd just graduated from high school and was working at this little coffee shop on Main Street called The Cosmic Cup. Is that still there?"

I shook my head.

"That's too bad. It was where the cool kids hung out. Bands sometimes played there. I thought I was so rad, serving coffee and flirting with the cute guys who came in. I really liked this one guy named Brant. He looked like the lead singer in Van Halen. You know, long blonde hair."

I ran my tongue over my teeth, hoping Tiffany didn't go too far down memory lane, as she sometimes enjoyed doing. "Uh-huh," I said, prodding her to continue.

She shifted onto the bench across from me, looking somehow both ethereal and world-weary at the same time. Her usually luminous eyes had dulled to a deep gray glow.

"Esmerelda started coming in regularly, always ordering a big coffee and sitting in the corner, scribbling in a vintage, leather-bound journal. She was a lot older, maybe in her late

171

thirties or early forties, but she had this aura about her. Like she knew secrets the rest of us could only dream of. She was cool for an older lady." Tiffany paused, a wistful expression on her face.

"I was totally intrigued. We started chatting whenever I brought her order, and she'd drop these little hints about magic and the supernatural. It was like, so cool to me. I'd always been into that stuff, you know? Ouija boards, tarot cards, all that. But Esmerelda, she was the real deal."

"She took you under her wing?" I asked gently, trying to understand their relationship.

Tiffany nodded vigorously. "Totally. She invited me to this group she was forming, said it was for young women who wanted to explore their spiritual side. I jumped at the chance. It felt like I was being let in on this exclusive club, you know? At that time, I wanted to be older, to get out of my parents' house. I wasn't even sure what I wanted to do with my life and I thought being a witch might help guide me."

I remembered those days, being young and adrift. So different from my daughter, who knew she wanted to go into graphic design since she was a freshman in high school.

I could see how a charismatic figure like Esmerelda could easily draw in someone impressionable and wayward. The allure of belonging, of being part of something secret and special, was a powerful thing. It was the engine of any good cult.

"At first, it was awesome. We'd meet at her house, do guided meditations, learn about herbs and crystals. Esmerelda knew so much, and she made us feel like we were tapping into this ancient wisdom. Like we were special, chosen. There was a core group of maybe five, six of us. She'd take us on little day trips to learn about sacred plants, or to museums to talk about the hidden meanings in paintings. Stuff we never learned in school."

Tiffany's voice faltered. I leaned forward, my heart aching. All the pain that woman caused. Anger began to bubble up in my chest.

"But then things started to get weird. Esmerelda became obsessed with this idea of eternal youth, of cheating death. She'd go on these rants about society's fear of aging, how women were discarded once they were no longer young and beautiful. She said she'd found a way to harness the vitality of youth, to steal it like a psychic vampire. Which is what she was. A vampire. Not like, a literal one, though. You follow?"

I nodded but shoved away a shudder at the metaphor. The woman I'd seen in my visions, presiding over dark rituals with manic glee, seemed a far cry from the cool, mysterious figure Tiffany had been drawn to.

"I didn't want to believe it at first. I thought maybe she was talking in riddles, you know? Sometimes she did that. Riddles and weird sayings. And she listened to a lot of Cher, but I figured that was her age. She never really liked my music because I enjoyed harder stuff. But then she started singling me out, saying I had this special energy, this *glow*. That I was the key to her eternal youth. That's what she called it. The key."

Tiffany met my gaze and the hair on the back of my sticky neck prickled. "I was flattered, at first. But also totally freaked out. It was like she wanted to consume me, to drain me dry. That was the feeling I got, but I wasn't sure whether to trust my instincts. I started making excuses not to go to the meetings, but Esmerelda, she wouldn't let up. She'd call me at all hours, show up at the coffee shop. I felt trapped."

"Oh, honey," I sighed, my heart breaking for the terrified girl she'd once been. "I'm so sorry. You must have been so scared. Where were your parents? Did you tell them about this?"

Tiffany shrugged. "They said I should go live with her. They wanted me out of the house from the time I turned sixteen. I felt like a loser because I was still at home. My folks had their own lives and were caring for my younger sisters. They didn't have time for me and barely noticed what my sisters were doing, much less me. I was like their roommate."

Ah, parents in the eighties. The ones that had to be reminded by a TV commercial to wonder, "It's 10 p.m., do you know where your children are?"

I thought about my own parents, who would shoo Mike and I out the door in the morning and tell us not to return until dark. Dad was working and Mom wanted to drink coffee with her friends and talk about how rotten my father was. My brother and I often did dangerous stuff, like the time we played Evil Knievel and tried to jump over a dumpster with our bikes. I successfully did it. Mike broke his leg and we still limped home.

Mom didn't believe him at first.

These days, Mike and I like to joke about how resilient and tough that had made us, but really, it only forced us to cope with a lot of loneliness and trauma at a time when we should've been kids. Should've been protected by adults.

My eyes began to water and I sniffled. "I'm sorry," I said.

Silvery tears tracked down her cheeks. "I didn't know how to get away from Esmee. And then, that night..."

Her voice broke, and she took a shuddering breath. I waited for her to continue, a pit of dread in my stomach.

"She told me she'd finally perfected the ritual. That it had to be me, that I was the only one who could help her achieve immortality. I tried to say no, but she wouldn't hear it. She dragged me to that awful altar room. I can still smell the incense, feel the heat of the candles on my skin."

Tiffany shook her head, as if trying to dislodge the memory. "I don't remember much after that. Only pain, and fear, and then...nothing. When I woke up, I was in the lake. I assume she dumped me there. Here. I was stuck. Alone. But it's not so bad now that I've made friends with the people in the In Between. And you. I like my existence, actually. A lot."

I reached out instinctively, my mom-instincts taking over. "Tiffany, I am so, so, so sorry for what happened to you. What Esmerelda did was unforgivable and she was totally out of line for wanting to sacrifice you in her quest to be eternally young. But I promise you, I will do everything in my power to bring her to justice. For you, and for and anyone else she may have hurt."

She leaned her elbows on the table, which was always distracting because it seemed as though half her arms were sinking into the wood.

"Do you want to know the true reason why I didn't want you investigating?"

I frowned. "Why?"

"Because I'm worried that if you confront Esmee, my situation will somehow change. That I'll be forced out of the In Between. Do you think that will happen?"

I swallowed hard. "I ... don't... know. That's above my pay grade. Don't you want to leave the In Between, though? I thought that was the goal?"

She shook her head. "I love where I am. It might not be perfect, but I adore the little family we've made down there. I don't want to go to someplace because it's new. I've had a lot happen to me in life, and I only want peace in death, or whatever this is."

Hmm. Who was I to talk her out of moving on in the afterlife? I didn't know squat about this life or any other. "Well, I can't make promises, but hopefully even if I confront Esmerelda, your, ah, status will be unchanged."

Tiffany offered me a watery smile. "Thanks. You're the first person who's ever really listened, who's cared enough to try and make things right. I've been alone with this for so long. I've told the people in the lake about it, but they have their own issues, too. We all kind of support each other, but it's not like we can do anything about the people who put us down there."

Maybe that could change, if I worked hard enough. If I managed to solve this situation. Sure, I could piece together what had happened, but how would I really get justice? It's not as though Chief Wolf could prosecute an elderly woman based on some visions, a bone, and a conversation with a ghost. I didn't want to say all that to Tiffany, though.

"You're not alone anymore," I said firmly. It was an attempt to boost my own confidence as much as hers. "I'm here, and I'm not going anywhere until the truth comes out. Esmerelda may have evaded consequences back then, but she won't escape them now. Not if I have anything to say about it."

We sat in awkward silence for a few minutes and I was about to wrap things up but a thought came to me.

"That reminds me. Who was Esmerelda's boyfriend? When I went to the Vine Street house, I talked with an older lady who lived there for decades. She said Esmerelda had a younger boyfriend. A 'boy toy,' she called him."

Tiffany rolled her eyes, something she often did. It was always fascinating because a trail of illuminated glitter followed her gaze. I adored those little sparkles.

"Oh. My. God. I haven't thought of that guy in a long time. That was Garrett. He was sooooo grody. I think he thought Esmerelda was rich, and that's why he was with her."

"How old was he? Was he from Cypress Grove?"

Tiffany shook her head. "He was from Tampa. I think he was about five or six years older than me, so mid-twenties back in the mid-eighties. At least fifteen years younger than Esmee. He was handsome, though, like Mickey Rourke in Nine and a Half Weeks." She paused and leaned in. "We all loved Mickey. Did he become a huge star? I'll bet he's good looking even as an older man."

This, I'd come to learn, was the most difficult part of talking to ghosts: deciding whether or not to break it to them that their teen heartthrobs had taken the express train to plastic surgery land. Or worse.

"Mickey had some hard times there for a while, but I think he's bounced back," I hedged, then quickly changed the subject back to the investigation. "What was Garrett's last name, anyway? Do you remember?"

Tiffany's form grew brighter. "Yes! I do. It was strange. Hickinbottom." She then spelled it. "We used to joke that his name was Hickey Bottom because of all the hickeys Esmerelda used to give him. Which was so gross."

"Garrett Hickinbottom," I murmured. "That should be easy to Google."

"Huh? What's that?"

"A research tool," I said. "Are you going to be okay for the rest of the day?"

I always worried about Tiffany when we parted, and wished she could come back to the inn with me, even if it meant her living in her ghost form.

"Yeah, I'll be fine. We're going on a swim with the gators tonight." She beamed.

Occasionally Tiffany threw in a detail about her life in the lake that was so weird that I was caught off guard. This was one of those times.

"Well, that's...rad." I chewed on the inside of my cheek,

trying to envision a nighttime swim with ghosts and gators. Usually, my mind simply couldn't comprehend any of it. "Thank you for telling me all this today. I know it wasn't easy."

I didn't want to leave her, but had to get back to the inn. Mom was probably there already, wondering where I was, and we had Oliver's concert tonight. I stood up from the picnic table, my knees cracking.

"I should get going. But I promise: I'm not going to let this go. We'll figure out what happened to you and the others. I have something tonight, but tomorrow afternoon I should be able to devote some time to this."

"What's tonight? A hot date with the professor?" Tiffany rose and floated over the table toward me.

I grinned. "Sort of. He's playing a concert."

She narrowed her eyes. "Don't trust guys in bands."

"Wise words. He's only sitting in for a night with his old group. Normally he's content playing acoustic guitar in his living room." *And sounding mighty sexy while doing so*, I declined to add.

Tiffany nodded. "Rad. And thanks. For listening. For caring."

Her words tugged at my heart. I wished I could give her a hug, but that was impossible. Instead, I settled for a smile and a wave. "I'll be back soon, okay? Stay out of trouble with those gators."

Tiffany grinned, a sparkle returning to her eyes. "No promises."

And with that, she glided over to the lake and dissolved into a million glittering particles, vanishing into the water. I stood there for a moment, staring at the spot where she'd been, my mind absorbing everything she'd told me.

Esmerelda's dark obsession, the terrifying ritual, poor Tiffany's fate: it was almost too much to handle for one woman. But I couldn't dwell on that now. I had to keep moving forward, piecing together the clues.

I turned and started power walking back down the boardwalk. The sun beat down mercilessly. A now-familiar wave of heat crashed over me, and I groaned. Another hot flash.

"Perimenopause can go duck itself," I muttered under my breath. Here, in the cypress forest, there was little breeze and even less relief from the sun. By the time I reached my car, my hair was plastered to my forehead and I'd tied it up in a messy knot.

I cranked the AC to the max as soon as I got in, sighing with relief as the cool air washed over me. I reached for a paper towel in the glove box and attempted to mop the sweat off my neck. So much better.

As I waited for the car to turn into a mini fridge, I pulled out my phone and typed a name into Google.

Garrett Hickinbottom.

What if he was involved in Tiffany's death, or Marigold's disappearance?

I shook my head. I had to know. I hit search.

To my surprise, the first result was a website for "Garrett Hickinbottom: Chicago-based Life Coach, Motivational Speaker, and Certified Sensuality Therapist." I raised an eyebrow. That old lady wasn't kidding. He'd gone from being a middle-aged witch's boy toy to a self-help guru — and, apparently, a sex instructor.

"Ewww," I whispered as I clicked on the link.

I was immediately assaulted by a garish website filled with flashy graphics, cheesy stock photos, and background music that grated at my ears. Front and center was a headshot of a tanned, grinning man with blindingly white teeth and gelled, thinning hair. He looked to be in his fifties, which tracked with my timeline of Esmerelda's life.

According to his bio, Garrett specialized in helping folks "unleash their inner power" and "manifest their deepest desires." He offered one-on-one coaching, group seminars, and even a line of branded essential oils. Not unlike what people sold and did here in Cypress Grove, but this somehow seemed more slick, more calculated.

But there, in a bright red, clickable bubble, was a contact number. I stared at it, my thumb hovering over the screen. Did I dare? What would I even say?

I took a deep breath. If this Garrett guy had been close to Esmerelda back in the day, he might know something about what happened to Tiffany and Marigold. It was a lead I couldn't ignore, no matter how much my gut was telling me to run in the opposite direction.

I summoned all my courage and tapped the phone number before I could change my mind. I figured it was probably better to talk to him here, in the privacy of my car. I didn't need Mom inserting herself into this conversation.

"Garrett Hickinbottom, how can I help you?" a rich, deep voice answered.

Oh, crap. I didn't expect him to actually answer. "Hi."

"Hello," he purred. "How can I help you today?"

I turned the air down a notch, worried that it probably sounded like I was in the middle of a tornado. "This is kind of an odd question—"

"There are no odd questions, my friend."

Well, we'd see about *that*. "Okay. My name's Amelia Matthews, and I live in Cypress Grove, Florida. I'm calling about an Esmerelda Blackthorn. I'm looking into some things here in town, and I heard that the two of you used to be quite close. Did you know Tiffany Ferndale? Or Marigold Wentworth?"

I paused for his response. Nothing.

"Hello? Hello? Are you there? Can you hear me?" I repeated my question, speaking slower this time. I was met with more silence. Then I checked my phone screen.

"He hung up," I muttered, longing for the days when people slammed phones down and you knew precisely when they had ended the call.

Now supremely annoyed, I called back. It went straight to voicemail. Duck. I wiped sweat off my upper lip, then was reminded that I needed to wax any peach fuzz that had accumulated there in recent days.

Apparently, there *were* odd questions, ones Garrett Hickinbottom wanted to avoid like a bad batch of gas station sushi.

Nineteen

Neither Mom nor the guests were there when I arrived back at the inn. Jimbo had come and gone and left a note saying that he and Sage would see me at The Cauldron later tonight for the concert.

As I stood in the lobby sorting through the day's mail, I heard a pitiful meow coming from the direction of the apartment.

"Be right there, Fred," I called out.

The mail could wait. My cat's stomach could not. I let myself into the apartment and Freddie came darting toward me. He rammed his head into my ankle, then did it again.

"You want to be picked up? Okay. Hello, sweet boy. I missed you." I scooped him up like a baby and planted a kiss on his broad, orange head. He rubbed his face on my chin and purred.

I noticed that whenever I had a vision, whether it was here at the inn or elsewhere, Freddie was extra affectionate afterward. It seemed impossible that he'd know when I went into a trancelike state, but stranger things had happened in town.

Perhaps he'd gone through his own transformation upon coming to Cypress Grove.

Or maybe he suspected that I'd give him more food if I was in a slightly altered state.

"You want to eat?"

"*Brrrrap.*"

"Okay. Let's get you an early dinner." I set him down and we went into the kitchen. While spooning wet oceanfish and turkey mix into his bowl, I mentally ran down everything I needed to do.

Since I was running late, happy hour was the first order of business. I had thirty minutes to get a spread together, since the inn advertised a nightly cocktail event for guests at 4 p.m. — and the couple from Michigan had vowed to return from their psychic adventures by then.

Freddie noshed, I washed my hands, and donned my apron. Then I got to work.

I turned on the radio, which was already dialed to WBOO, the local station. Saturdays were devoted to 80s and 90s music, and I bopped around the kitchen, singing along to Stevie Nicks.

As difficult as this day had been, as scary and troubling and angering, I wasn't in a terrible mood. No, I was determined, which was my default setting.

Determined to get to the bottom of this Esmerelda situation.

Determined to make things right for two, maybe three, young women.

Determined to set out a spread of tasty food.

I had purpose, and that was way more than I had in my final years in California. I also had an amazing home base here at the inn.

I couldn't help but smile at the cozy familiarity of my new

kitchen setup. Sure, it was smaller than the expansive, state-of-the-art one I'd left behind, but it felt more like home. I'd taken my Aunt Shirley's well-stocked and organized space and made it my own, adding personal touches and rearranging things to suit my needs. I'd also splurged on a commercial-style stove and oven, my one major purchase I'd bought after the sale of my West Coast home.

I loved that oven almost as much as my only child and Freddie, I swear.

I pulled out a platter and began assembling an array of happy hour snacks: cubes of sharp cheddar and creamy brie, plump grapes, crisp apple slices, and a selection of artisanal crackers. I added a few goat cheese stuffed dates for good measure.

As I arranged everything, I couldn't help but think how far I'd come. A year ago, I never would have imagined I'd be running a quirky old inn in Florida, let alone investigating paranormal mysteries on the side.

Next, I turned my attention to the wine offering. I had a nice variety on hand, thanks to my aunt's impeccable taste and my own love of collecting interesting bottles. I drummed my fingers on my chin as I inspected the choices.

After a moment's deliberation, I chose a Sauvignon Blanc. It was Florida and seventy-five degrees outside, perfect for a crisp white. By now I was really belting out the tunes because I knew every word to the three-song block of The Cure on WBOO. Freddie scampered around, batting a mouse toy.

While I was setting out the glasses on a table in the library, I heard the front door open and the excited chatter of Maude and Steve, the couple from the Midwest. They burst into the room, their faces pink from the Florida sun and their eyes sparkling.

"Amelia, you won't believe the day we had in town!"

Maude said, practically bouncing on her toes. "The psychic we met was absolutely incredible. She knew things about us that no one else could possibly know!"

Steve nodded while petting Freddie. "She even predicted that our grandson would get accepted to his dream college next year. We can't wait to tell him!"

I grinned, feeling a surge of pride for my adopted hometown. I loved when guests returned with excitement in their voices. "That's awesome! I'm so glad you had such a fantastic experience. We have some truly gifted people here."

As I poured them each a glass of wine, Maude and Steve regaled me with more details of their day, from the fascinating aura readings to the cute shops on Main Street. I listened intently, marveling at how Cypress Grove had a way of bringing out happiness in everyone who visited.

Perhaps that was the true magic of this place.

"We can't thank you enough for hosting us," Steve said, raising his glass in a toast. "It's already been a trip we'll never forget and we've only been here one night! In fact, we're planning on returning for a longer weekend in the summer. We want to stay here, of course."

I clinked my glass of sparkling water against theirs, feeling a warm glow replacing my earlier fierce determination. "I'm so glad to hear that. And the best part is, there's always more to discover in Cypress Grove. What are your plans for tonight? Dinner? Jazz club? A séance at the library? They usually hold those on Saturdays."

"We're not sure. We wanted to ask for your recommendations," Maude said.

A stack of local, glossy tourist magazines sat on a table, and I reached for one.

"Well, there's a talk about birth charts at the bookstore on Oak Street," I said, flipping through. "Or a crystal skull demonstration at a restaurant. If you're in the mood for live music, my friend's band is playing tonight at The Cauldron. They do classic rock covers."

Maude's eyes lit up. "Oooh, The Cauldron sounds intriguing! What kind of place is it?"

Before I could answer, Mom swept in, looking absolutely giddy. Apparently, her time with Marisol had been fun. She set down five shopping bags.

"Amelia, you won't believe the day I've had!" she gushed, helping herself to a glass of wine. "Marisol is an absolute delight. We went to this darling little bistro and then spent hours browsing the cutest shops. I found the most adorable scarf."

As Mom launched into a detailed description of her purchases, I caught Maude and Steve exchanging an amused glance. They politely listened for a few minutes, then made noises about wanting to rest up before dinner in town.

"We're thinking of trying that new Italian place," Steve said as they headed towards the stairs. "But we'll definitely keep The Cauldron in mind for next time."

After they'd retreated to their room, Mom turned to me with a mischievous grin. She was positively vibrating with joy. "So, what are you wearing to impress Oliver tonight?"

I rolled my eyes. "I was thinking my black jeans and that green top."

"Oh honey, no," she cut me off, shaking her head. "You need something more alluring! How about that little red number I saw in your closet? Wear it with some new pantyhose and some black heels. You do have hose, right? And maybe some Spanx to suck it all in?"

"I don't wear hose anymore. Don't even own a pair. And no to Spanx. When did you go through my closet? Mom, it's a bar, not the opera. Casual." I pushed out a breath, resigned to an evening of unsolicited advice. "Let's focus on getting ready, okay?"

An hour later, after much debate and a minor mascara mishap, we were seated at a table at Burgatory, a casual bar and grill. Mom picked at a meager salad while I happily devoured a mushroom burger.

Mom was still focused on my outfit choice. I'd managed to win that skirmish, opting for a tight black tank top with lace accents paired with skinny black jeans, ankle boots, and a dramatic long black cardigan that went to my calves. I topped it all off with a drapey scarlet scarf. It was witchy and Stevie Nicks-esque and I did not give one whit if I looked too over the top. I had my aunt's ruby pendant around my neck and frankly, I felt pretty badass.

"I still say you should've gone with the red dress," Mom sniffed, shuffling a cherry tomato around her plate. "Men appreciate a woman who puts in some effort."

I bit back a retort and suppressed the urge to roll my eyes. Instead, I focused on the deliciously greasy fries and sipped my soda. We'd used Uber tonight, because I wanted to be responsible. Although I wasn't drinking now, I knew I'd have a cocktail or two at the club.

"This is perfectly appropriate attire. Plus, it's kind of my signature look now. Witchy, yet comfortable. Eileen Fisher meets Practical Magic. You look cute, by the way." She'd worn a pair of white jeans, tan flats, and a silky, colorful blouse (probably Lilly Pulitzer). Truthfully, it wasn't that different her usual attire, but I thought a compliment would get her off the subject of my fashion choices.

Mom pursed her lips but let it drop, choosing to interrogate me about Oliver instead.

"How old is he?"

"About my age."

"Does he have a job?"

"Yes, he's a history professor."

Relief washed over her face. "Does he have children?"

"Not that I know of." He didn't, but I couldn't help being a little snarky.

"Rent or own?"

"He owns a beautiful house in town. He grew up here."

"Does he have a drug problem?"

I paused and rubbed my lips together. "Not that I've seen."

"Alcoholic?"

"No! Geez."

"He must have some problem or personality defect if he's your age and single."

Now I did roll my eyes. "Thanks, Mom. That's the only kind of man who would be interested? A guy with a *personality defect*?"

"You know what I mean." Her brows furrowed. I was giving her nothing to criticize. "Does he have, er, powers? I tried to get Marisol to dish the dirt about him but she was unusually vague."

I smiled. Marisol had my back. "Oliver doesn't have any powers or abilities. Not everyone in town does, you know? He's a smart, talented guy who also happens to be kind and sweet."

"Hmph. Sounds like he might be on the ugly side. Although Marisol insisted he was good-looking. What kind of music does he play?"

"Rock. I've mostly heard him on acoustic guitar. He's quite good. This is his old band, who hit it big in the 90s. Oliver left right before that to go to grad school. They're doing a special benefit concert tonight to benefit a children's charity in town."

"Well, at least he has his head on straight. Who would want

to be married to a rock star? By the way, have you heard from you-know-who?" She shot me a knowing glance.

"My ex-husband?" I didn't even like to say his name, and I immediately knew who she was talking about.

She nodded.

"No. I haven't."

"Don't you miss those days, you in that beautiful house, overlooking the hills and vineyards?" Mom looked wistful. "You had so many stunning holiday parties, with that big Christmas tree and that beautiful long table with your legendary spread of food…"

"Mom," I said sharply, trying not to remind her that Chad had cheated and broke my heart. Somehow Mom always thought that was the tradeoff for a glitzy life in California. As if it came with the territory. "That's the past. I'm through with that life. I've moved on. New chapter. New book, even. Whole new genre."

Fortunately, Mom took the hint. She changed the topic to my daughter Jenny's grades at university (which were excellent, thank goodness). While she talked, my mind was off in its own world, racing to the next challenge in solving the Marigold mystery: getting the members of the coven together to strategize about Esmerelda.

We needed to form a plan, and soon, especially if we wanted to break this case open before the coven's anniversary celebration next weekend. There was no way I could confront Esmerelda on my own. Even if she was an elderly lady in a 55-plus retirement community, I had to assume her powers were still formidable.

I wanted to help the coven, but I didn't want to risk injury, or worse, in the process.

"…And when Jenny came to visit for the weekend, I

showed her how to do laundry. Amelia, why did you not teach her how to wash clothes?"

"I did, but she probably wasn't paying attention. Hold that thought." I picked up my phone. "Need to send a quick text before I forget. Sorry."

I started a group chat with Liz, Julia, Renee, and Sage — the four women in the coven who I knew.

> Hey, I've uncovered some important things about Marigold's case. I think we need to strategize about what's next. Is there any way we can meet tonight at the concert and talk?

I had no sooner snarfed down a few more fries when the responses made my phone vibrate like the spin cycle of a washer. Sage and Liz popped up first, then Renee.

> You know I'll be there. My brother has reserved the upstairs VIP for all of us.

> I'm coming with my date…but I'll send him for drinks when we need to discuss our business.

> The Cauldron? I'm doing a big grocery shop for a customer and should be done about eight-thirty. Let's plan on chatting after the band's first set.

> See you all there. Can't wait to hear what you've found. Amelia, I'm so impressed with how quickly you've tackled this situation.

That last message was from Julia. I smiled as I read it a second time.

"Who are you texting?" Mom asked, trying to peek at the screen.

I looked up. "The coven. They're meeting us tonight at the bar so we can go over Marigold's case."

"Oh, well." Mom focused on a cucumber. "Did you find any little incriminating details on that? Ready to solve the crime, Agatha Christie-style?"

From that one statement, I knew she still wasn't taking me seriously. Whatever.

I decided not to launch into a lengthy explanation of everything I'd discovered. Mom clearly wasn't in the right headspace to absorb the gravity of my findings. And frankly, I didn't have the spoons to convince her. I needed to conserve my energy. I was too excited about seeing Oliver play — and to meet with the coven.

"Oh, a few little things here and there." I dunked a fry in ketchup. "You know, the basics. Clues, suspects, possible human sacrifices. We'll get into it as a group tonight."

Mom's eyes widened and she opened her mouth, then closed it again. I could practically see the gears churning in her brain as she tried to determine if I was joking.

I smiled innocently and sipped my soda. For now, I'd focus on the positives: good food, a cute outfit, and the promise of seeing Oliver rock out on stage. I held my glass up as if I was toasting Mom.

"To a memorable evening in Florida. May it be filled with music, magic, and minimal motherly meddling." I winked at her.

Mom rolled her eyes but couldn't hide her smile. "Cheers to that. Now let's settle the bill and get this show on the road. I can't wait to meet this Oliver fellow and see if he's worthy of my daughter. He's got big shoes to fill."

Clown shoes, if we were comparing him to my ex. I could

never understand why Mom liked the man. I guess it was because he'd always accommodated, no, *encouraged* her quirks and benign narcissism. For some reason, this was only dawning on me tonight.

But it didn't bother me, like it would have years ago. Instead, I let everything all wash over me, like water off a duck.

I laughed and flagged down the server for the check. Yes, this would be a night to remember. I could feel it in my bones, and not just the ones hidden in old library books. Cypress Grove had more secrets, and I was ready to spill them all.

Twenty

Our Uber pulled up to The Cauldron, Cypress Grove's premier spot for live music, craft cocktails, and dart tournaments.

The place was housed in an old Art Deco theater, complete with a grand, lighted marquee that read "Stardust Riot Reunion Show feat. Oliver Everhart - One Night Only!"

I beamed at the sight of Oliver's name. He deserved this moment in the spotlight, and I was thrilled to be here to witness it. During dinner together once, he'd told me how conflicted he felt for years about leaving the band, which later went on to be moderately successful.

As we walked toward the entrance, I grabbed mom's arm and pointed. "Look. Pretty cool, huh?"

We stopped and stared at the exterior of the old theater, which was a mix of 1920s architecture and occult-inspired decor. The ticket booth had been transformed into a tarot reading stand, and the poster cases showcased upcoming events like "Coven Karaoke Night" and "Potion Mixology Class."

"Everybody's so creative here in Cypress Grove," Mom

remarked, eyeing a window display featuring a crystal ball and a neon sign that read 'Get Your Hex On.' "Who owns this place, anyway?"

"A lovely couple, Fern and Teagan," I explained. "They've created a really welcoming space for everyone in town. And their craft cocktails are out of this world."

Mom raised an eyebrow but said nothing as we made our way to the door. I had a feeling she was in for more than a few surprises tonight.

There was a line to get in, and we joined at the end. It took us a few long minutes to reach the front.

The door woman, a tall, striking person with a shock of purple hair and a septum piercing, greeted us with a warm smile. "Welcome to The Cauldron! Can I get your names?"

"Amelia Matthews and guest," I replied.

The woman consulted her clipboard and nodded. "Ah, yes. Oliver put you on the list. Right this way, please. You're in the VIP section upstairs."

Mom's eyes sparkled at this development. There was nothing she adored more than being treated like she was special. I found the trait kind of embarrassing. Probably it was part of the reason I'd wanted to blend into the background for most of my life.

As we walked through the back of the club to the stairs, I soaked in the Cauldron's vibe. The stage was set up at the far end of the space, with an impressive array of sound equipment. Roadies scurried around, testing microphones. Purple and blue lights illuminated a sign at the very back of the stage that sported the band's name in gothic letters.

The main floor was dotted with red tables and booths, all oriented towards the stage — but also with a small dance floor. The bar ran along one wall, its shelves lined with colorful bottles and wrapped in what looked like ivy vines. The downstairs was absolutely packed. I recognized several people in town and waved at a few.

But once we were upstairs, it was the balcony that truly took my breath away. Plush, red velvet couches and armchairs were arranged around low, black tables, creating an intimate, lounge-like atmosphere. Twinkling fairy lights and flickering candles cast a warm yet slightly ethereal glow.

"Wow," I breathed, taking it all in. Perhaps Fern and Teagan would like to consult on the décor of one of the rooms at the inn, because this was totally my vibe. "Amazing."

The door woman led us to a prime spot opposite the stage and handed us each a drink menu. "Oliver wanted to make sure you had the best seats in the house. Your server will be right over to take your order. Enjoy the show, ladies. It should be starting in about fifteen to twenty minutes."

Mom turned to me. "Well, well, well. Looks like your professor knows how to pull out all the stops."

I grinned, settling into a plush armchair and scanning the crowd below for any sign of the coven members. "What can I say? He's full of surprises."

Mom and I checked out the drink menu, which listed cleverly named concoctions like "Siren's Song," "Pixie Dust Punch," and "Crystal Elixir." Each one sounded more intriguing than the last, and I found myself torn between the Mermaid Margarita and the Phoenix Rising.

The server came, a young, skinny guy in all black and a shaved head. I went with the Mermaid Margarita. Mom opted for an extra dry martini, two olives. The server left.

I leaned into Mom, suddenly uneasy. "Are you sure you're okay with all this? We can go anytime you want. It might be loud."

"Amelia! I'll have you know that Hal and I saw the Rolling

Stones last year in Phoenix. My generation invented rock music." She let out a huff.

As I was trying to picture my mom rocking out to Mick Jagger, a familiar voice called out from the stairs. "Amelia! There you are!"

I turned to see Sage, Jimbo, Liz, and Chief Wolf making their way across the balcony, drinks in hand. Sage was in a flowing, tie-dyed dress and cowboy boots, while Jimbo sported his signature trucker hat and a Stardust Riot t-shirt.

"I had no idea you were such a fan," I said while giving him, and everyone else, quick hugs.

"Oh definitely, they were my favorite back in the day," Jimbo drawled. "I know the words to all their tunes."

Liz had gone full Gothic glam in a black lace gown, black talon-like nails, and dark lipstick. Chief Wolf was in a button-down dark blue shirt and black jeans. I introduced everyone to Mom, and I could tell she was already enamored with Wolf. Of course.

As everyone settled into the seats around us, Mom leaned in and whispered, "Is that the werewolf police chief you were telling me about?"

"Shhh. Let's not mention that." I put my finger to my lips, trying not to giggle at the absurdity of it all.

Here I was, sipping magical cocktails with my mother, my witchy, quirky friends, and a potentially lycanthropic law enforcement officer, all while waiting for my history professor boyfriend to take the stage with his rockstar buddies. Later, I'd convene a coven meeting to discuss solving a mystery.

My life was ducking amazing. Why would I ever want to trade it for a return to suburbia?

A few minutes later, our cocktails arrived. Mom seemed pleased with her gin and tonic, and my eyes nearly popped out of my head when I saw the Mermaid Margarita. The electric blue concoction was in an oversized mason jar, with a salt rim, stacks of tropical fruit on two sticks, and a twisty straw.

We all toasted with our drinks and chatted while waiting for the band. I was in between Mom and Liz on a sofa. At one point, Liz leaned into my ear and whispered, "Jimbo's going to distract Christopher at the break so the coven can meet."

"Excellent."

"And Julia is reaching out to the owners of The Cauldron so we can take over a back room for the meeting."

While sipping the margarita, my eyebrows shot up. I swallowed. "You all think of everything, don't you?"

"Wait till you see the coven handle a bake sale. We do it with military precision."

The two of us dissolved into laughter, but that quickly stopped when the lights in the place dimmed. My heart began to thrash around. I didn't know what to expect from, or for, Oliver.

Honestly, I was nervous on his behalf. I knew he was an excellent guitarist and his voice was smooth and strong. But I also realized he hadn't performed in years. Could he pull this off? Or would it be embarrassing? He'd practiced with the band all week, but was it enough? There were so many people here.

I was worried for him because I knew how excited he was, and anticipation swelled in my chest.

After a few notes of a guitar, a white spotlight illuminated the stage, revealing Oliver.

In a low, raspy baritone, he belted out the first line of a familiar song.

My jaw dropped. Gone was the nerdy history professor who wore faded t-shirts, cargo shorts and white sneakers around town. In his place stood a lean, mean, muscle machine, with a goatee that looked positively foxy. His black hair flopped over his forehead in a way that made my stomach flip. The spotlight glinted off his silver Jim Morrison belt buckle as his strong fingers gripped the microphone.

Leather boots?

My jaw dropped. Liz grabbed my knee. "Oh my word," she yelled. "He's so... so..."

"Hot?" I glanced at her and met her shocked gaze for a second. "Sexy?"

"Yeah, that."

Those jeans. Holy cannoli, those painted-on skinny black jeans. I stood, gripping the balcony rail at the sight. His tight black t-shirt clung to his muscular chest in a way that made me feel warm, and not hot flash warm. He crooned a few lines and undulated around the stage as the beat picked up. The crowd went nuts, and I think someone in the front — a female someone — threw a rose on stage.

Goodness.

When he got to the chorus of the song, I realized it was a familiar 80s tune: Whitesnake's "Slow and Easy."

And he was looking directly at me as he sang. Oh, my.

I felt a blush creep up my neck as Oliver's voice, rough and sensual, seemed to wrap around me like a caress. Was he really serenading me, here in front of everyone, with an '80s power ballad? He pointed toward me, grinned, and winked as the drumbeat thundered.

"I think he's trying to send you a message," Liz yelled into my right ear, making my eardrum vibrate. "It's not subtle, but girl, it's scorching. I also think he might be wearing eyeliner. And the synth player is wearing pink frosted lipstick."

I was about to enthusiastically agree with her about every observation, but Mom made a choking sound. I tore my gaze away from Oliver long enough to make sure a martini olive hadn't lodged in her throat.

She was staring at the stage, eyes wide and mouth agape. Oliver and the band looked like an exact replica of an 80s hair band (except the bassist was going bald and the guitarist had a silver shag).

"That's him?" she gasped. "The singer?"

"That's him. Yes." At first, the look of shock on her face made me feel a little embarrassed. But why? This was the best time I'd had in years.

Watching my normally mild-mannered love interest sing like a rock star while shocking my mother at the same time? Rebelling against my mother like I was sixteen again? Knowing that the man onstage was employed, smart, and kind — and a rock god?

Priceless.

Oliver rasped something about wanting a *superstitious woman*. I felt like pointing at myself and saying, "who, me?" I stifled a giggle. Maybe I was overtired from everything that had happened over the last few days. That had to be it.

"Did he thrust his hips at us?" Mom hissed in my left ear.

"I think so." A grin was spreading on my lips, and I began to sway to the tune.

Oliver was gyrating to the beat in what could only be described as a lascivious manner. He was great at it, actually. Shockingly so.

And did he wag his tongue at the guitarist?

I bit my lip to keep from dissolving into hysterical laughter at Mom's expression. Or from drooling over Oliver. This was both the most mortifying and thrilling moment of my life.

He continued to croon, and the music was so infectious that I couldn't help but dance and sing and clap along, tossing my hair to the beat. Liz joined me. At one point during a guitar solo, the spotlight shone on us and I pointed down at Oliver then blew him a kiss. I didn't care what I looked like, or who saw me.

He captured my air kiss in his hand and pressed his palm to his heart. Then continued singing. While moving his hips in a *very* suggestive manner. When the song ended, a roar went up from the crowd.

"Thank you very much," Oliver growled into the mic. "That sure felt good, singing again. What did you all think?"

More cheers, and a few people hollered Oliver's name.

He grinned. "Welcome to a very special performance of Stardust Riot. We've got a great show planned for you tonight, in the town where we started it all. And that last song, by the way, is dedicated to a very special woman."

Eeep. I wasn't sure my heart could take all these crazy, sexy emotions.

While still beaming, I took a peek at mom. She'd sank into her chair, aghast, as if the corpse of Hugh Hefner had reanimated before her very eyes.

She clutched the strand of pearls around her neck for dear life, and the band launched into another song.

I kept on dancing.

Forty-five minutes later, after Oliver had stepped down from the microphone and taken up a guitar to play several more '80s metal covers, the band announced it would take a half hour break before their second set.

"They are so good," I gushed to Liz. "That Def Leppard cover was something else. Mom, what did you think?"

Mom was on her second gin and tonic and took a fortifying slug. "It's not exactly my kind of music, dear. You know that.

But he does have, ah..." she paused to fake cough, "a certain presence on stage. It's a tad... racy."

Yes, if one defined "certain presence" as *the sexiest silver fox who is not named George Clooney.*

I wasn't sure how Oliver could be racy but Mick Jagger wasn't, but I suspected it had something to do with the fact that her daughter was not romantically linked with Mick.

I peered over the balcony. People were flocking to the bar and the restrooms. I spotted two familiar faces working their way through the crowd: Julia and Renee. I pulled Liz and Sage over.

"Okay, the others are here. I think we need to get Jimbo to distract Wolf."

They both nodded. The plan was in motion. Or it was, until Oliver suddenly appeared on the balcony, looking even better up close. His cheeks were flushed, and his eyes sparkled, probably from the adrenaline of playing live.

"Oliver, that was incredible!" I gushed, throwing my arms around him in a tight hug. "Your voice was so good! And those guitar licks? Amazing!"

He chuckled, his breath warm against my ear. "Thanks, Amelia. It felt good to be back on stage. Especially since I knew you were up here, watching."

We pulled apart, and I couldn't stop smiling. It was as if everyone else on the balcony had faded into the background. We stared at each other.

"Hey," he said in a low, growly voice.

"Hey," I whispered.

Out of the corner of my eye, I saw Julia and Renee coming to our part of the balcony. Ugh, ok, I needed to set my libido aside for coven business. I also needed to introduce Oliver to my mother, because even though I was juggling a lot tonight, I didn't want to be rude.

But before I could say a word, Oliver cupped my face in his hands and pulled me in for a kiss. Right there, in front of everyone. My eyes widened in surprise, but then fluttered closed as I melted into his warm body. His lips were soft yet insistent, and I could taste the faint sweetness of Coca-Cola. Tongue was involved.

He'd never kissed me this passionately before, and *definitely* not in front of others.

Someone let out a low whistle. Others, Liz and Sage if I had to guess, hooted. I think I heard Jimbo yell "Get 'er done!" And then, from somewhere to my left, came the unmistakable sound of my mother clearing her throat.

Loudly.

Oliver and I broke apart, both of us slightly breathless and grinning like fools. I turned to face her, my cheeks burning.

"Mom," I said, my voice a bit high-pitched and giddy. "This is Oliver. My boyfriend. Uh, man friend. Friend. Special friend. And Oliver, I didn't get a chance to tell you, not with everything else going on. My mom's in town. Oliver, meet Linda."

Oliver extended his hand, an adorable smile on his face despite the obvious awkwardness of the situation. His cheeks grew pink. "It's a pleasure to meet you, Linda. Amelia's told me so much about you."

Mom shook his hand, her grip firm and her gaze steely. "Likewise, Oliver. Though I must say, Amelia neglected to mention a few key details. Like your penchant for tight pants and public displays of affection."

I winced, but Oliver merely laughed good-naturedly. "Well, the pants are a special occasion for tonight only. Usually, I opt for something more comfy. As for the PDA, I apologize. I got caught up in the moment, seeing Amelia's beautiful face."

Mom's expression softened a little, but I could tell she was still sizing him up. "So, a history professor by day and a rock star by night. That's quite the double life you lead."

He shrugged, his arm sliding around my waist. "I like to keep things interesting. And really, the rock thing is more of a hobby. Teaching is my true passion. Mostly I play guitar for friends or to relax."

"Hmm." Mom took a sip of her drink, her eyes never leaving Oliver's face. "And what are your intentions with my daughter?"

"Mom!" I hissed. "*Please.*"

But Oliver squeezed my hip reassuringly. "It's okay, Amelia. I'm happy to answer." He met my mother's gaze head-on, his expression sincere. "My intentions are to make your daughter happy, Linda. To support her, learn from her, and grow with her. She's an incredible woman, and I feel lucky to be a part of her life. I'm honored to be her special friend."

I felt tears prick at the corners of my eyes. Oliver's words were so genuine, so heartfelt. I leaned into him, grateful. I saw Liz put her hand over her heart and make an *awwww* face.

How had I gotten so lucky with this group of people?

Mom stared at us, her face unreadable. Then, slowly, she nodded. "Well, I suppose that's all a mother can ask for. But let me be clear, Oliver: if you hurt my only daughter, I will haunt you for the rest of your life. I may not have powers myself, but I know people who do."

Wow, I'd never heard Mom sound so fierce when it came to my well-being. What was going on with her?

Oliver blinked a few times but managed a smile. "Understood, ma'am. I promise you, hurting Amelia is the last thing I want to do."

The tension broke as Sage giggled at the exchange. Julia and Renee, who had been watching the whole thing, wore amused expressions.

I let out a breath I hadn't realized I'd been holding. Crisis averted. Sage whispered into Jimbo's ear.

For now, though, it was time to get down to witchy business. I pulled Oliver aside. "Hey, we're convening an emergency coven meeting in a back room to discuss Marigold's case. Jimbo's going to bring Wolf downstairs so he doesn't poke around our meeting. I'll see you after the show?"

Oliver nodded. "Definitely. I'll help Jimbo get Wolf downstairs."

"Thanks."

He brushed a quick kiss over my lips and I went over to Julia and Renee.

"Ready?" I asked them.

"Ready," they replied in tandem.

Once Oliver and Jimbo had ushered Wolf downstairs for a beer, the rest of us followed Teagan, one of The Cauldron's owners, to the back room. Even Mom trailed along, and I wasn't in the mood to question her. Time was of the essence.

Teagan stopped in front of a door adorned with a glittery unicorn cut-out and turned to face us. "Okay, witches, here's the room. But, heads up, we're hosting a birthday party tomorrow and the decorations are already up. Try not to touch anything, yeah?"

She swung the door open and we all filed inside. I blinked, startled, when I saw the explosion of pink, purple, and rainbow decorations. Streamers hung from the ceiling, balloons bobbed in the corners, and a large banner that read "Happy Birthday, Princess!" stretched across one wall. In the center of the room was a table set with sparkly plates and cups, a piñata in the shape of a pony dangling from the ceiling.

Liz let out a snort. "Well, this is an interesting vibe."

Sage grinned, picking up a tiara from the table and putting

it on her head. "This is my kinda scene, honestly. Maybe I'll have my next birthday party here."

"Don't touch that," Teagan warned. "Have fun, ladies. And remember, the walls aren't soundproof, so keep the chanting to a minimum. We don't want to overshadow the band."

With that, she slipped out, closing the door behind her.

Julia cleared her throat, settling into a chair wrapped in white tulle. "Amelia, why don't you fill us in on what you discovered the past couple of days?"

We all pulled the other chairs away from tables and sat. I took a deep breath, the whimsy of the room doing nothing to calm my nerves.

"Right. Earlier, I visited Esmerelda's old house on Vine Street. It's abandoned now, but I met an elderly neighbor who remembered her. She said Esmerelda was always hanging around young people, and she remembered Tiffany. Oh, and here's a detail: Esmerelda apparently had a much younger boyfriend named Garrett Hickinbottom."

Renee snapped her fingers. "That name sounds familiar. Is he an actor? The Sherlock guy?"

"That's Benedict Cumberbatch," Sage piped up.

"Hickinbottom, Cumberbatch. Sorry. Never mind. Carry on." Renee waved her hand.

I nodded. "From what I found online, he's based in Chicago, as a life coach and motivational speaker. I tried calling him, but he hung up on me as soon as I mentioned Esmerelda, Tiffany, and Marigold."

"Sus, as the kids say," Liz murmured.

We all looked at her, confused.

"It's short for suspicious," she quickly added. "My kids use the word all the time on TikTok."

"Definitely sus," I said with a smile. "But get this: I also snuck into Esmerelda's old place with some neighborhood kid, and we found an altar room. It was creepy as heck, with all these occult symbols and candles. And there was a dagger..."

I shuddered at the memory of the vision and swallowed a lump that had formed in my throat. "I had a psychometric vision. I saw Esmerelda performing some kind of ritual on Tiffany, talking about how they'd both stay young forever. And then I saw her wrapping a body in a rug."

"That's not just a red flag, but Six Flags amusement park," Sage said. "I don't like it at all."

"Wait, there's more." I explained every detail of my conversation with Tiffany at the lake. I added a few details about how I'd come to meet the ghost, and how she lived in the water with others like her, in the In Between.

The room fell silent, the weight of my story hanging in the air. Even Mom looked disturbed, her brow furrowed.

"I don't think this is a good idea to continue this investigation," Mom piped up. "I thought you all were joking at first, but you're not. This sounds like dangerous stuff."

"This isn't a game, Linda," Liz said gently.

"Goddess above," Julia murmured. "It sounds like Esmerelda was doing spell experiments on young women, seeking eternal youth. It goes against everything I've ever learned about witchcraft. We're supposed to evolve beyond that, accept and embrace being older."

Mom made a horrified face. I don't think anyone but me noticed.

"We have to confront her," Sage declared, slamming her fist on the table and making the paper pony plates jump. "She can't get away with this."

Renee held up a hand. "I agree, but we need to be smart about it. Esmerelda is clearly dangerous, and if she's been able to evade consequences for this long, she's probably got some serious power."

"Not to mention connections," Liz added. "Didn't you say her dad was a cop, Amelia?"

I nodded, my stomach twisting. The more I learned about Esmerelda, the more daunting the task of bringing her to justice seemed. "I'm assuming he's probably dead by now, though."

"What if we went to the police with what Amelia saw?" Mom suggested, surprising me. I hadn't expected her to have any suggestions at all about this situation.

Julia shook her head. "Visions aren't exactly admissible in court. And this Garrett guy clearly isn't going to talk. We need solid evidence, or a confession. Or we need to get across our main point: no more spell experiments. Then there's also another issue."

"What?" Renee asked.

"We know where Tiffany is. She's in the lake, in the In Between—"

"What's that?" Mom interrupted.

I leaned in. "I'll tell you later."

Julia continued. "But the question remains: where is Marigold? Her body was never discovered. Where did she bury the body? Where is Marigold's spirit? And now I'm not so certain Tracy's death was really a car accident."

In the short time I'd known Julia, I'd never seen her look so fierce.

"So we make her confess," Sage said, a glint of determination in her eyes. "We confront her as a united front, use our combined power to break through whatever defenses she has up. She's got to be weaker now, right? It's been decades. We can gather the entire coven as backup."

"Sage is right." Renee shifted forward, lowering her voice.

"If we can get Esmerelda rattled, catch her off guard, she might let something slip. It's risky, but it might be our best shot."

I chewed my lip, my mind racing. Renee and Sage's plan made sense, but the thought of facing Esmerelda, even with the support of the coven, made my gut churn.

"I believe we can use Marigold's bone in a spell, to work against Esmerelda," Julia said, her tone businesslike. "I've been doing some research and I think we can persuade the witch to turn herself in — or face the consequences from our coven. We can be quite persuasive, but we'll need a lot of support and a solid plan. Also, we need to do this as soon as tomorrow morning."

We continued to debate strategy. But even as we hashed out the details of our confrontation, I couldn't shake the feeling that we were about to poke a very dangerous bear — er, witch.

By the time we filtered back out to the club, I was a jangle of nerves. Jimbo and Wolf were deep in conversation by the balcony. The band hadn't resumed playing yet, and Oliver stood, sipping a soda. His eyes lit up when he saw me, and I mustered a smile.

"Everything okay?" he asked when I reached him.

I reached for his hand, twining my fingers into his. That simple touch was enough to anchor me. "Yeah," I nodded. "I think so."

"I have to get back on stage. I'll see you later? We're grabbing a beer after, a quick one, since Denny has his colon prep tomorrow. Want to join us?"

"Sure," I said, giving him a quick hug.

I watched as Oliver bounded back downstairs and onto the stage. A roar of applause rippled through the room. Despite my hesitation about tomorrow, I felt a swell of pride and affection. At least I had this perfect moment before plunging into the unknown.

I ordered a second Mermaid Margarita, wanting to soak the night in — in case it was my last.

My only hope was that, come morning, the coven's strength and my own budding powers would be enough to finally get answers for Marigold and bring Esmerelda to justice. Or, at the very least, get her to stop any spells or experiments — if she was still doing them.

But as I watched Oliver shred on his guitar under the stage lights, part of me wished we could stay in this magical bubble of music and laughter and pony piñatas forever, the evil kept at bay by the beat of an '80s power ballad.

The next day was Sunday. The entire coven was scheduled to meet in the parking lot of an abandoned grocery store down the street from the Willow Oaks retirement community.

I was there, in the cracked and dilapidated parking lot, with mom. Slightly hungover. The two Mermaid Margaritas and one beer after the show with Oliver had left me feeling off-kilter. The status of my stomach was best described as *sour*.

Or perhaps that was because of what we were about to do. I let out a small moan as I killed the car engine.

"I told you to always drink gin. No hangovers with gin. And never mix beer with liquor. But you never listen," Mom chided. She'd stopped drinking after her martinis and had spent the hour after the show grilling Oliver about his work.

"I don't need a lecture," I grunted. "Why is it so bright out?"

"Because it's seven-thirty in the morning? Because it's Florida?"

I curled my lip and reached for my extra-large coffee. Somehow, we were the first ones here, probably because I was nervous and had barely slept. Thank goodness the inn's two guests had planned to leave early, so I'd crawled out of bed at five and gotten breakfast on the table for them by six-thirty.

Mom and I got out and leaned against my car, sipping our coffees. The air was moist. My skin was on the verge of sticky. How could one be too hot, yet simultaneously be cold and clammy at the same time?

"Mom, what do you remember about perimenopause?"

She waved her hand dismissively. "Oh, you know. Some hot flashes. No big deal, really."

"Really? Because it sucks."

"Everyone's experience is different, dear. You'll get through it."

I stewed for a few minutes in silence about Mom's unwillingness to commiserate. I had to let her reaction go, if I wanted to stay sane. Especially today.

We watched the parking lot slowly fill up with a parade of minivans and SUVs. It was like a soccer mom convention, except instead of hauling kids to practice, these women were gearing up to confront a potentially murderous witch.

Carpools arrived, women spilling out in twos and threes. A few small buses even pulled in, disgorging what looked like entire groups. I began to wonder if it was safe for Mom to be here, given that she wasn't a member of the group and that she didn't have powers.

"These must be the coven members," I said between sips.

Mom glanced around, half-alarmed, half-impressed.

I marveled at Julia's ability to mobilize such a large group on short notice. The woman had a gift for organization that rivaled a presidential visit.

Mom nudged me as I exchanged waves with a few people. "Do you know all these women?"

I shook my head, still trying to process the sheer number of witches assembling. "No, only a handful. I recognize some from town, but a lot of these faces are new."

"Well, they certainly mean business, don't they?"

I nodded, feeling a swell of awe. These women had shown up in force to support the coven and seek justice for Marigold. It was a powerful reminder of what could happen if we stuck together as a sisterhood.

As the parking lot reached capacity, I spotted Julia, Renee, Liz, and Sage climbing out of a Volvo station wagon. They all wore windbreakers in eye-popping aqua and pink hues.

Liz and Renee sauntered over, their colorblock jackets practically blinding me in the morning light. I couldn't help but grin, though. It was perfect Gen X '80s style.

"Nobody's fighting harder against the wind than you two," I joked, pulling Liz into a half-hug while still keeping a grip on my coffee.

"We have one for you," Liz said. Sage held out a folded windbreaker.

"We can't have you facing down evil without proper attire, pardner." Sage wore the windbreaker with skinny jeans that were tucked into aqua cowboy boots.

I accepted the jacket and set my coffee on the hood of my car, then shrugged it on over my T-shirt, zipping it to my chin. The slick material crinkled with each movement and I knew I was going to sweat something fierce.

"I feel like I'm ready to solve mysteries and Jazzercise, at the same time."

Julia strode over, her own windbreaker a vibrant aqua that perfectly matched her steely eyes. She carried a clipboard and nodded at Sage, who stuck two fingers in her mouth and whistled loudly. The shrill sound carried across the lot, and a hush fell over the place.

"Good morning, coven sisters," Julia said, her voice

carrying across the lot. "I see we're all ready for action. Hang tight while I give the mission captains instructions. Remember: we want today to be a success without anyone getting hurt. That's our main goal today. Everyone got that?"

Applause and cheers rung out. I watched, rapt, at how well Julia commanded the group.

She pulled out her phone and fired off a quick text. "Come with me," she said, gesturing.

We all followed her. As Julia greeted people with a cool professionalism while still walking through the crowd — similar to a general or president — I heard snippets of conversation as we marched past.

"Diane couldn't come today. She had Disney tickets with her grandkids."

"I heard Esmerelda was the most powerful witch in town at one time."

"Yeah, the hair on my upper lip curled so I looked like Salvador Dali. That's when I got laser removal."

We stopped at a minivan, where six women in aqua windbreakers stood, coffee, clipboards, and pens at the ready. Everyone made little *pfft-pfft-pfft* noises from the synthetic fabric as they clustered around. These were the mission captains, no doubt.

"Is this a common thing, getting everyone together like this?" I asked Sage under my breath.

She shook her head, then leaned in and whispered, "Only once, when we had to get a coven member out of a domestic violence situation. Julia tries to use her powers only for good and will only open a can of whoop-ass in extreme circumstances."

My eyes widened. So this was serious.

"Come close, everyone, gather round," Julia called out.

Liz handed her a map, and Julia unfolded it, spreading it

across the hood of the van. We all clustered together, the scent of coffee and patchouli in the air.

Julia tapped a bright red circle on the map. "This is a map of the Willow Oaks retirement community. These are the condos, and this area is the single-family homes. Esmerelda lives here, on a corner lot, and we're out here." She circled our location. "Thankfully she's not in a condo, which means we'll be able to surround her home. If any neighbors ask what we're doing, we say we're there to celebrate Esmerelda's birthday. A team of us have those flamingos for the lawn, and will be putting those up while we're inside."

She looked up, her eyes scanning every one of us. "Team leaders, you have your assignments. Everyone else, check in with your group. We move out in ten."

As the women marched off, Julia turned to me, her expression softening slightly. "Amelia, you're with me. Your psychic abilities will be key in confronting Esmerelda, as we discussed last night. Linda, I think you should stay here."

Mom shook her head. "No way. I'm not letting Amelia do this alone. I know I'm a lot older and you all probably think I'm incapable—"

"Nope," Julia said sharply. "We don't do ageism here. I simply didn't think you'd want to see Amelia in the middle of something like this. It can be disturbing to confront someone who possesses dark witchcraft, much less watch someone you love confront them."

Mom pursed her lips and the two women sized each other up for a beat. I held my breath.

"I've seen a lot of disturbing things in my day," Mom said firmly. "I want to be there to support my daughter."

Julia turned to me. "Amelia? This is your call."

I glanced from Mom to Julia, then back at Mom. "She can

come with us. She needs to witness my new life, all of it. Including this."

"Okay, then." Julia nodded. "Amelia and Linda? You're with me and Renee in the van. Sage and Liz, follow us closely. The five of us will go inside first. This is a pretty big community, so it's going to take us at least five minutes to get to the house."

We all climbed into the minivan, with Renee driving, Julia in the passenger seat, and Mom and me in the back. A faintly familiar, earthy smell hung in the air.

Renee twisted around in her seat. "Sorry it smells like dog in here. I have a lab who's overdue for a bath."

"No worries," I said.

When Renee started the engine, the dramatic opening chords of Phil Collins' "In the Air Tonight" filled the van. She reached for the volume knob, but Julia held up a hand.

"Wait, keep it on," she said. "I like this song."

Renee shrugged and put the van in drive. We pulled out of the parking lot, leading the other vehicles toward our destination. The moody synth beat pulsed through the speakers as we drove in tense silence.

My neck started to sweat. The familiar, dramatic song transported me back to my childhood, sprawled on the shag carpet with my brother Mike, eyes glued to Miami Vice on the TV screen. I couldn't have been more than ten or eleven. I remember thinking how cool Crockett and Tubbs were as they drove a Ferrari while this song played.

How had our parents let us watch that show at that age? I pondered this, trying to stave off thoughts of Esmerelda for another few moments.

We passed by shuffleboard courts and a pool. Then Renee slowed at a crosswalk.

"Oh crap," Julia sighed.

A parade of older men in golf carts streamed past our vehicle. Evidently the golf course sprawled on both sides of the road.

"It looks like it's some kind of amateur tournament," Renee said.

One of the carts, filled with four men that had to be at least eighty, slowed to a crawl. The men turned their heads to look at us. They grinned. One man waved. Another man winked and held up his cell with a gnarled, wrinkled hand, as if he wanted to exchange numbers. The four of us sat, stone faced. When the guys saw that we weren't reacting, they shook their heads and glided away.

"Men never stop trying, do they?" Mom said.

"As long as they're breathing, they'll keep trying," Julia said, her tone resigned and annoyed.

Once the parade of dudes had ended, Renee gunned the engine and we were off again, Phil Collins and his drum solo thundering in the background.

"Take a left here," Julia murmured to Renee. We turned down a street, filled with identical beige stucco houses that sported red, barrel-tile roofs. Every home here was the same, which meant the homeowners' association must be quite powerful if they managed to lay down a law of conformity like this.

"Slow down. Okay. It's at the end of this block. Corner house." Julia's voice was steady.

Mom sat up a little straighter. I craned my neck to get a good look. I wasn't sure what I was anticipating, but as we approached, it wasn't what was before us.

Esmerelda's home was nothing like I anticipated. It was like every other home here. To my surprise, we pulled into the driveway. A team of coven members were nearby, taking out flamingo lawn ornaments from the back of a pickup.

As Renee turned the engine off, Julia turned to face Mom and me. "I want you both to follow every one of my directions. Do not wander off, understand?"

Her voice was so sharp, so steely, that all Mom and I could do was nod.

"Okay, let's do this." Julia opened her door, and we all followed suit. As we made our way up the small walkway to her door, I noticed two things.

One was that the dozens of cars in the parking lot were now parked on the street. There was no available parking space anywhere. Women were climbing out of the vehicles with determined looks on their faces.

And two, my eye caught on the only thing that set Esmerelda's home apart from all the others: a flag, flying high from a pole on the lawn. But instead of the U.S. Flag, or something cute that said "Hello Spring" or "Welcome Friends," it had a symbol.

The same one I'd seen in the altar room in the house on Vine Street. The same one that was etched on the bone, and on the knife. I didn't know what the symbol meant, and it looked like a few squiggly lines and a circle — but I suspected it was nothing positive.

As we were about to open the door, it flew open. Mom made a strangled gasp, and I reached for her arm. We all stopped at the front door. By now, Sage and Liz had joined us.

"Hi Julia," the woman said. This was not Esmerelda. A home health care aide, perhaps? She was young, maybe in her twenties, and wore scrubs, like a medical professional. "She's inside, in the back room. Good luck."

The woman slipped past us with a small, triumphant smile.

I caught Liz's attention. "Who was that?" I whispered.

"Julia has sources. Her son's girlfriend is a home health care aide and she connected us to Esmerelda's nurse."

I nodded, but Liz's answer only confused me more. Esmerelda needed a nurse? I didn't have time to dwell on the questions racing through my mind, because I was stepping through the doorway, following the coven leaders into a world that I didn't understand.

From the street, sidewalk, and lawn, I heard a noise. It was the low, eerie chanting of the coven members, giving us the support we'd need to get through this.

Twenty-Two

Ordinary.

That was all I could think as I walked into Esmerelda's house. It was so... boring.

The living room looked like it belonged to any other Florida retiree: seashell-adorned lamps, mermaid figurines, and pastel-colored throw pillows were the accents. A white leather sofa, which had seen better days, sat against one wall, flanked by a walker and a stack of AARP magazines on the side table.

The walls were a soft, non-threatening shade of pale yellow, decorated with a few generic landscape paintings that looked like they'd been purchased from a discount store. Lace doilies covered the end tables, and a vase of faux flowers gathered dust in the corner. It was all so sparse and unremarkable, a far cry from the eccentric, witchy den I'd been expecting.

I glanced at Mom, who seemed equally surprised by the mundane decor. She raised an eyebrow at me as if to say, "This is the big, bad witch's lair?"

Julia, however, remained unfazed. She strode through the living room, leading us down a narrow hallway. Framed photos lined the walls, but they were all generic stock images of sunsets and beaches, not a single personal picture in sight. Did we have the right house?

As we neared the end of the hall, a strange scent wafted towards us, a mix of medicinal ointments and something sharper, almost metallic. My stomach clenched.

Julia paused outside a closed door, her hand resting on the knob. She turned to face us, her expression grave.

"Remember," she said in a low voice, "follow my lead. If I give you instructions, do everything I tell you."

"Of course." I swallowed hard, my mouth suddenly dry.

With a deep breath, I nodded at Julia. She turned the knob and the door swung open, revealing a small, dimly lit bedroom. And there, propped up in a hospital bed amidst a tangle of blankets and pillows, was Esmerelda Blackthorn herself.

She looked nothing like the vibrant, charismatic woman from Tiffany's stories, and nor was she the gorgeous, confident woman I'd seen in the photo. Her once wild mane of dark hair was now thin and white, her skin pallid and heavily lined. She seemed shrunken, diminished, a mere husk of her former self.

But when her eyes locked onto mine, I felt an icy shiver run up my spine, cooling even my sweaty neck. Because even in her frail state, those dark eyes still burned with a fierce, unsettling intensity.

Her eyes were hungry.

An 80s song cliché, perhaps, but that was all I could think when she stared at me. It was as if she radiated envy and a deep urge to consume everything in her path.

"Well, well, well," she rasped, her voice like sandpaper. I flinched. "Looks like the slacker coven has come to pay their respects to a true genius. And you must be Amelia Matthews, the town's newest star psychic."

Her thin lips curved into a smile that was more mocking

than friendly. "I've been expecting you, dear. Come closer, let me get a good look at you. My eyesight isn't what it used to be."

I looked to Julia, who nodded. Apparently, that meant I should approach.

With a deep breath, I stepped forward. She appraised me haughtily, craning her head to take in my outfit. Which, admittedly, wasn't much. Mom jeans and my usual white Keds, along with the colorblock windbreaker. My hair was swept up into a messy bun and I hadn't bothered with makeup this morning.

"Hmm," she murmured, her lips twisting into a smirk. "You're not quite what I expected. A bit rough around the edges, aren't you? And those crow's feet. You could use some Botox. I know an excellent dermatologist in Winter Park who works wonders."

I bristled at her catty remark, my cheeks flushing with a mix of embarrassment and indignation. How dare she criticize my appearance? Still, it stung, especially after I'd felt smokin' hot last night. Duck her. Between this and my hangover, I was becoming more irritable by the second.

"I'm not interested in beauty tips, Esmerelda," I said, trying to keep my voice steady. "We're here about Marigold Wentworth. And Tiffany Ferndale. We're here to seek justice."

At the mention of those names, something flickered in Esmerelda's eyes. A flash of recognition, maybe even a hint of fear. But it vanished in an instant, replaced by a mask of cool indifference.

And arrogance. The one thing I despised in people.

"Marigold and Tiffany? Those names do ring a bell. But it was so long ago, and my memory isn't what it used to be." She waved a hand dismissively, the liver spots stark against her pale skin. "What about them?"

I glanced back at my companions for support. Mom gave

me an encouraging nod, while Julia's expression remained stony. I turned back to Esmerelda, squaring my shoulders.

"I know what you did to them. The rituals, the spells, the dark magic you used in your twisted pursuit of youth and beauty in the late 80s and early 90s. Tiffany told me everything. And I saw things, in my visions."

Esmerelda's eyes narrowed to slits. "Tiffany? But she's dead, in a watery grave. Has been for decades. I'm sure you know all about that, with your psychometry."

How did she know that about me? Oh boy, this was way creepier than I imagined.

"Tell us what happened," I said through gritted teeth. Now I was irate. Although I hadn't known what to expect from her, I wasn't anticipating this kind of attitude.

I glanced at Renee. Her eyes were shut and her lips were moving.

Same with Julia.

They both seemed in some sort of a trance, and I suspected they were doing a spell on Esmerelda. I pressed on.

"What did you do to Tiffany? Start with her." I tried to summon my most stern voice, channeling Mom, Julia, and the few times I'd been truly upset with my daughter. "I need to know, now."

Julia and Renee's chanting grew louder. Somehow, Esmerelda either couldn't hear them, or was successfully ignoring the sound. Mom looked terrified, and Liz didn't look too calm, either. Sage stood like a sentinel by the door, her gaze like a laser on the woman in the bed. I edged away from the dark witch.

Esmerelda shifted uncomfortably in her bed, wincing as she tried to adjust her sitting position. Her face was growing a grayish pale and her bottom lip began to tremble.

"My hip," she groused, more to herself than to us. "The

surgery was supposed to fix everything, but the pain. Oh, lord, the pain! It never really goes away, does it? If only I could be twenty again."

Her voice was tinged with bitterness and regret. I almost felt a dash of pity for her, but then I remembered the horrible things she'd done. The lives she'd destroyed in her selfish pursuit of eternal youth.

As Julia and Renee's chanting reached a crescendo, Esmerelda's eyes widened in panic. She clutched at her chest, gasping for breath. She looked like a cornered animal, desperate and afraid.

To my shock, Mom stepped forward. I tried to reach for her, to pull her back, but she was too quick. "Listen, I'd do what they ask you," she yelled, over the chanting. "There's at least a hundred witches outside, all doing some mumbo-jumbo. You don't stand a chance against my daughter and her friends."

I appreciated Mom's vote of confidence, but now wasn't the time. I reached for her arm and yanked her back with me.

Judith and Renee hadn't seemed to notice Mom's attempted intervention. Their chanting continued, loud and insistent. Then Julia, without opening her eyes, reached into her windbreaker pocket.

And took out the bone. Marigold's bone.

Julia's eyes snapped open, fixing Esmerelda with an icy glare as she held the yellowed finger bone aloft. "Do you recognize this, Esmerelda? It's all that remains of Marigold Wentworth after your wicked spell."

Esmerelda smiled for a second, as if she'd remembered something lovely in the midst of her pain. "You found it."

Julia continued, her voice low and dangerous. "You brutally severed Marigold's finger as part of your dark ritual. Her blood is on your hands!"

Esmerelda began to tremble, whether from fear or rage I couldn't tell. "You have no idea what you're meddling with, you foolish girl! The forces I've channeled, the entities I've bargained with, they're beyond your wildest nightmares!"

I seemed to stop breathing in that moment, holding my breath. Mom and I held onto each other tightly as we watched.

Julia took a step closer to the bed, still holding the bone. "You sacrificed an innocent young woman for your own vanity and greed. And now, you will answer for your crimes, one way or another. Marigold's spirit cries out for justice."

Esmerelda let out a harsh, wheezing cackle that made me rethink my life here in Cypress Grove. "Justice? There is no justice in this world, only power. Raw, primal power. You're all insignificant worms compared to what I was!"

The chanting from Renee intensified. Esmerelda began to writhe on the bed, clawing at her throat as if an invisible hand were choking her. Julia watched impassively, the bone still raised.

"Last chance, Esmerelda," Julia warned. "Confess your crimes or face the consequences. Marigold's restless spirit demands retribution. Do what we ask."

"Stop," she wheezed, her voice barely above a whisper. "Please, stop. I'll tell you what you want to know."

I clutched Mom harder, my heart pounding in my chest.

"Tiffany," Esmerelda began, her voice quaking and low. "She was an experiment. I thought I had perfected the ritual, the spell to harness youth. But something went wrong. So wrong."

She closed her eyes, as if the memory was too painful to bear. "Everything backfired. Instead of transferring Tiffany's youth to me, it, it drained her completely. She withered before my eyes, aging decades in mere moments until she was nothing but a husk. That's why Garrett and I did what we did. We were so afraid she'd come back to hurt us. The spell was supposed to allow us to share her youth, but it failed."

My breath hitched. Dear, sweet Tiffany.

Esmerelda swallowed hard. "She died right there on my altar. I panicked. I didn't know what to do. So we wrapped her body in a rug and dumped her in the lake."

I felt bile rise in my throat. The casual cruelty of it, the callousness. It was obscene, like something out of the bleakest horror movie.

"And Marigold?" I pressed, my voice shaking with barely suppressed rage. "What did you do to her?"

A single tear rolled down Esmerelda's cheek. "Marigold. She and the other girl started poking around into Tiffany's life and death. I had to stop her, otherwise I might get caught, and Garrett, too. I thought with her, I could finally achieve what I'd been seeking for so long. Eternal beauty, eternal life. When I saw her, I knew I had to try the spell once again. I needed her fingerprint, which was why I did the amputation."

My rage was threatening to boil over, and I couldn't help but blurt, "Why didn't you get a face lift? Botox? A chemical peel? There are alternatives to stealing another woman's youth!"

Liz nodded. "They also have those vampire facial things. Seriously."

"I tried all of those, but they were only surface level. They didn't make me *feel* young." Esmerelda's voice was tinged with regret.

"Why the duck would anyone want to feel young?" I cried, throwing up my hands in exasperation. "You killed two people. That's unforgivable."

She let out a choked sob. "I was more careful with the ritual with Marigold. And it worked, or at least I thought it did. She gave me some of my looks back, until about five years ago. Then I began aging again. I thought the spell would keep me young until I died. It's hell, you know that? Aging is awful."

"It's only awful if you allow it to be," I snapped. My mind raced. "But where is she? Where is Marigold's body? Where is her spirit? Tell me!"

Esmerelda patted at her wet cheeks with a crumpled tissue. "Her spirit is here in this house with me. That's all that matters. She'll be with me until I pass, and then? Who knows. I'm sorry it all worked out this way."

I stared at her, this feeble old woman who had once been so fearsome, so formidable. And I felt nothing. No pity, no forgiveness. Only a cold, hollow ache where my heart should be.

"It's too late for apologies, Esmerelda," I said softly. "You can't undo what you've done. But you can help us bring some measure of peace. To the coven. To Marigold's family. Where is she?"

Julia and Renee began to chant again, this time with more fervor. Esmerelda shivered and retched.

"I'll do whatever I can. Whatever you need. Just...please. No more magic. No more spells. I can't...I can't bear it. I want to live. I can't stand this pain! It's everywhere!"

Suddenly, she began weeping. Was it all an act?

"How did you meet Marigold? Did you lure her in with the promise of community?" I asked.

Esmee shook her head. "She showed up at my house one day. Claiming to be a reporter for her college newspaper. Said she was looking into the disappearance of Tiffany and that I was one of the last people to see her."

Somehow this made me even angrier. "So you killed her because you feared she was about to expose you."

"No," Esmee yelped, pointing at me with a shaky hand. "I

asked her if she wanted to experience what Tiffany had, and possibly become forever young in the process. She was such a curious girl that she said yes."

"Oh my goodness," I whispered, horrified. What do we do with that information? I looked to Julia for help. "Where is she?"

Julia slowly put the bone back into her pocket. "Go. Look around the house and see if you can find anything that's a vessel for Marigold's soul. We'll take care of the rest."

I nodded and shot another glare at Esmerelda. Mom handed her a box of tissues, and she took one.

"You know what to do, Esmerelda," Julia said, handing her a cell phone. "You know who to call."

I couldn't tear myself away from the scene, even though I had my orders.

"I don't want to go to prison," Esmerelda whispered. "I'll never survive a trial."

"Too bad," Julia growled. "Call the cops."

Renee's hands clenched into fists and Esmerelda gasped. "Oh, my hip! The pain!"

She let out a scream of pure anguish. I stood, gaping, half expecting her to melt or evaporate or burst into flames. But she stopped to gulp in a few breaths. I couldn't help but notice that Renee was staring at her, unblinking and furious. Whoa. She must be pretty powerful to cause pain like that.

"Okay, okay! I'll call the police," Esmerelda said between sobs. "Please stop the spell. Lord, I didn't think your generation had this kind of powerful magic."

"You misjudged us," Julia said in a voice so low and menacing even I was frightened. "That was your biggest mistake. You had to know we'd come for you eventually. It's the biggest sin you can commit against a coven."

Eeep. Terrified, I quickly turned away, scanning everything in the bedroom. "What am I looking for?" I asked aloud to no one in particular. Mom seemed frozen from fear because for once, she didn't have a witty comeback.

"Anything that seems out of place," Julia said. "Go. Now."

I moved quickly around the room, feeling confused and useless. My legs seemed to be disconnected to my brain, and I hustled out of the bedroom.

What could possibly hold Marigold's spirit after all these years? I didn't even know what I was searching for, but I had to try.

The living room was my best bet. I tore through the space like a tornado, opening drawers, flipping couch cushions, and rummaging through the few knick-knacks on shelves. Seashells, cheesy Florida souvenirs, old TV Guides — nothing jumped out at me as a potential vessel for a trapped soul. I hoped my psychometry would take over once I started touching things, but everything my fingers grazed yielded nothing.

Why wasn't my psychometry working in here? Did Esmerelda have some sort of force field over her house?

Frustration mounting, I moved into the kitchen. The room was spotless, almost sterile, with outdated white appliances and faded linoleum. I yanked open cabinets and rifled through drawers, sending utensils clattering. Nothing here, either.

I raced back into the bedroom. Liz was on the phone, giving our address.

"Hurry," Julia hissed to me. "We need to find it before the cops get here. We don't want them to take Marigold into evidence. We'll never get her back."

I rifled through the closet, which was mostly house dresses and worn slippers. Then I scanned the bureau. A line of pill bottles, an asthma inhaler, one of those blue bulbs to extract ear wax...

And a jewelry box.

Not the kind an adult would own, but a small, white box with faded pink flowers on the side. I recognized it immediately, because I had one as a child. Long-buried memories of my grandmother — the witchy one — giving it to me one Christmas came flooding back.

With trembling hands, I snatched it up. The gold clasp shone in the ray of sunshine beaming through a crack in the curtains. The edges of the box were worn, as if it had knocked around during several moves over the decades. This was the only thing that seemed out of place.

Holding my breath, I carefully opened the lid to reveal an empty interior, covered in pink satin. An eerie, tinkling melody began to play, the notes thin and slightly out of tune. And there, in the center of the box, was a tiny ballerina figurine, turning in circles in front of a small oval mirror.

"That's her," Esmerelda cried. "Don't take her from me!"

As Swan Lake played, the ballerina began to turn slowly, her porcelain face frozen in a serene smile, her painted-on tutu a faded pink. Around and around she spun, the mechanism clicking softly and the song shrill and spooky.

As the ballerina twisted in slow motion, I swore I heard a voice, faint and distant, like a whisper within the breeze. At first, I thought it was my imagination. But then I heard it again, louder this time, and unmistakable, an echo in my mind.

"Help me."

"Marigold?" I whispered to the ballerina. I mean, duh. Who else could it be?

"Yes. Please help me."

I hauled in a ragged breath, wanting to cry. But I needed to stay strong. "I'm here. We're here. The coven's here. The coven you started. You're safe now, with your sisters."

I snapped the lid shut.

An hour later, Renee was being questioned by police. I was outside Esmee's home with Julia.

She nestled the ballerina jewelry box containing Marigold's spirit into the back of Julia's Volvo station wagon, inside a reusable Publix shopping bag and behind a box of beach toys for her step-grandkids.

She pulled off her windbreaker and loosely wrapped it around the jewel box, almost as if she was tucking a child into bed.

"There." She snapped the trunk shut. "That'll be safe for now."

We were on the street, outside of Esmerelda's house. The coven members who had been chanting outside had left before cops arrived, leaving behind only those of us who had been in the house.

"Julia?" My voice was still shaky, as was my stomach. "I have to ask. What exactly did you do with Marigold's bone in there? It seemed to have quite the effect on Esmerelda, almost as if it compelled her to confess."

Julia gave me a thoughtful look. "The bone turned out to be a potent talisman. It's imbued with Marigold's essence, her spirit. When I held it up and Renee and I focused our energies, it amplified the coven's power. Plus all of the people outside. They were channeling their positive energy as well."

She paused, glancing at the house. "Esmerelda couldn't deny the truth any longer, not when faced with such undeniable proof of her crimes. The bone acted as a conduit, a way for Marigold to reach out from beyond and demand justice. It was the magic of the coven. Our power, combined with hers, was no match even for a dark witch. That's what happens when women work together."

I nodded slowly, trying to wrap my mind around the complex magical workings. "So, it was like Marigold herself was forcing Esmerelda to come clean, through the bone and with your help?"

"With *our* help," Julia said firmly. "Renee's chant helped weaken Esmerelda's defenses, making her more susceptible to the bone's influence. It was a team effort, a show of the coven's strength and unity."

She placed a comforting hand on my arm. "You played a crucial role too, Amelia. Your psychic gifts allowed us to see what happened to Marigold, and that set you and us on the path to the truth. Without you, we might never have been able to confront Esmerelda like this."

"But why would Esmerelda hide the bone in the library book in the first place?" I was still so confused. "And how could she have done it, given her age and condition?"

Julia blew out a breath. "It's possible she used magic to conceal it. A teleportation spell, perhaps, or an enchantment to make the bone invisible until the right person found it. Or she could have had an accomplice. Someone who shared her dark interests or was under her influence. Garrett perhaps. They might have placed the bone in the book on her orders. We still don't know his full role in this."

"But why?" I pressed. "Why leave such incriminating evidence behind?"

"To mislead us, perhaps," Julia suggested. "Or to send a message. Esmerelda's motives have always been twisted. We may never fully understand her reasoning. She wasn't rational."

"That's a difficult pill to swallow, possibly never knowing."

Julia nodded somberly, but pasted on a tight smile when a young officer in uniform approached.

"Ma'am," he said, staring nervously at Julia. "We're going to need you for questioning now."

"Of course." Julia smiled tightly. "We'll talk soon, Amelia."

I watched her walk away.

Esmerelda was whisked off to the county hospital, where regional law enforcement had a few rooms for medical inmates. A judge would arraign her via video.

Cops crawled her place for evidence, and Chief Christopher Wolf was in his glory, marching around in his starched uniform, giving orders and acting like he was in command. I mean, he was in charge since he was the chief, but I couldn't help but feel that some of his demeanor was for the benefit of Liz.

Who was watching his every move from a chair on the porch with a small smile. I walked over and I sank into an empty chair next to her. Mom was there, too, already sitting on a bench.

"Where's Julia and Renee?" Mom asked.

"They're being questioned by detectives. Geez, it looks like the entire force is here," I said.

Liz nodded. "Well, Marigold's disappearance was a sore spot for the department. They got a lot of heat back in the day for not finding her or solving the case."

"They must be thrilled that Esmerelda confessed," Mom said.

Liz sucked in a breath. "I know I am. She made me so angry in there. Can you imagine not wanting to get older? I'm having the time of my life now. No worries about pregnancy, no kids to raise, no real responsibilities other than retirement, but that's not ever going to happen so I'm going to enjoy the ride."

"I'm with you. Even with hot flashes and the occasional migraine and some weird brain fog, I'm happier than I ever was when I was young," I agreed. "I know myself better and that means more than anything."

Mom stared at us like we'd both sprouted extra eyes. "Are you two crazy? Who wants to be old? I don't condone what Esmerelda did, not in the least. But I understand the impulse. Looking like a hag is dreadful."

"Why, though?" I asked. "It's a privilege to age. To reach the point where you don't care anymore, where you can let go of all the expectations you had and live in peace. I don't even care if I look like a hag. I only want happiness. And maybe fewer chin hairs."

Liz nodded enthusiastically. "I love the start of my crone era. Someday we're not even going to care about the chin hair. Laser's not a bad idea, though."

Mom shuddered. "To each her own, I guess."

Just then, Chief Wolf came out of the house. "Good news, ladies. I think we've found some financial records to link her to Garrett Hickinbottom. We'll have to send them to a forensic audit, of course. But I hope we'll soon have enough for a warrant for his arrest, too."

"You are amazing," Liz said.

The chief grinned, showing all his pearly whites. "Thanks."

"Does anyone have any water?" she asked. "I'm parched."

"I have a case in my car. Want to come with me to grab some bottles?"

"Sure."

Mom and I watched as they walked off together, to the chief's car that was parked down the street.

"They make a nice couple," I remarked.

Mom cleared her throat. "Amelia?"

"Yeah?"

Mom stared out at the street, where curious onlookers had started to gather behind the police tape. She sighed. "I owe you an apology."

I turned to her, shocked. Apologies usually weren't in Mom's bag of tricks. "For what?"

"For not being more supportive of your new life here. Of your abilities. I didn't know what to think, at first. Honestly, I was always skeptical of your aunt when she said she had powers, or when she said *you* had powers. Then when I arrived and you had bought into everything, well, I thought you'd lost your mind."

I held up a hand. "Trust me, I thought I was losing my mind at first. It's pretty weird here. But in a good way, I've discovered. I've found my people. After decades of moving and trying things, I've finally found my place in the world."

"Yeah, I know. I can sense that." She laughed softly. "I was scared at first, because it was all so foreign to me. But seeing you today, the way you handled Esmerelda and helped find justice for Marigold? *Wow.* I was proud of you, honey. So very proud. You kept your composure. I was ready to run out of there. My goodness."

Tears pricked at my eyes. Mom had never been one for emotional heart-to-hearts, being a Boomer and all. Her words and her expression carried so much weight, so many years of unspoken emotion that I'd longed to hear. "Thank you, Mom. That means a lot."

She patted my hand, her eyes shining. "You've found your calling here in Cypress Grove. I can see that now. And as much as I wish you were closer to me in Arizona, I understand why you need to be here. Florida is where you belong. But I have Hal and Jenny nearby, at least."

My throat tightened with emotion. "I'm happy here, Mom. Happier than I've been in a long time. But that doesn't mean I don't miss you or need you in my life. I promise to come visit. Maybe even with Oliver."

"Oh, I know. I'm your mother. You'll always need me to keep you on your toes." She winked, and we both chuckled. The tension that had hung between us for so long had finally started to evaporate. "And yes, I would like to get to know Oliver better."

"He'd like to get to know you, too. I think he feels bad that your first impression of him was singing a sexy rock song while wearing tight pants."

Mom snickered. "Oliver is quite handsome, I have to admit. And speaking of men, Hal will be here later today to pick me up. I got a text from him about twenty minutes ago. He wants me to go to that golf tournament with him." She picked an invisible piece of lint off her pants. "But I hope we can talk more, going forward. I want to hear all about your witchy adventures. And I'll probably return soon without Hal, because Marisol wants me to take one of her tea classes. If you'll have me at the inn."

"I'd love to have you."

"And one other thing." Mom's gaze was serious. "I'm going to leave it to you to tell Jenny and your brother about your abilities. I promise I won't say a word."

"I appreciate that. Truly." I grinned because my heart felt

lighter than it had in years. Mom and I still had our differences, but for the first time in a long while, I felt like she was actually seeing me. The real me.

And that was a magical feeling all on its own.

***

Later that afternoon, after I'd downed an Advil and what felt like a gallon of water, Oliver and I stood on the wraparound porch of the Crescent Moon Inn, watching as Mom and Hal loaded up their rental car. The Florida sun was beginning to dip low in the winter sky, casting a wan, golden light that made the palm trees look extra-lovely.

Mom came up the walkway, a small smile playing at her lips. "Well, Amelia, it's been quite a visit. I never imagined I'd do anything that I've done these past few days. Never in a million years. I thought we'd drink wine and bicker a little but this was much more fun."

I laughed. "Just a typical weekend in Cypress Grove."

Hal bounded up the porch steps, grinning from ear to ear. "Linda, you ready to hit the road? I can't wait to show you around the golf tournament. Did I tell you we're in the same hotel as the caddies?"

Mom rolled her eyes good-naturedly. "Sounds thrilling, dear."

I got the distinct impression that she'd prefer to stay here with me.

I handed Hal a paper bag filled with the orange shortbread cookies. "For the drive."

Hal's eyes lit up as he accepted the bag. "You're the best, kiddo."

"You two have fun, okay? And Hal, try to stay away from the ponds on the golf course. That's where the gators are."

"I heard that," he said, and winked.

Mom turned to Oliver, quirking an eyebrow. "And you, Mr. Rock Star Professor. You take good care of my daughter, you hear me?"

Oliver grinned, sliding an arm around my waist. "Loud and clear. Scout's honor."

"He was never a Boy Scout," I stage-whispered to Mom, and we all laughed. "He was into the X-Files."

With a final round of hugs and promises to stay in touch, Mom and Hal went to their car. Hal climbed in the driver's side.

Before Mom got in, she turned and waved. "I love you, Amelia," she called out.

"Love you too," I said.

As the engine roared to life, Oliver and I stepped back, our arms around each other. We waved until the car disappeared down the street.

"You know, that's the first time she's ever told me she loved me at the end of a visit." I tilted my head. "Huh."

"Interesting. What do you think changed her?"

"Dunno. Cypress Grove, maybe? Or perhaps Marisol's tea?" Whatever it was, I was here for this new era of my relationship with Mom.

"The town does work in strange ways," he said in a low voice.

We turned to go back inside. I spotted Freddie staring at us out a window. We locked eyes, and he meowed.

"What are you doing the rest of the day?" Oliver asked, his hand on the small of my back.

"Oh, lots of excitement. I was going to clean the rooms, check my emails, and maybe schedule some posts for the inn's Instagram. You?"

He gently pulled me close and drew me in for a kiss. It was

like the one on Saturday night: passionate and intense. When we broke apart, I was breathless.

"Can I possibly talk you into procrastinating a bit?" A small smile played on his lips, but his eyes were filled with pure desire. Probably mine were, too.

I grinned wide. "I would love nothing more than to procrastinate with you."

And with that, I reached for Oliver's hand and pulled him inside.

Epilogue

One month later

The full moon was climbing in the clear night sky as I walked up the steps to the coven house. The Mediterranean Revival mansion was even more impressive up close, with its stucco walls, terracotta roof tiles, and ornate wrought iron details. The place sat on the edge of town, down a dirt road past an orange grove. It was so remote that I feared I'd gotten lost a few times.

Before I could knock, the large, wooden door swung open. Renee was on the other side.

I stepped over the threshold, my insides quivering with anticipation.

Julia and Renee greeted me, their faces glowing with excitement. They were dressed in long silver caftans sporting beautiful, crystal bead-embroidered V-necks. Renee wore Birkenstock sandals with hers, while Julia had on spiky black heels.

I also had on the same caftan; Julia had one sent to the inn from an expensive store in Miami, with a note saying I should wear it tonight. She'd also included a pair of sparkly silver flip-flops, which fit perfectly and looked amazing with my red toenail polish.

"Amelia, welcome, welcome!" Julia said, pulling me into a warm hug. "It's the night we've been waiting for."

"This is some house. Wow." Julia released me and I did a little spin to take in the curved staircase and the antique-looking Spanish tile on the floor.

"We'll give you the full tour later," Renee promised, guiding me down a long hallway. "But first, the ceremony."

"Here, let me take your things." Julia held out her hands and I gave her the canvas tote bag and a paper bag with twine handles. The first held Marigold's basket. I'd kept it safe for the last month, but now it would reside here in the coven head-quarters. The second bag held a few bottles of wine for the party.

"Thanks. This place is incredible. Wait. Why am I whispering?"

Julia laughed. "Everyone has that reaction when they first see the place."

"Do people live here?" We started to make our way down a long hallway.

Julia shook her head. "I was fortunate to buy this some years ago when it went into foreclosure. The entire coven pitched in to renovate, and now we use it for meetings, parties, events...oh, and if members need a safe space or temporary housing during emergencies. We also use it as a hurricane shelter."

"What a great idea," I murmured.

As we walked, I couldn't help but marvel at everything as we passed open doors, giving me a peek at designer showroom-worthy décor. The plush Persian rugs, the intricately carved wooden furniture, and the crystal chandeliers that cast a soft, enchanting glow — everything was strangely beautiful and relaxing.

It was like a high-end spa.

We came to a set of double doors at the end of the hall, and Renee pushed them open with a dramatic flourish. My breath caught in my throat as I took in the sight before me.

It was a grand ballroom, with soaring ceilings and scarlet velvet curtains that draped gracefully from the windows on one side of the room. Painted portraits of women, some with punk rock hairstyles and others with 90s bobs, lined one wall. I assumed they were former coven leaders, since Julia's portrait was up there, too.

The room was filled with around a hundred women, all chatting and laughing, their voices blending together in a friendly hum. In the background, a New Age song with flutes played softly in the background.

This was kind of like a cocktail party. With witches.

I scanned the crowd, marveling that everyone was wearing the same silver caftans as Julia and Renee. All of the women were around my age, some with gray hair, others with obvious Botox, still others with funky, cat-eye glasses on chains around their necks. There was a sense of camaraderie and excitement that hung in the air, a palpable energy that made my skin prickle.

As I stepped further into the room, I spotted some familiar faces: Liz and Sage. They moved toward us while waving and grinning. They, too, were wearing the caftans. Liz wore sparkly flip-flops like me, and Sage had on bedazzled cowboy boots. Renee and Julia squeezed my arms.

"Hang tight with them. We'll start the ceremony in about ten minutes," Julia said. She and Renee melted into the crowd.

"Amelia, you made it!" Liz exclaimed, pulling me into a fierce hug. "Are you ready for this?"

I nodded, my heart swelling with a mix of nerves and excitement. "As ready as I'll ever be."

Sage draped an arm around my shoulders, her cowboy boots clicking against the polished wood floor. With her other hand, she handed me a champagne glass. "You're going to do great, pardner. We're all here for you. Here, drink this. It's a special concoction that one of the members created. It'll calm your nerves."

I sniffed the drink. It smelled like sweet champagne, with a hint of lavender. I took a sip and a thousand bubbles exploded in my mouth.

"What a week, huh?" Liz said. "Between the court hearing, the alligator downtown, and now this ceremony, I can't think of a more exciting time in Cypress Grove in years."

I shook my head. "Unreal. It's been nonstop, right?"

Liz and Sage started talking about the gator, which had been discovered early one morning by Shawnda, the owner of Cheesy Does It. She'd shown up at her normal time of five in the morning only to find the gator on the doorstep to her business.

That happened on Monday. On Tuesday, two things occurred at the local courthouse that sent the town abuzz.

Most importantly, Esmerelda took a plea deal. She agreed to a second-degree murder charge. Her sentencing would come later, but Chief Wolf told me that it effectively meant she'd be in prison for the rest of her life.

She'd told the judge that she felt great remorse and shame for what she did to Tiffany and Marigold — and that she felt it was her duty to atone for her crimes. We'd also gotten to the bottom of what had happened to Tracy: Esmerelda had nothing to do with her death. It had been a random accident on the interstate during a rainstorm.

I'd been in court the day Esmerelda pleaded guilty, then

had raced to the lake to tell Tiffany all the details. Although she was happy that Esmerelda had finally been brought to justice, she was even more pleased that her status in the In Between hadn't changed.

I wished she could be here tonight, and Julia and I had even discussed holding the ceremony at the lake, but Tiffany politely declined, saying she'd rather not meet the coven yet. She wanted her private life to stay private, and I had to respect that.

The second thing that happened this week was that Garrett Higginbottom was arrested and extradited from Illinois to Florida on charges of being an accessory to murder. That had been big news, with his case drawing reporters from around the country since he was a well-known motivational speaker. I'd even hosted a couple of the journalists at the inn for a few nights.

"I heard a rumor that gator was a shapeshifter," Sage said.

Liz and I looked at her skeptically.

"Seriously, my dudes! If witches and psychics are real, why not shapeshifters?"

"And what, the shapeshifting gator was looking for some of Shawnda's famous chicken salad?" Liz joked.

"Why not?"

We all cracked up.

A large clock on one wall, chimed eight times. Tonight's ceremony was supposed to last until ten. As a middle-aged woman, I appreciated that the coven's business began and ended at a reasonable hour. No howling at the midnight moon for us.

"Oh, it's starting," Sage said excitedly, and Julia gently elbowed us both. A hush fell over the room because Julia and Renee had made their way to the small stage at the front of the ballroom.

In their matching caftans, they stood tall, their presence

commanding everyone's attention. Julia raised her hand, and the chatter died down to a roaring silence.

"Sisters," Julia began, her voice carrying across the space. "We gather here tonight under the light of the full moon to welcome a new member into our coven. Amelia Matthews has proven herself worthy of joining the Sisters of Hecate through her dedication, her bravery, and her unwavering pursuit of truth and justice."

Renee nodded, a proud smile on her face. "Amelia's gifts of psychometry and her keen instincts have already served our community well. Her tireless efforts in solving the disappearance of our founder, Marigold Wentworth, have brought long-awaited closure and healing to our sisterhood."

A murmur of approval rippled through the crowd. Liz and Sage squeezed my hands in support.

"Now," Julia continued, "we ask that everyone join hands and form a circle. Let us create a sacred space to welcome Amelia into our ranks."

The women moved gracefully, their clothing swishing as they clasped hands, forming a large ring around the perimeter of the ballroom. I found myself between Liz and Sage, their palms warm against mine.

Julia and Renee stepped down from the stage, each holding a white taper candle. They approached me, their faces glowing in the flickering light.

"Amelia Matthews, please step into the circle," Renee said.

My heart was in my throat as Liz and Sage gave me a small nudge. I found myself inside the circle of beaming women. And then, I felt something. Like a vision, only I wasn't touching anything.

Pure, radiant, happiness.

"Oh, wow," I whispered.

Julia and Renee stood in front of me.

"Amelia, do you pledge to uphold the values of the Sisters of Hecate? To use your gifts for the good of our Generation X sisterhood and the wider world? To protect and support your fellow witches, and to keep our secrets sacred?"

I took a deep breath, feeling the weight of the moment. "I do."

Julia smiled. "Then repeat after me: 'By the powerful light of the moon and its power within, I bind myself to this coven, heart and kin. My gifts I will share, my sisters I'll defend, our magic and mysteries, I'll protect to the end.'"

As I recited the words, a tingle of energy raced up my spine. The molecules in the air seemed to hum and shimmer around us.

"Welcome, Amelia Matthews," Julia and Renee said in unison, "to the Sisters of Hecate."

The room erupted into applause and cheers. I found myself enveloped in a sea of hugs, my senses overwhelmed by the scent of sage, lavender, and sisterhood.

I didn't even notice that Julia and Renee had climbed back on stage.

"Sisters!" Julia said.

Everyone quieted and ceased their hugs. We all looked to the stage. I knew what she was going to say, and it made me more nervous than any initiation ritual.

"We have another special milestone tonight. As you know, we postponed our anniversary celebration last month because of the events involving our founder. We needed time to determine the best course of action for our dearest Marigold. After much discussion amongst the coven's board, and after consulting with some of the world's top witches, we determined what we need to do. Amelia, will you do us this honor?"

Nodding, I wove my way through the crowd and climbed on stage to join Julia and Renee. I thought my neck was about to heat up with a hot flash, but the silk caftan was keeping me surprisingly cool. This was the part of the night I was truly nervous about.

Renee went to a silk cloth bag with a drawstring top that was sitting on a table on the stage. She opened it and extracted the little jewelry box, the one that I'd found at Esmerelda's. The one that contained Marigold's spirit. Renee handed it to me.

I clutched the jewelry box, feeling its weight in my hands. This was the moment we had all been waiting for: the chance to finally give our coven's founder the recognition and peace she deserved after so many years trapped by Esmerelda's dark magic.

I turned to face the gathered witches, their eyes shining with anticipation in the candlelight.

"Sisters," I began, my voice trembling slightly with emotion. "Tonight, we honor Marigold Wentworth by releasing her spirit from this vessel where it has been confined for far too long. With the power of our combined magic and love, let us guide her into the light."

Renee stepped forward and placed a hand on my shoulder. "I will join my astral projection abilities with Amelia's psychometry. Together, we will open a pathway for Marigold to cross over."

We focused, reaching out with our minds and hearts. I felt the now-familiar tingle of my psychic gift activating as I touched the sides of the jewelry box. Renee's astral energy merged with mine, amplifying the connection.

The box began to vibrate and glow in my hands, a light pinkish hue that almost hurt my eyes with its brightness. Gasps echoed through the room as the lid to the box opened, revealing more pink light — and Marigold's bone, nestled in the satin. The eerie tune began to play, making everyone fall silent.

The ballerina began to spin.

No visions came, however. Only wave after wave of pure energy surged through me. It was a little like getting an oxygen infusion while drinking a triple espresso. My mind felt clearer than it ever had.

Then, a shimmering, translucent form rose from the box.

It was Marigold's ghost, appearing to us at last. She was radiant, her face filled with joy and gratitude. She waved her hands, and I noticed that all of her fingers were there.

She was whole again.

"My sisters," Marigold spoke, her voice like a whispering breeze. "I cannot thank you enough for your tireless efforts to find the truth and set me free. Amelia, your courage and gifts have brought me such peace. I am forever in your debt."

Tears streamed down my face as I basked in her presence. "It was my honor, Marigold. Your story deserved to be told. Your legacy, remembered. Justice, sought. Also: Tiffany Ferndale sends her love."

Marigold smiled, her ghostly form growing brighter. "Though my earthly time was cut short, I long to remain with the coven in spirit. To watch over you all and shower you with light and love. If you would have me, I wish to stay, no longer trapped, but as a joyful presence you can turn to in times of need. I do not have the energy to return to life, and I'm not ready to fully cross over, either."

Julia grinned, an idea sparking in her eyes. "Sisters, we would like suggestions for a new vessel for Marigold. It should represent her eternal light, and it should be something we can display proudly here in the coven meeting house. We must do this tonight, as Marigold has been in the jewel box for far too long."

"Wait! I know just the thing, it's in the storage room," a

familiar twang called out. It was Sage. "Hold your horses, I'll be right back."

Sage said something to a woman next to her, and the two of them power-walked out of the room. The sound of Sage's boots striking the tile floor echoed and bounced off the walls. I glanced at Renee, then at Julia, then at Marigold.

"Even if it's a temporary location, I'm fine with that," Marigold said. "I hated the ballerina box. I mean, like, I never wanted to be a dancer."

The room erupted into giggles.

More laughter and chatter bubbled up from the assembled witches as we waited for Sage to return. I couldn't help but smile at Marigold's quip about the ballerina box. It was strangely comforting to know that even in the afterlife, or wherever she was, a woman could retain her sense of humor.

"You know," Marigold mused, her ghostly eyes twinkling, "being trapped in that jewelry box for decades really puts a cramp in your social life. I'd love to let loose and listen to some tunes with my sisters. If that's a possibility."

Renee leaned over and whispered to me, "I heard she loved Motley Crüe. She would've adored Oliver's band."

Before I could respond, Sage burst back into the ballroom, slightly out of breath but grinning from ear to ear. In her hands, she held a large, mirrored disco ball. The crowd parted so Sage was in the middle of the floor. Behind her was the other woman, holding a step ladder.

"Ta-da!" Sage exclaimed, holding it aloft. "I knew this beauty was tucked away in storage. It's perfect, don't you think?"

Julia clapped her hands in delight. "Sage, you're a genius! Marigold? What do you think?"

Marigold grinned and laughed, doing a little ghostly spin

that left glitter in her wake. "It's perfect," she squealed, clapping her hands and creating a shower of sparks.

Sage carried the sphere over to me and Renee. We shared a knowing look, ready to work our magic. Meanwhile, a few of the women set the ladder up in the middle of the room. Sage climbed up with the ball and somehow hooked it to the chandelier.

"Looks solid to me," she said, then stepped down. She and a few others whisked the ladder away.

The coven joined hands once more as Renee and the witches began to chant, their voices rising and falling in an ancient rhythm. I didn't know the words yet, so I focused intently on Marigold's spirit, gently guiding it towards a new, glittering home.

As the last words of the spell left their lips, Marigold's essence swirled and danced, coalescing into a brilliant orb of energy that floated towards the disco ball. In a flash of light that was almost blinding, she merged with the mirrored surface.

Julia waved her hand. The room plunged into darkness and everyone gasped aloud.

"Let the healing light of the moon guide us all," Julia commanded.

The heavy scarlet curtains parted, allowing silver moonlight to stream into the ballroom. It hit the disco ball, which started to turn.

Then, the moonlight fractured into a dazzling display of spinning, sparkling beams that painted the room in a kaleidoscope of ethereal light.

A cheer went up from the gathered witches as the first notes of Madonna's "Holiday" began to play over the sound system. Laughter and whoops rang out as my new sisters began to dance around the drops of light that came straight from Marigold's heart.

I looked up at the disco ball, the joy of her spirit washing over me. She was free now, a guardian and guide for the coven she started all those years ago when she was a young woman.

As I shimmied and twirled beneath the sparkling light, surrounded by the laughter and love of my new witchy, middle-aged sisters, I felt a sense of peace and belonging settle deep into my soul.

I was home, at last.

---

*Thank you for reading **EVERY HEX YOU TAKE!** I truly appreciate all of the love you've given this series.*

Make sure to turn the page for Tracy North's shortbread cookie recipe!

Tracy North, a young and talented witch and baker, was known in Cypress Grove for her extraordinary baking skills. Her candied pecan orange shortbread and dark chocolate cookies were the stuff of legend among her friends, who liked to joke that the cookies paired well with both boxed wine and fine champagne.

The secret to Tracy's magical cookies lay in a cherished recipe that she created with her dear high school friend Mary Jo, a fellow witch from the sun-drenched state of Florida. Mary Jo had inherited the recipe from her great-grandmother, a powerful woman known for her enchanting culinary creations.

Tracy and Mary Jo's friendship blossomed over their shared love of baking and witchcraft. They would spend hours in Tracy's cozy kitchen, experimenting with new twists on the recipe, infusing each batch with a pinch of magic and a dash of love.

Tragically, Tracy's life was cut short in a devastating car crash. As a tribute to her memory, Mary Jo decided to share the precious recipe with the world, ensuring that Tracy's legacy would live on through her beloved cookies.

Now, every time someone bakes a batch of Tracy's candied pecan orange shortbread and dark chocolate cookies, they are not only indulging in a heavenly treat but also honoring the memory of a talented baker who touched the lives of so many with her kindness and culinary magic.

It is said that on certain moonlit nights, the scent of Tracy's cookies wafts through the streets of Cypress Grove, a gentle reminder of the enduring power of friendship, love, and the magic of sharing something sweet with those around us.

INGREDIENTS for cookies

3.5 cups flour

1 cup cane sugar

1.5 cups candied pecans roughly chopped

2 tsp orange extract

1 tsp salt

3/4 pounds unsalted European butter (Substitute Earth Balance for Vegan)

For Chocolate Dipping:

Dark chocolate discs (Hu for Vegan)

1tsp coconut oil

Sea salt

Zest of 1 orange

INSTRUCTIONS

Gather Your Ingredients: Assemble all the components for these enchanting cookies because Tracy loved an organized kitchen. Preheat your oven to 350 degrees, as if stoking the flames of a mystical furnace.

Conjure the Butter and Sugar: In your cauldron (a standup mixer), combine the unsalted butter (or Earth Balance for a vegan spell) and cane sugar using the paddle attachment. Mix until just combined, as if blending the elements of earth and sweetness. Add the orange extract, which is a burst of citrusy magic.

Sift the Dry Ingredients: In a medium bowl, sift together the flour and salt. Add this mixture to the butter and sugar concoction, along with the roughly chopped candied pecans. Mix on low speed until the dough comes together, as if weaving an incantation.

Chill the Enchanted Dough: Pour the dough onto a lightly floured parchment paper and knead it into a flat disc. Wrap it in plastic and chill for 30 minutes, allowing the flavors to meld and the dough to firm up.

Roll and Cut the Cookies: On the same parchment, roll out the chilled dough into a round circle about 1/2 inch thick, as if creating a base for a mystical symbol. Use fluted round cookie cutters to cut out 2-2.5 inch rounds.

Bake the Shortbread Spells: Place the cookie rounds onto an ungreased baking sheet and bake for 20-25 minutes, until the edges are slightly brown. You are imbuing them with the power of the oven's mystical heat. Remove to a baking rack and let cool completely, allowing the magic to settle.

Optional Chocolate Dipped Enchantment: For an extra layer of sorcery, melt dark chocolate discs (Hu for vegan) with 1 tsp of coconut oil in a microwave-safe bowl, stirring until glossy. Using tongs, gently dip half of each cooled cookie into the chocolate and place on parchment paper to cool. While still warm, sprinkle with sea salt and orange zest. As you do this, think thoughts of joy, infusing the recipe with love and sisterhood.

Enjoy the Magical Delights: Savor these candied pecan orange shortbread and dark chocolate cookies, each bite a journey into a world of culinary sorcery. Share them with friends and family, spreading the joy of your magical baking prowess.

Acknowledgments

A massive thank you to MJ Landry, my dear college friend who lovingly created the cookie recipe in this book. If you are ever in Marin County, California, check out her business The Board Shop Mill Valley for all of your delicious charcuterie needs!

I must also thank my husband Marco for giving me all of his love and support. Without him, I wouldn't be able to do any of this. I love you, honey bunny.

About the Author

Tara Lush is a Florida-based author and journalist. She's an RWA Rita finalist, an Amtrak writing fellow and the winner of the George C. Polk award for environmental journalism.

Previously, she was a reporter with The Associated Press in Florida, covering crime, alligators, natural disasters and politics.

Tara is a fan of vintage pulp fiction book covers, Sinatra-era jazz, 1980s fashion, tropical chill, kombucha, gin, tonic, seashells, iPhones, Art Deco, telenovelas, street art, coconut anything, strong coffee and newspapers. She lives on the Gulf Coast with her husband and two dogs.

Click HERE to sign up for Tara's newsletter.

Also by Tara Lush

CRESCENT MOON MYSTERIES

Eat, Pray, Hex

I Want Your Hex

Every Hex You Take

Cattitude and Charms (coming Sept. 13, 2024)

Serving Up Hex (coming January 2025)

THE CRITTERS AND CRIMINALS SERIES

Gator Queen

Swamp Princess (coming August 2024)

THE COFFEE LOVER'S MYSTERY SERIES

Grounds for Murder

Cold Brew Corpse

Live and Let Grind

A Bean to Die For

www.ingramcontent.com/pod-product-compliance
Lightning Source LLC
Chambersburg PA
CBHW021414010826
48972CB00014B/2135